Steel Shadows

THE STEEL EMPIRES SERIES BOOK FIVE

Steel Shadows © 2019
by J.L. Gribble

Published by Dog Star Books
Bowie, MD

First Edition

Cover Image: Bradley Sharp
Book Design: Jennifer Barnes

Printed in the United States of America

ISBN: 978-1-947879-14-0

Library of Congress Control Number: 2019941297

www.RawDogScreaming.com

For Erik, again.

Also from the Steel Empires Series

Steel Shadows

J.L. Gribble

DOG STAR
BOOKS

SHADOW

"You're sure this will work?"

Despite the evidence of Victory's enhanced senses over the past week, putting her faith in time travel remained difficult. She stood with Toria in the museum's basement, clutching Toria's warm fingers within her cool hand.

But putting faith in her daughter's magical ability was effortless.

"The spell worked. I have no idea about this next part," Toria said. "But wherever we end up, this time we'll be there together."

Victory closed her eyes. With any luck, the next time she opened them, they would stand in the ruins of Nacostina, decades after the Last War. Decades in the future. Somewhere close to their own time.

She hadn't prayed in a long time. She wasn't sure who or what she should pray to now, so instead, she focused on one idea. *Home.*

Without warning, a mysterious force jerked Victory away. The stillness pressed in, like invisible hands grasping at her clothing and limbs. The silence screamed in her ears. The voices she'd heard in the shadows when they first traveled to Nacostina coalesced into words. Not Loquella, not Qin, nor any of the other languages she'd learned and forgotten over her lifetime. But she understood nonetheless. Her body obeyed no orders, else she'd have clawed at her ears to force out the voices.

One comes.

We know this one.

One is too early.

One does not know us.

Shock reverberated through the impenetrable void, as if the entire universe experienced outrage at such an oversight.

The oppressive touch shifted. Now, hands caressed her in mingled curiosity and affection. No difference between the pressure on her clothes, on her body, within her skin.

One will.

Victory's entire sense of self spun away, twisting itself inside out.

Scenes played out, overlaying her twisted vision. The visions spooled out of the void and pummeled her with images. Dreams, memories, scenes—familiar and not. A life both lived, and unlived.

Campfire light haloed Asaron, the wild man with tangled red hair, as he kneeled above her in the darkness. Gentle hands pushed her against the bedroll, in counterpoint to his gruff voice. "Don't panic. Your body is still healing."

"I don't know who you are."

"I'm Asaron. What's your name?"

"I… don't know."

"That's okay. We'll find you a good one."

The scene shifted. Asaron moved away, the world twisting around her and night stars shimmering into a mosaic pattern. Brilliant colored tiles spiraled on the wall opposite the couch where Victory lounged. Gentle fingers touched her wrist, and she accepted the goblet of blood from the demure serving girl. When the servant scurried away, her cotton robes fluttered in the nighttime breeze that came through the narrow windows under the eaves.

"I've done well for myself since you've been gone, Victory."

She shifted her attention from the departing servant to the woman who reclined across from her, garbed in black fabric that should have seemed drab next to the tile wall. Her progeny smiled under her hooked nose.

Victory raised her goblet in a toast. "I didn't expect this sort of welcome, Fatima."

"You're always welcome in my home, Mother. None of this would exist without you."

The tiles behind Fatima's waterfall of black hair took on a life of their own. The many-hued mosaic swirled together, blending into new patterns, and Victory fell forward among them.

The carriage jolted on the unpaved road. Her spine would need days to recover, but her progeny Jarimis had insisted they could not afford to turn down this hunting party invitation. He patted her knee, and his golden rings glinted in the full moonlight. "We're almost there, Mum."

"I imagine this is less about finding potential clients and more about access to the viscount's library, isn't it?" Victory shifted on the carriage bench, glad she never traveled in a corset and dreading the change into appropriate evening wear when they arrived at the estate.

Jarimis caught her fingers with his. "For once, it's not about a book. I heard the viscount's daughter had need for a security detail to accompany her to Londinium for the season. I may have promised an introduction."

"Oh, Zvi." Victory drew her handkerchief to her face. "I've already heard the rumors about that woman."

But when she lowered the slip of cotton, the jolting travel had stopped. She stood alone on a flat, gray surface. The colorless sky melded with the ground on the horizon, difficult to distinguish even with her vampiric eyesight. Jarimis' cool hand in hers had returned to Toria's calloused grip, but her daughter was nowhere to be seen outside that solid connection.

The invisible, searching caresses returned, and Victory shuddered away from the touch. "Hello?" Her voice fell flat against the blank expanse, as if she stood in a sound-proofed booth. "I need to get home."

Toria's hand twitched in her own, but she held fast. What did her daughter see in this weird space between time?

The creeping hands never faltered, but the voice echoed through the air.

We will return one to whence one came. We will wait for one.

The tugging sensation behind her sternum closed its grip, yanking her out and away.

LIMANI

The voice kept its promise.

Victory returned to the barren ruins of Nacostina, Toria at her side. From the perspective of her daywalker Mikelos, they had been gone for a single day.

However, Victory had been trapped in the past, in a city on the verge of destruction for almost a week. Her adopted daughter Toria had lived there for six months, unsure whether she'd ever make it home again and terrified every action might destroy the future she'd come from.

Victory had never found such a stark landscape so welcoming.

They had no reason to stick around, now. Toria declared the mission complete once she wrapped the time-travel artifact in multiple layers with their winter coats, useless now in the summer warmth. They left Nacostina and the Wasteland behind, returning to Limani. Entering the city-state's territory had no physical effect, but it seemed to Victory as if her home embraced her soul, welcoming her return to her proper time and place.

Toria insisted on bringing the artifact straight to the Mercenary Guildhall before she and Kane returned to the mage school. Though she acted cheery, the dark bags under Toria's eyes belied the truth. Her daughter needed to be home, and home was no longer at Victory's house.

An anxious hum pulsed under Victory's skin as she approached her own house. Though she'd shared the important details of her experience with Mikelos—traveling to the past, reuniting with Toria, and making their way home with the artifact—Victory needed to talk to someone else. He would either confirm she was going insane, or worse, agree something more was going on.

She left Mikelos with the bags in the foyer and sprinted to the basement apartment. She stopped in front of the couch where Asaron sprawled with a book and planted her hands on her hips.

Her sire lifted his chin in greeting, not bothering to glance from his book. "You weren't gone long. How did it go?"

Victory had a million possible answers to that question, ranging from "Holy shit, time travel is real," to "I saw Jarimis again and I need a hug," and ending with "I beat the crap out of my past self, so I need you to tell me I didn't fuck up the timeline."

Instead: "I'm seeing strange shadows, and I think I spoke to them."

Asaron lurched at her words, fumbling his book. "You what?"

Victory collapsed next to him on the couch. She reclined against the cushions, shielding herself from any disdain her sire might show at how insane she sounded. "I thought I was imagining things for a long time. That I was going crazy."

She had expected Asaron's silence, but when it dragged on for longer than she could stand, his pain-wrenched expression shocked her.

"We thought it was just us."

"Just who? What are you talking about?"

"The shadows. The darkness that shouldn't exist, leeching into our world."

Victory grit her teeth. If it wasn't a problem limited to her own mind, then it was something real, something tangible. Something that could be measured. Could be reasoned with.

Could be defeated.

"Tell me everything you know."

Asaron retrieved his book from where it had fallen between the couch cushions and set it on the coffee table, square to the corner.

Victory held herself still. He'd draw in if she pushed further, and then getting any information would be like wringing water from stone.

"There's not much we know." Asaron propped his elbows on his knees. "I've seen the shadows, off and on, for a few years now."

"Ever since the kids arrived home from Parisii the first time, right?"

"Exactly right."

"But who's 'we'?" Victory asked. "If it's more than you and I, this isn't limited to Limani's vampires." Who consisted of she and Asaron, and no one else.

"Daniel and Kahina." Two vampire Masters of the City in the southern Roman colonies. "Daniel approached me first, though I'd assumed it was just me before that. I made an oblique comment to Kahina the next time I passed through Fort Caroline. She latched on quick, grateful for confirmation she wasn't losing her mind."

"But you didn't talk to me?" A tiny hurt jabbed her, despite how she hadn't confided in her sire either.

"The three of us are over a thousand years old. I assumed it was age-related."

Fair assessment. Three unofficial milestones existed in a vampire's life after death: one year, one hundred years, and one thousand years. Victory needed close to two more centuries before she crossed the final threshold. Asaron sometimes joked he'd stopped counting once he'd hit a thousand, a time long before he turned Victory. "But I've seen them, too," Victory said. "Daniel and Kahina are the only ones you've discussed it with?"

"If not age, perhaps location. We all live on the New Continent. Proximity to the Wasteland?"

Asaron liked to play the grunt, but a man didn't live to his age without a few tricks up his sleeve. However, she found a flaw in his theory right away. "Except the first time I saw them was south in Jiang Yi Yue. Thought it was the *kitsune* harrying us on our way out of the city, but it kept happening once I came home." She paused, her brain running through the last crazy week. "I really did think I was going insane. But then they spoke to me."

Asaron pointed at Victory. "Full report, now."

Victory rose from the couch to pace the room. She did an about-face at Asaron's storage chest and crossed her arms over her chest in a primal urge at defense. She did not want to have this conversation, but it was an integral part of the story. "The artifact in Nacostina the kids were hired to find sent us back in time. Toria was there for close to six months. I was there for a week. We escaped before the Qin bombed the city." It sounded like a fairy tale, or pure insanity, and Victory braced herself for Asaron's reaction. "On our way back, I was stuck in a sort of in-between place. I saw visions out of the past, and a voice told me it wasn't time for me to be there yet. In the real world, I appeared next to Toria, but she doesn't remember anything from the trip either way."

Silence from her sire again. "Visions?"

"Moments with you and Jarimis and Fatima." Victory picked up a crude clay pot, crafted by Toria in grammar school, and traced the purple whorls etched in its surface. "Even you, right after you turned me."

"Interesting. And something talked to you?"

"Around me. Words in a weird speech pattern, as if I was getting a bad translation." Victory flinched away from the memory of the invisible hands running over her body. "So, where do we go from here?"

Asaron stood and plucked the clay pot from Victory's hands. After setting it next to a pile of books on knife care and urban warfare tactics, he rested both hands on Victory's shoulders. She met his moss-colored eyes for the split second manageable, before his age and power overwhelmed her, then let her gaze slide to his cheek. She didn't pull away when Asaron tugged her to his chest. She settled her temple on his shoulder as the muscles in her shoulders loosened. She had needed a hug. Though his calluses caught on the fabric of her cotton shirt, Asaron's touch on her back grounded her.

"I think it's time to talk to the experts." Asaron's voice rumbled through her chest.

"How the hell are we supposed to find an expert in something this crazy?"

"Maybe we should start with someone crazy."

The next evening, Victory sat with Asaron in the guest seats across from a battered antique desk. Notebook paper and scattered fist-sized mineral samples warred for space on its surface, but the rest of the cozy office was neat as a pin. Someone, perhaps Kane, had left a houseplant in the fireplace for the summer. Across from them, Archer Sophin reclined in his chair and propped his leather boots on his desk.

Sitting across from a grizzled mercenary with years of experience and the mother of his partner did not appear to disconcert him. The master-level water mage and director of Limani's mage school flipped a handful of dreadlocks over his shoulder. A crystalline unicorn horn spiraled out of his forehead, refracting a rainbow prism across his dark olive skin from the light of the desk lamp.

Asaron waggled his fingers in front of his own face. "New fashion statement?"

"No. Sorry about that." Archer clapped his hand to his forehead. It passed through the horn, which disintegrated with a flutter of silver sparkles. "The pranksters always go nuts once they figure out the illusion charms."

Victory had many memories of the previous mage school teachers sending home note after note as Toria and Archer, and then Toria and Kane, got up to such mischief in their younger days, and she snickered at seeing the tables turned. "At least you know the worst they can manage."

"Yeah, because I've already done it." Archer's smirk lit his face more than the rainbow. "But you two didn't drop by to relive memories or laugh at my students' petty revenge against their difficult teacher. What can I help you with?"

Victory shot Asaron a glance, but he gestured for her to speak. She was in the hot seat first.

Despite Archer's relative youth, he was a talented mage who had received the best education possible in New Angouleme's former magical academy before taking over the local school here. If anyone, perhaps he could explain what Victory had experienced between time. "Did Toria tell you what happened to us in Nacostina?"

"Up late into the night, and we talked about it again this morning." Archer raised both hands. "I already know I'm going to need a beer for this. Either of you want one?"

Both accepted the offer. Archer fetched bottles from a miniature fridge tucked in the office corner, popped the caps into his waste bin, and handed them over. When he settled in his chair, he waved for Victory to continue. "This whole thing makes my brain hurt."

"You and me both, kid." Asaron toasted with his beer. "And we haven't even reached the crazy part."

"That does not encourage me. I still can't believe we're using terms like 'time travel' about something other than a thought-experiment."

"If you're both done?" Victory asked. The men fell silent at once. "On the trip home... I saw visions from my past. Which makes sense, considering the circumstances of time travel. But I also heard a voice speak to me. It told me I wasn't supposed to be there, and that it would send me home."

Archer scratched his brow, as if reassuring himself the illusionary horn hadn't returned. "Did you see anything other than the visions?"

"At the end, I stood in a sort of empty space. Nothing there. No colors other than a lot of blank gray." Victory tilted one shoulder. "I don't suppose that rings any bells? Or did I imagine it all?"

Archer chewed at his bottom lip. "I'd rather not insinuate that you imagined anything. Barring blunt-force trauma to the skull, we have to assume it all happened."

"I guess we're here to find out if you know where I was," Victory said. "Or what spoke to me. This is so far outside my realm of experience that it might as well be another world." Which it might even be, crazy as that sounded. Making it into a joke distanced it enough for Victory to be able to talk about it.

She noted Asaron's silence. Getting Archer's help would require telling him the full story about the shadows.

Archer scratched his neck, under his scruffy goatee showing hints of gray. Even though he was a few years older than Kane, it reminded Victory that her kids were growing up whether she liked it or not. "I'm not a doctor, but maybe your brain reacted to the time travel and tried to make sense of what it was experiencing. Random neurological firings to compensate for sensory overload. Or underload."

Victory had not expected Archer to go down this path. She nudged Asaron. They had to tell the entire truth, or they would get nowhere.

Proving he wasn't the director of a school for no reason, Archer picked up her cue. "There's something you're both not telling me."

"You're right." Asaron placed his half-empty bottle on the floor next to his seat. He clasped his hands across his stomach, slouching in his chair as if this wasn't the biggest revelation since, well, time travel. "Ever since you kids took on the elves and vampires in the Parisii Catacombs, vampires have seen shadows in the real world, too."

"And by shadows, you mean…?" Archer rolled his hand for more details.

"Blurry figures at the edge of my vision. Like a person is standing where they shouldn't be. I can't get a good look, and when I turn, nothing is there."

Victory straightened in her chair. "But that's not what it looks like at all! For me, it's a sort of drifting darkness. Patches of shadow where there shouldn't be shadow. And they move."

"Doesn't surprise me," Asaron said. "In Newport Hill, Daniel says they look like plumes of smoke where there's no fire. And Kahina told me she saw them as holes of pure darkness against any bright light."

Archer retrieved a pad of paper and pen from his desk. "So Kahina seems to be seeing them the most clearly."

"Kahina is the oldest." Retrieving his beer, Asaron toasted Archer's startled expression. "Yes, older than me. She retired from the Senate in Roma but never lost her taste for power. Retirement as the Master of the largest city in the colonies suits her."

"I expected her to go back after the invasion nonsense and set the Emperor straight." Victory rolled the glass bottle between her palms. "She even sent me a lovely apology note for allowing General Octavian to travel through her territory without learning the truth about why he was there. Promised it wouldn't happen again." Limani might not be a large or powerful city, but at least the local Masters in the Roman colonies to the south valued its position as neutral ground between them and the British.

Archer waved his notepad to get them back on topic. "Dark shadows where they shouldn't be. I wish I could ask you how they feel, but I know vampires don't feel magic."

"I still don't know how *you* feel magic, much less manipulate it." Victory exchanged a wry glance with Asaron, a long-lasting sense of mutual confusion that the closest people in their lives had access to something so alien to them. "But you're the expert, so that's why we came to you."

"I'm not the only expert, though." Archer's attention lingered in the middle-distance between them, then snapped to the present. "Be right back."

He rose from his desk and strode across the office, his thick-soled boots squeaking on the wooden floor. Poking his head out the door, he called to someone unseen. "Fee! Can you send a message to Kane and Toria that I need them in my office?"

"I must remind you, sir, that Master Connor has requested I not summon her, because—" The woman's bland voice shifted to a perfect mimicry of Toria. "—It makes my brain itch, damn it."

"I remember, Fee, thank you. Can you please ask Kane to fetch her?"

"Yes, Master Sophin."

"Do you know where they are right now?"

"Yes, Master Sophin."

"Every damned time. Right. Can you please tell me where Kane and Toria are right now?"

"Master Nalamas is in your suite, reading. Master Connor is in the living room, helping Journeyman Sjolander and Apprentice Lukis study."

"Thank you, Fee." Archer drew back into the office. He returned to the fridge and withdrew two more beers, which he readied at the edge of his desk.

"Doesn't it creep you out, her knowing where you are all the time?" Asaron asked.

"She doesn't have enough power to reach beyond the physical limitations of the mage school grounds, and access to her privacy settings are limited to me, Kane, and Toria." Archer popped the caps of the beer bottles and tossed them into the trash bin with the others. "Those sorts of duties are tied to her original crafting. Lack of work to do or information to process causes problems, so we figured it was better to have her function as a sort of security measure instead of leaving her to her own devices."

Archer had brought the simulacrum known as "Fee" back from New Angouleme after shutting down the school there, declaring that leaving her unsupervised was both inhumane and courting disaster. The pale, emotionless-being disturbed Victory. Based on the overheard exchange, Fee unsettled Toria as well.

Footsteps trotted down the hallway, and two figures soon passed through Archer's office door. The taller was the dark-skinned, muscled figure of Victory's foster son and Archer's significant other, Kane Nalamas. His lighter shadow was Kane's warrior-mage partner and Victory's adopted daughter, Toria Connor. Magic had linked the two since adolescence, allowing them to pursue a career as mercenaries along with their magical studies.

Kane dragged a stool from the corner and sat next to Archer, accepting his beer with a kiss, while Toria perched on a corner of the desk. She snagged the other beer and drowned a long swig. Though less than two days had passed since they arrived in Limani after the adventure in Nacostina, Toria had embraced the return to modern dress standards, as indicated by her crop top and ragged jeans. "Thank you for not having Fee talk in my brain. Hi, Mom. Good evening, Grandpa."

Archer moved the bottle, damp with condensation, away from a stack of papers. "You're welcome. A bit thirsty?"

"If I'd remembered how much I hate tutoring ward theory, I might have stayed in the past."

"I'll get Maggie to sit with me tomorrow to see where she's getting hung up. Anyway. Your elders are here to pick our brains." With the practice of years of teaching, Archer outlined what the vampires had relayed to him, with Victory interjecting once to correct his description of what she'd seen when traveling forward through time.

As Archer finished, Toria said, "I was in the storage room at the museum. And then I was on the ground in Nacostina. There was nothing between."

Kane picked at the label of his beer bottle, shredding it into a tiny pile on Archer's desk. "And you've both been seeing the shadows for how long?"

"Sounds like since we ruined the ritual in the Catacombs." Toria stared into the distance, emotion darkening her face. With a disconcerting shift in attention, she stared at Victory. "Why didn't you say anything?"

Victory held her daughter's gaze for two beats, then turned away before her vampiric power forced Toria to bend first. "Same reason Asaron didn't say anything, probably. It's hard to accept feeling crazy when you're supposed to have seen and done everything already. There's always a rational explanation for everything. Until there's not."

"Pretty much." Asaron patted Victory's knee.

"So, seeing the shadows is linked to the broken ritual in the Catacombs." Kane stretched one arm with the pop of a wrist joint, then the other. "But when

Victory heard them talk to her, it was when the artifact transported her through time. Sounds like we need to examine the artifact."

"No." Toria slid off the desk and loomed over them all, hands braced on her hips. "We're destroying that thing."

The muscles in Kane's shoulders bunched, but he remained seated. "We can't destroy the object that might have some answers without doing our due diligence."

"It's too dangerous." Toria stared Kane down, and the warrior-mage partners might have been alone in the room.

How would this play out? Victory had come to Archer for advice, not to cause a fight.

"You told me it was physical touch that activated the time travel," Archer said. "I can't believe I said that with a straight face. You said it let you cast an illusion on it without fighting back. So passive examination should be safe enough."

Kane pulled Toria toward his stool and tucked her against his side. "It'll be okay," he said. "We can bring it here from the Guildhall. Honestly, it might be safer here under wards than in Max's safe."

As if a valve had opened, the tension drained from Toria's body and she slumped against Kane. "I hate it when you're rational. We'll have to get Liam's permission. The contract is fulfilled, so the stupid rock belongs to him now."

In a twist of fate, the man Toria had fallen in love with in the past was the same who'd set the mercenary contract that sent them to Nacostina in the first place. Despite her lack of magical acumen, Victory had to agree that the mage school was a securer place for a dangerous magical artifact than a safe in the heart of Limani's Mercenary Guildhall, even under the protection of its Guildmaster. "Do you have a way to contact Liam?" It boggled her mind further that the man she'd known for years fell in love with Victory's daughter before Victory ever met him.

She hated time travel.

"We're, uh, having dinner in a bit," Toria said. "We decided it was better for me to get settled at home first, and take things slow. But Kane met him yesterday."

"Seems like a stand-up guy." Kane hugged Toria once more, then allowed her to detach from his side. "He's a scientist, like you. I can't imagine that he won't want to learn more about the artifact before it's destroyed."

"But it is getting destroyed." Toria's tone brooked no argument. "It's too dangerous. If anyone else touches it, they'll be sent back to a horrific war. I'm not letting that happen."

"Right." Victory rushed to reassure her daughter before the debate continued. "I won't let that happen either. We need answers first, though, and this is the best clue we have."

Toria blew out a huff of air, causing shaggy locks of her hair to fly up for a beat. "Okay. I'll talk to Liam tonight. Because this won't already be the most awkward not-first-date ever."

Victory returned to the mage school the next evening, with Asaron and her daywalker Mikelos in tow. The summer weather hit its peak, swamping Limani in oppressive humidity.

As they crossed from the small parking area to the school's front entrance, Mikelos said, "I'm glad we're not still camping in this."

If Victory and Toria hadn't stumbled over the artifact the kids had been contracted to find, they all might have still wandered the ruins of Nacostina, searching foot by foot. Small favors, but Victory's mere days in the past did not compare to Toria's months, so she wasn't one to talk. "Me, too."

"I was bummed that you got home early." Asaron held the front door open for Victory and Mikelos, waving them ahead of him. "Had a big party planned."

"When's the last time you had a party that didn't consist of you and Max drinking alone in the dark?" Many things described Victory's sire, and "party animal" did not make the list.

"A party is a party."

"Where's the party?" Kane asked in the entryway, next to a small study room. One of the young heads bent over the table raised in interest, but Kane pointed to her book. "No party for you until you finish your reading on cantrips."

The second student in the room peered at the newcomers in interest. "Can we have a party when Tasya's done?"

"No parties!" Kane threw up his hands. "Forget I said anything. Finish your reading." He gestured, leading the visitors away from the room before the apprentice mages goaded him into further conversation. "Kids, I tell you."

Kane escorted them into the depths of the original mansion that held the mage school, past the industrial kitchen and down steep stairs into the cellar. From Victory's perspective, he'd also been a kid too short a time ago. She stepped behind Mikelos into an underground room. The cool air prickled the hair on her arms, a temperature much lower than the bathwater air outside. The steady glow of mage-lights in each corner dispelled any sense of gloom. A minty smell touched the air.

Asaron nudged her to the side with a gentle tap to the wrist. With eight adults along the walls, the room seemed smaller than it was. A box about two feet square sat in the center of a ritual circle embedded into the ground in a lighter slate. Whoever had packaged the artifact had not gone light on the packing tape.

Archer clapped his hands. "And the gang's all here!" Kane joined him along the wall opposite the door.

Toria stood on Archer's other side, staring at the package with the fierce gaze of a hungry hawk. Liam completed the set with hands shoved in jean pockets, face hooded under the mage-light above him. He met Victory's gaze and quirked his lip, which tugged at the thin scar that slashed across his face.

Victory crossed the room, skirting the artifact, and extended her hands to Liam. "Now I know why an elf kept hanging around my bar all those years ago. Keeping an eye on us?"

Liam pressed a kiss to her cheek, and said, "It's such a load off my shoulders that we've come full circle. It's been a weird few weeks for you, but it's been a long century for me."

"And it's not over, yet, it seems." Victory waved Mikelos closer. "Mikelos, you already know Liam. But I'd like to introduce you to the man who helped Toria in Nacostina."

Mikelos clasped Liam's hand. "Good to see you in town again. Guess this explains why you disappeared on us thirty years ago."

"I imagine it would be weird to see your girlfriend grow up from a distance." Toria's snark cut through the friendly conversation like a knife. "Or your great-great-grandson."

A complex set of emotions crossed Kane's face, and he tugged at his ear. "Yeah, that's not going to stop being weird. My partner is dating my adopted great-great-grandfather."

Toria glanced away the artifact long enough to waggle her eyebrows at Kane. "Your partner was also friends with your actual great-great-grandmother."

Asaron's deep voice rumbled from the room's entrance. "All of this is weird. Can we get this show on the road?"

The room's occupants scattered to the edges of the ritual circle, leaving it clear. Liam moved to the side with the vampires and daywalker, exchanging a short greeting with Asaron.

After the three mages conferred in the opposite corner, Archer sank to his knees inside the circle, on one of the abstract designs Victory assumed had some arcane meaning. Kane kicked his boots off and tucked his socks inside them, then he and Toria stood on either side of Archer, their bare feet connected to the floor.

Sparing a short glance to the onlookers, Archer returned his attention to the artifact and set his hands on the ground on either side of the package. Liam inhaled next to Victory, but the water mage left inches of space on either side.

Then—nothing. The three mages' eyes moved as if they saw a different world inside the ritual circle. Even Liam seemed intent on an unknown view.

Asaron had fallen into a variation of parade rest, where he'd be content to wait for hours, if necessary. Mikelos dug a notepad and pen from his jeans pocket and soon music notes and other shorthand flew across the page, occupying his attention during the wait. Victory shifted her weight from her heels, onto her toes, and back again, unable to look away from the tableau before her.

Minutes later, the kids still hadn't moved.

After all the hype, and Toria's dramatics, this was a bit of a let-down. No reason for all of them to be here after all. She turned to Asaron, but his hand flashed out to grip her elbow. "Look."

In the ritual circle, the edges of the packaging that encased the artifact grew fuzzy. Victory rubbed her face, clearing her vision. But it wasn't her eyesight. Dirty fog flowed from the package and drifted across the circle. Tendrils flicked toward the mages, but Toria snapped out an upraised palm. The fingers of shadow licked up and down the invisible barrier she maintained. Shimmers of violet rippled around the circle with each touch.

"You got it?" Kane's deep voice seemed over-loud after the silence, but the strain in his words told Victory more was going on than she saw.

Toria bared her teeth. "For now. Liam, any help would be useful. Hurry, Archer."

Archer didn't respond, still intent on the package before him, but Liam's hands flew in an unfamiliar pattern. Victory had no concept of whatever he did, but when Toria lifted her other hand, tension no longer trembled in her fingers.

Asaron's grip on Victory's elbow never wavered as they faced the mysterious scene. Even Mikelos had dropped his pen and paper to his sides.

With a strangled gasp, Archer flew backward, shoved away by an invisible force. Kane caught Archer's arm before he slid across the slate floor. Toria yelped in mingled surprise and pain, and the invisible barrier surrounding the shadows cracked and failed.

The shadows surged away from the artifact. Victory stepped forward, but now two sets of hands tugged her away. Mikelos' fingers wrapped around hers, and her sire's hand never left his iron-tight grip on her arm.

Toria and Kane stepped into the circle, her left hand caught in his right. They exchanged unreadable glances before turning their attention to the circling shadows. Kane closed his eyes, but Toria's stare never wavered. Ozone scented the room, and the hair on the nape of Victory's neck raised under the sudden onslaught of static electricity.

Kane must be feeding Toria power. She was going to destroy the artifact.

"No!" Victory ripped herself away from Asaron and Mikelos and lunged into the circle, ignoring their cries behind her.

"Back off, Mom! This has to happen!" Toria flung her outstretched hand at her mother, and an invisible shove pushed Victory away. Electricity crackled in the air, and the magical lights in each corner flared.

The shadows at the ceiling froze in an eerie inverse topography of grays. The room stilled.

It's you again.

The words reverberated in Victory's skull as the shadows dove toward her. She threw her arms out, crossing them in front of her face, to no avail. The shadows swept around her, closing off Toria's horrified face. One by one, her senses failed. A dull darkness overwhelmed her. A now-familiar grip tightened around her sternum, then yanked her up and out and away.

SHADOW

Victory wasn't sure, at first, whether she'd opened her eyes.

When she blinked, the view didn't waver. A solid gray sky, like the thickest fog reflecting street lamps on a winter night. She blinked again, but the scene didn't change. Definitely not the depths of Limani's mage school. A hard surface supported her, and she raised herself on her elbows. Grit from the ground beneath her coated her bare arms. She dug her fingers into the surface, but they met bedrock under a fine layer of gray sand. Everything was flat, like the surface of a smooth lake. No breeze disturbed the scene, and the only difference between ground and sky was a thin line in the distance.

Her body ached when she pushed herself to her feet, as if she'd run for miles. She turned a slow circle while brushing sand from her hands but found no variation on the horizon in any direction. She filled her lungs through her nose, but the air's scent was as flat and empty as the ground. The generic harshness of rock under particles of dust. No hints to where she might be.

Not Limani. Back in Nacostina, in the past after the hydrogen bomb destroyed the city? But even that could not have caused this complete desolation.

A sharp pop displaced the air behind her. Victory whirled and dropped into a defensive stance. Asaron had appeared in the same spot where she arrived.

Victory nudged him with the toe of her boot. "You absolute moron." But she grabbed the hand he extended to haul him to his feet.

He brushed dust from his jeans. "You disappeared."

"So, you decided to follow me? Even knowing what happened last time?"

Jutting his chin, Asaron said, "You're the one who ran toward the shadows, when you are also aware of what happened last time."

Victory threw up her hands as a second *pop* sounded. "Damn it."

"Ouch." Mikelos rubbed a hand to the side of his face. "That was not pleasant."

"We have a new contender for the title of moron," Asaron said.

The vampires helped Mikelos stand, and Victory considered and rejected half a dozen exclamations before settling on, "What the hell were you thinking?"

Mikelos examined their unexpected surroundings. "You and Asaron disappeared. Wasn't about to let you get into trouble without me."

"Now all three of us are trapped here." Victory ran her fingers over her scalp, displacing more gray dust.

His survey completed, Mikelos stood at the third point in their triangle. "And where is here?"

"No idea." Victory twined her hair into a thick braid, and Asaron answered with his own silent lift of one shoulder. "But we're not mages. We're stuck here, with no supplies, inappropriate clothing, no weapons—"

Asaron snorted. "Speak for yourself."

"Right, no weapons other than the two knives my maniac sire keeps on himself at all times." Victory spread her arms wide. "Any suggestions?"

Mikelos pointed in the distance. "There."

Victory squinted, but that particular point on the horizon seemed as empty as the rest. "There's nothing there."

"Either we sit here and wait for the kids to track us down while I die of dehydration and then you two starve to death." Mikelos brushed past Victory in the direction he'd pointed. "Or walk and hope we find something different."

"Man has a point." Asaron followed Mikelos.

Victory peered into the blank sky. Not sunlight. But not night, either. Wherever they were, it wasn't any place she recognized.

In any time period.

They walked for hours.

Asaron kept dropping into a march pace, but Victory resisted the urge to lengthen her stride and fall into step with him. They both wore sturdy boots, but Mikelos had on colorful summer-weight sneakers, with flimsy rubber soles and no ankle support.

Her daywalker would keep up with them without complaint, but his ego wasn't worth ruining his shoes, or worse. She kept the speed to a more casual stroll.

Not like they were going anywhere.

The light above never shifted, the sky maintaining its soft, gray light. In a gradual change over the course of a few miles, the landscape grew rougher.

The flat plain of gray dust transformed to gravel. Later, pebbles and larger rocks cropped out of the ground. Their straight line transformed to a meandering path.

The rocks grew from handball sized, to the height of Victory's knees, then her waist. By the time Mikelos demanded his first break, they had convenient places to sit and rest.

"You're only going to get thirstier." Asaron flipped one of his knives end over end, staring into the distance. "The break won't help."

"I'm sorry, did you have someplace to be?" Mikelos glared until Victory placed a hand on his knee. He acknowledged Victory's silent request for restraint with a half-shrug.

"We're not on a schedule." Victory fingered the rock's rough texture. But she was no sort of geologist. "Ever seen this type of rock before?"

"Do either of us look like Kane?"

Victory didn't dignify Asaron's snide retort with a response. Her foster son, the earth-aligned mage, would be handy right about now. Any of the kids, with their magical ability, would be handy, and she prayed they were searching for a way to find their parents and Grandpa as soon as possible.

Mikelos hopped off his rock and stretched his calf muscles. "I'm blanking on any myths or legends that might explain where we could be."

"What would legends be able to tell you? They're legends for a reason." Asaron set forth once again. Mikelos and Victory trailed behind.

"It's been hours, but the light hasn't changed," Mikelos said. "We're not still in our world. The likeliest explanation is some sort of alternate space, perhaps the realm of the shadows that you've both been seeing."

Asaron glanced over his shoulder, brows furrowed. "You think we're in some sort of magical dimension?"

"What do we know about magic, really?" Mikelos had his lecture voice on, which he often used during his music lessons. His students learned about the history of their instrument and the language of music along with how to play. He didn't wait for an answer to his rhetorical question. "We know about elemental magic. Kane's element of earth, Archer's of water. There's also fire and air. Then there's primordial magic, which is embodied by storm, Toria's alignment. But when you get down to it, that's all we know."

"You don't think the mages know more?" Victory asked. "It's their job."

"I would hope they know more. But knowing more about their specific abilities and more about how magic exists in the world are two different things, right?"

27

Asaron's voice rumbled. "I'm not sure where you're going with this."

Mikelos spread his arms, encompassing their bleak surroundings. "Everything we know about magic does nothing to explain this." He pulled his hand in before it smacked a boulder.

The rocks continued to grow as they progressed, now almost to Victory's shoulders. The path Asaron picked around the rocks deviated more and more from their original straight line. The flat horizon became a jumbled mess of boulders and crags they had to veer their way through. Her nerves tightened as her field of view narrowed to a smaller space around them.

"It's too bad we don't know anything about magic," Asaron said.

Victory needed to nip Asaron's attitude in the bud, before the sarcasm war worsened. "Enough, gentlemen. Let's conserve energy." She assumed their silence signaled assent and continued to trudge along at Mikelos' heels.

Measuring distance in this field of rocks grew difficult because of their irregular path, but Victory estimated that she achieved at least a few miles worth of quiet. Not peace, because the unnatural silence broken by their sliding footsteps on loose gravel disconcerted her almost as much as the unchanging sky.

"I don't want to start any arguments—" Mikelos continued over Asaron's exasperated groan. "—But I have another theory."

"Okay," Victory said. "What's this one?"

"I'm trying to remember it all." He hummed a few bars. "There was a series of hymns dedicated to the original Roman gods. I found them in a library in Veneti when we wintered there one year between tours."

Her daywalker made no sense. "What are you talking about? There are no Roman gods."

Asaron halted, steadying Mikelos when the other man almost ran into him. "There were, though. A long time ago."

Taking advantage of the break, Victory rested against the nearest boulder towering above her, easing her weight off each foot in turn. "Are you talking about the first Senate members?"

"No, not those vampire assholes who thought they could deify themselves with enough statues. Real gods. With worshipers. Human and vampire alike." Asaron clipped his words. He knew more than he let on but waved Mikelos to speak instead.

Mikelos sagged against the boulder next to Victory. "Right. The hymns referenced places of reward and punishment. Heaven and hell, but not the nebulous places advertised by the spiritualists of the modern age. These had specific details. But damned if I can remember now."

Asaron didn't rest, standing braced on both feet with his arms crossed over his chest. "What are you getting at?"

Mikelos waved one hand in dismissal. "We might not know where we are. But at some point, someone might have."

A female voice sounded beyond the boulder they rested against. "Huh. You're closer than you think."

Victory lunged away. She caught a flash of the edge of a body behind Asaron, but her sire's taller bulk blocked her view. He lurched in surprise as well, spinning in place and lashing out with one arm. Flesh connected with flesh with a sickening crunch, and the figure staggered away from Asaron.

A feminine silhouette had both hands clapped to her face. "Son of a *bitch*." Between her fingers, blood dripped onto a white tank top, a vivid scarlet stain against their dull surroundings. The rest of her—pale skin, white-blond hair, and gray denim jeans tucked into dust-stained boots—was as washed-out as everything else.

Then the woman pulled her hands away, shaking them out. Her nose reset itself with another shudder-inducing crunch, but the woman herself already distracted Victory.

The woman she knew.

The woman she knew to be *dead*. "Syri?"

Syrisinia, Toria's elven best friend who'd died in the Parisii Catacombs half a decade ago, tucked a loose strand of hair behind one pointed ear with a hand now clean of blood, though the stain on her shirt remained. "Hey, guys."

Syri settled herself cross-legged between two boulders, facing Victory and Mikelos on the ground. Victory tugged at the hem of Asaron's shirt until he deigned to rest his feet. He knelt a few feet to the side, keeping wary attention on the newcomer. Victory didn't blame him.

"I bet you're wondering why I summoned you all here today," Syri said.

The joke fell flat.

"How are you even here?" Victory asked. Of all the unexpected things to happen to her in recent weeks, this had to be the most insane. People didn't come back from the dead, and she was sure Syri wasn't a vampire.

Syri's eyes unfocused, as if she sorted through how to answer the question. "This is where my people are from. I guess everyone thought I died. Instead, I was pulled home when a breach opened between the worlds."

Asaron loomed forward. "Did you summon us to this place?"

"No, no." Syri's hands flailed in time with her response. "I didn't actually summon you here. Sorry."

"Explain yourself."

"What, no apology for punching me?" When the vampire didn't respond, Syri traced lines in the dusty gravel next to her knee, avoiding their gazes. "Okay. Long story short. You're in the realm of the shadows. You know, the things that have been stalking vampires for a few years."

"Since you died," Victory said, unable to help the words that tumbled from her lips

Syri flinched. "Yeah. Something like that." She brushed dust from her fingers on her knee, but the pants seemed to absorb the vanishing grit. It was as if the elven woman was part of the landscape. "Mikelos was on the right track. Magic used to be a lot more prevalent in the world, even before the world spell fucked things up. Storm was never the only primordial energy. Storm isn't even purely primordial energy at all, or else humans like Toria wouldn't be aligned with it. Storm is the energy that links the elemental and primordial magics."

"What does that have to do with the shadows?" Mikelos leaned forward, as if to absorb Syri's every word.

He didn't seem freaked out by the girl's presence. Victory swung between nervousness that she'd come back to life and assuming that her daughter's dead best friend was a vivid hallucination, and that they'd all passed out from thirst and exhaustion.

"The shadows are part of the primordial energies," Syri continued. "Just like you have air, water, earth, and fire on the elemental side, there's life, death, light, and shadow on the primordial side. With storm connecting the whole she-bang."

They all stared at her. "I was right," Mikelos said. "There is more magic the mages don't know about."

"Right. There's a lot human mages don't know about. It's like the more things become codified and academic, the more things get lost if they can't be slotted into existing beliefs," Syri said, with more gesticulating. "The reason magic is so out of whack is because the world spell is powered by primordial magic. As it draws more and more power, it's overwhelming elemental magic. But even primordial magic was suffering, and as new elves were born, they were sacrificed to power the world spell."

"We knew some of that already," Victory said. "Toria and Kane told us that's why you were kidnapped in New Angouleme. So that you could be sacrificed in Parisii."

Syri stared past them into the rocky distance before speaking. "Yeah. Because I was one of the Broken. Like every elf born after the world spell was cast."

"I don't know that Toria ever figured out what that meant." Victory kept her voice steady, as if calming a skittish horse.

"The life magic elves use stopped being born with the new elves." Syri stared past them. "We were different."

"So, are you not an elf?" Mikelos asked.

That seemed to snap Syri back to herself, and her scathing expression of disdain was so familiar that it caused a sudden ache deep in Victory's chest. "Don't be an idiot." The accompanying eye roll proved to Victory more than anything that this was Syri, somehow with them, somehow as alive as Mikelos.

"Anyway," Syri continued, "it didn't help that the vampires have been forgetting their own magic."

Unnatural silence reigned at Syri's pronouncement. Mikelos' heartrate increased.

Asaron recoiled, lip curled in a snarl. "What the hell are you getting at?"

"Like I said. If it can't be easily explained, it's forgotten."

Syri's flippancy grated on Victory's nerves. The girl summoned memories she didn't like to revisit. "What do you know about after you—after you died?"

This gave the elven woman pause. "Nothing, obviously."

"Kane died, too."

Mikelos lurched to his feet. "What? I didn't know about this."

"It took years for Toria to tell me," Victory said. "And she was very, very drunk. A vampire fed from him, then broke his neck. But the vampire gave Toria a choice. She could bring Kane back, or Syri." Victory halted, claws of fear strangling her voice.

"Toria made the right choice," Syri said.

"Toria said there was only one vampire there." Mikelos' voice was ragged. He and Victory stared at each other, until Mikelos broke away.

"I never knew who she was," Syri said. "What am I missing?"

"It was Serena. One of the vampires I was bonded with before Victory," Mikelos said. "And I don't remember Serena having any sort of magic."

31

Victory caught Mikelos' hand to draw him back down, and he didn't avoid her touch. "You hadn't seen her for a long time. Things may have changed." She cast a glance toward Asaron. "You've been pretty quiet."

"Because this is absurd." Asaron's incinerating glare targeted Syri. "Vampires can't do magic."

"Never say never." Syri waved her fingers. "We're surrounded by it now. You're old enough. Give it a shot."

"What does age have to do with it?" Victory asked.

"Far as I can tell, it's easier to access or something. But seriously. This is the perfect time. Go for it."

Asaron sat still as a statue. "Go for what? What parlor trick do you expect me to be able to perform?"

"In the real world, you'd be able to manipulate your internal energy to drain a person's life essence along with their blood." Syri hesitated. "Something like that."

"You volunteering yourself for a snack?"

"No, of course not." This time, Syri waved her arms with purpose, encompassing the surrounding rocks. "This isn't the real world, so you can do a hell of a lot more. Try to move one of the rocks."

Victory studied the boulders. Each must weigh multiple tons. "We couldn't manage that with our bare hands, much less with our minds."

Syri selected a stone the size of a fingernail from the ground. She tossed it to Asaron, who plucked it out of the air. "Try that."

Asaron cradled the stone in one large palm. "You're kidding."

She propped her elbows on her knees, as if ready for a show. "Move the rock, old man."

He growled.

"We're in an environment of pure magic. You're talking to a dead person. Suspend your disbelief and—make it move."

Syri's words of encouragement faded around them. But Asaron raised his palm higher, bringing it eye-level.

Victory's fingers dug into her knee, and she forced herself to relax. Next to her, Mikelos held his breath.

Nothing—

Did it move?

No, Asaron's hand trembled with the force of his will. The rest of his body stilled, coiled with tension.

Everything moved, then. The ground beneath them shuddered, and a rumble echoed across the sky.

Syri bolted to her feet. "Shit! They shouldn't have noticed that."

"Who?" Victory scrambled up as well. "What's going on?"

Asaron dropped his rock. One of his knives appeared in his hand, a more familiar sort of magic. The four of them circled, facing outward, but the source of the noise beyond the towering rocks remained unseen. Asaron called over his shoulder, "Any help would be good, kid."

"It's the shadows. They sensed your magic."

"I didn't do magic!"

As a screaming unseen mass approached, Victory wanted to shove Mikelos behind her. But from the noise that grated against her enhanced hearing, they'd need all hands against what was coming. "Not helpful, Syri." She had to pitch her voice above the noise.

"Don't worry. We do have weapons!"

Victory turned away from the oncoming storm at the glee in Syri's voice. She did a double-take at the knives in Syri's hands, twin silver blades the length of her forearms.

The set of knives Toria kept on the wall of her apartment, just like she kept Syri's leather jacket wrapped in a trunk.

More importantly, the twin blades Syri could not have had hidden in her form-fitting clothing. "How did you do that?"

Syri twisted her wrists, and the knives glinted in the flat light. "We're surrounded by magic. We can do whatever the fuck we want."

"You mean Asaron can," Mikelos said.

"I said I didn't do any magic!"

"Not important right now, old man!" Syri held out her knives. They vanished, then reappeared again. "Nothing here is real. Like I said, suspend your disbelief." She paused. "But you can still die. Don't forget that bit."

This was ridiculous. But the ominous sounds grew louder and louder, so Victory held her hands in front of her. Should she emulate how she'd seen her daughter and foster son do magic? Close her eyes. Wave her hands around to manipulate unseen magical energy. But if she couldn't sense the energy, that would do no good.

What did she want? Her sword. Her trusted, beloved bastard sword, which had been by her side for years. It had never failed her. Not like reality seemed to have.

So, she kept her hands steady and instead, *wished*. Wished against all hope that her sword would join her in this battle against an unseen, unimaginable foe.

In the space between one moment and the next, it appeared. The worn leather hilt, contoured over the years to fit her fingers better than any glove. The brushed-metal cross guard. Forty inches long from tip to pommel. Like it had always been there. Victory forced her hands to curl around the sword rather than drop it in shock. "What the—?"

Asaron's shout of glee distracted her from her own shock. He brandished his own basket hilt Schiavona, as familiar to Victory as her own blade. Would Mikelos have bothered to summon a blade of his own? He had trained in the basics of combat, which he used most effectively in drunken brawls.

"You're kidding me." Asaron's words echoed Victory's own confusion.

Mikelos supported a strap attached to what appeared to be a semi-automatic rifle—but none Victory had ever seen before. The stock was familiar, a British model. The barrel resembled one of the Aragonian weapons she'd used in the short war with Castille before the Romans absorbed both countries. Like a hybrid weapon created by someone who knew nothing about them other than vague memories of weaponry used in a war decades past. Which, she supposed, described Mikelos. "I know how to shoot," he said, defensiveness coloring his words.

True. He wasn't a half-bad shot, either. "Is that thing even going to work?" Victory asked. Mikelos might blow his own arms off, or worse, if it jammed and exploded in his face.

"Guess we'll find out!" Nervousness tinged Mikelos' bravado.

She followed his cue. Releasing the hilt of her sword, she held out her free hand. Another weapon appeared out of nothing in her palm. She tucked the small pistol into the waistband of her jeans, at the small of her back. Not the way she'd ever carry a weapon in normal circumstances, but these were far from normal circumstances. Victory elbowed Syri. "It's getting louder, but where are they?"

"This place doesn't make sense." Syri raised her knives higher. "Sound sometimes travels faster, or slower, than it should. But trust me, they're coming."

Victory hoped the adrenaline surging through her body didn't cause her to crash before the fight even commenced. They drew their circle tighter, each taking a field of view to cover the craggy forest. Behind her, rustling noises indicated that Mikelos' crazy idea had inspired Asaron. She shoved away the curiosity that dared her to turn and see what absurd weaponry her sire now carried.

There. At the base of a boulder in the distance. A tendril of shadow, the gray matching the boulder's bland hue. But Victory was a predator, and movement drew her attention the way a single drop of blood drew her nose. She hissed a warning to her companions and raised her sword.

The shadowy fingers wrapped around the boulder, with other tendrils appearing around more and more rocks.

Then, the figures came.

Not humans. No sentient being Victory knew. These were caricatures of a person on two legs, stumbling on unformed joints between the rocks. No detail distinguished the figures' hands and the weaponry they held. But there was no mistaking the swords, knives, clubs, and various other blades or bashing weapons they carried.

Three of them. Five. Nine.

The first wave reached Victory before she counted higher, and Mikelos' semi-automatic roared. She screamed her own aggression and crossed blades with the lead figure. The shadows Mikelos shot blew apart, and she had no more attention to spare for her daywalker.

She always expected the worst when joining battle with a new enemy. They might be better than her. Quicker, stronger, more experienced. But this shadowy figure? None of those things.

The strength behind the first blow of her bastard sword obliterated the magical weapon the shadow creature held. The blades hit with a sharp crack, then the force of her follow-through cut through the air left behind. Her second blow severed one of its arms, like cutting through dense foam or a thick head of beer. The arm dissipated into nothingness, along with the sword. The shadow kept coming, and in three more hacks, it lost all cohesion and evaporated.

She dodged behind Mikelos, avoiding his area of fire, to join with another shadow creeping for his open side. This one, wielding a club resembling a deformed frying pan, wasted no effort on defense. It ran straight up her blade and swung its weapon toward Victory. She released one hand from her sword hilt to block with her forearm. But where striking the shadows with her sword felt like nothing, getting struck in return was being punched by a boulder.

She hissed in pain as the blow glanced off her arm, ripping a gouge through her skin and spraying thick, black blood across the nearest rocky surface. When the shadow swung again, she caught the weapon in her hand and wrestled the blow away. Her fingers sank into the shadow where she gripped with claw-like fingers, like clutching at sponge cake. But the weapon clanked against the nearest towering rock where she pushed it to the side, and even in the midst of battle, Victory remembered one of her daughter's explanations about magic.

It was all about intention.

With a burst of inspiration, she channeled her aggression into the blade of the sword she'd conjured, coating its blade with fury. Her intention made reality, the blade burst into flames. The impaled shadow reared in silent shock, but its attempt to writhe away from the fire at its core spread the heat faster. Then, the shadow faded into nothing.

Victory hefted her flaming blade and lunged at the nearest shadow trying to sneak up on Syri. Syri cackled in glee as the impossible blade shattered yet another shadow, and in the midst of her own fight, her twin blades lit with bright blue flames of their own.

Back to back with Syri, they fought off more shadows with their magic weapons. Mikelos' rate of fire slowed on occasion, but never stopped. He never took the time to reload. Perks of a magical firearm.

But the waves of shadow creatures showed no sign of stopping, and flesh and blood creatures wielded this magical weaponry. Or whatever Syri was. One by one, Victory collected more minor injuries. A cut on her forearm. A mighty blow that cracked at least one rib. A slice to her forehead that dripped no blood to blind her, signaling her nearness to the last of her energy reserves.

She held her sword high as the next shadow creature advanced.

Minutes seemed stretched into hours during the brutality of battle. They'd backed into the lee between two large crags, which helped Victory and Asaron protect Syri and Mikelos but also forced them to coordinate their actions to stay out of each other's way. Syri had abandoned her knives for the pistol Victory had summoned, and Victory's ears rang with the continuous gunshots Syri and Mikelos aimed behind them.

She spun toward the next attacker, noting her reduced speed with the part of her brain not focused on combat. But this was no half-formed shadow. An elven man wearing gray-hued, modern-day urban assault attire half-saluted her with an arrow, then nocked it to his longbow and shot past Victory's shoulder.

"Looks like we arrived in time, Syrisinia." His bass voice reverberated in the small space.

"About damned time," Syri said, cocking the pistol that never needed reloading. "Get caught in the badlands?"

"No. They moved again last week." The newcomer loosed two more shots in quick succession.

Victory never saw where they hit as she finished off a malformed shadow with too many joints and not enough limbs. "Hi, who are you?"

"My apologies. Brawleyn, at your service. We're going to get you out of here."

That was the best news Victory had heard since they'd appeared in this crazy place. Between Brawleyn and Mikelos, who'd maintained a steady rate of fire, Victory found a moment to just be. The shadows also seemed to retreat—or at least didn't send any of their fellows to be slaughtered for the moment.

A cluster of shadows blew apart in a silent explosion, and three more figures in body armor dashed across the empty space. Syri flung out her arm before Mikelos fired on them. "They're with Brawleyn."

A breeze stirred the tendrils of hair that had escaped Victory's braid in the melee. Since no air flowed in this weird plane of rocks and shadows, she craned her neck to see behind her.

A shimmering sphere of light spun itself up from nothing. Rainbow hues reflected on its surface, colorful brightness in this pale world. With a rate of exponential expansion, it soon grew from the size of Victory's palm to large enough to encompass a person.

"What is it?" Asaron's voice was rough, to match a body littered with injuries. Blood the color of tar soaked his pant leg, and the remnants of his shirt encircled his one forearm. Slashed flesh and mottled bruising decorated his chest.

Mikelos slung his hodgepodge weapon over his shoulder. "Back to Limani?"

"That's the plan." Brawleyn loosed another arrow. "Is it ready yet?"

Syri stared at the sphere. "I think so."

"You think so?" Asaron bared his teeth in frustration. "I'm not letting that thing touch me."

"You don't have a choice." Brawleyn lowered his bow and jabbed one finger toward the sphere. "I didn't risk the lives of my people to argue. Go now."

Fear added to the pain of Victory's numerous injuries. "But you said—"

Mikelos gasped as Brawleyn's three fighters approached, and a strong hand gripped Victory's wrist. "You have to go, Mum."

Victory ripped her hand away and forced herself to face the owner of the voice. The voice she'd said goodbye to in Nacostina several decades and mere days ago. "Zvi?"

Jarimis, her vampire progeny, pushed her toward the spinning sphere. Its rainbow shimmers reflected in his dark eyes. "*Go.*"

He shoved her again, and it seemed like gravity pulled her toward the sphere. Unlike when she'd traveled through time, or when the artifact brought them to this strange place, this transition was painless, like nothing at all.

One moment, she hid among the rocky crags of their defensive position. Now, she stood in a cobblestoned alleyway, lit by a distant street lamp.

Mikelos appeared next to her, then Asaron. Neither of them held weapons, and the flaming sword she'd clutched had not traveled with her. But her injuries had, and that awareness caused the pain in her arms and torso to flare to life again.

"Where the hell are we?" Asaron inhaled, scenting the air around them. "This isn't Limani. Damn it."

Victory echoed his action. Even in the center of town, Limani never smelled this "urban." The press of too many people in an enclosed space. Of a city that rivaled Asaron in age, whereas even Victory predated Limani's founding.

The scents of fresh bread, seared meat, and spiced vegetables overlaid the inherent smell of wherever they'd ended up. They had arrived near a kitchen.

Mikelos approached the entrance of the alleyway when a doorway swung open nearby, revealing a man dressed in chef's whites.

He paused midway through the act of lighting a cigarette, peering at Victory and Asaron's bedraggled states. At least the darkness hid the blood.

"We don't put out the leftover food until closing. Two more hours." He lounged in the doorway as light and cooking sounds spilled out, signs of a restaurant during evening rush.

"Sir, can I ask where we are?" The question sounded ridiculous even as Victory asked it.

The chef scowled. "Behind Café Paix. Off the Boulevard Capucines."

"Parisii." Mikelos' voice carried into the alleyway, a mingle of wonder and horror. "We're not in Limani. We're in Parisii."

Ignoring the chef, Victory joined Mikelos where the ancient cobbles met the smooth pavement of the sidewalk. She followed the line of Mikelos' arm, where he pointed above the rooftops.

The Tour Exposition Universelle towered over this section of the city, the fanciful metal tower built to commemorate the hundredth anniversary of one of the multiple Roman takeovers of the city.

Parisii. On the Europan continent.

Across an entire ocean from Limani.

PARISII

The three of them stared into the street, lined with tall buildings of residences above shops and cafés and crowded with parked cars. Café Paix hosted outdoor tables filled with diners enjoying a late dinner, now that the air had cooled after sunset. Though many Parisii residents fled the city during the warmer months for vacations along the coast of the Mare Nostrum, not everyone could afford to leave their work and homes.

Asaron growled low in his throat. "How did we get here, instead of Limani?"

"Oh gods." Mikelos covered his face with his hands and groaned. "It's my fault."

"How could this be your fault?" Victory asked. Her biggest fear was *when* in Parisii they were, but so far nothing seemed to indicate they were outside their contemporary time. She hesitated to voice her concern and panic the men without reason.

"When we were walking, before we found Syri. Or Syri found us, whichever. I got hungry. Started thinking about food, obviously. And my brain stuck on macarons, and I remembered the best macarons I'd ever had, obviously from Parisii." Mikelos trailed off. "And I suppose Parisii never left my mind, and here we are."

Asaron seemed close to beating his skull against the alley's brick wall. "Indeed."

A couple strolling arm-in-arm approached, and Victory tugged Mikelos back. Asaron froze in the shadows, and the women passed without noticing them.

Once the women had entered the restaurant, Asaron spoke again. "No supplies, no Roman currency, no real weaponry. We won't make it halfway down the block without someone calling the police on us, considering the way Victory and I look."

Mikelos studied their torn and bloodstained clothing, then gestured to himself. "But I look fine."

True. A small splatter of blood, from Victory or perhaps Syri, didn't stand out much against the dark red of his worn T-shirt. He'd be presentable enough in public. And they had an option, albeit one that grated on Victory.

"We have to make it to either the Master of the City or the Mercenary Guildhall." Asaron shoved his hands in his pockets, hunching his shoulders forward. He held himself so tense that his injuries must bother him more than he showed. "But Mikelos can't show up at either without us."

Mikelos coughed, a delicate dissent. "Not true. We have a third option."

And there it was. The unavoidable.

Asaron steamrolled on, his frustration and pain presenting in unusual verbosity. "And when was the last time you were in Parisii?"

Victory clenched a fist but released it when a new wave of pain flowed from her forearm. Her daywalker would have more patience for the needed explanation. "We haven't been to Parisii. We just have… an unexpected resource."

Mikelos saved her from further explanation. "One of the vampires I bonded to before Victory didn't disappear when I thought she did. She died a few years ago, but it turned out most of her local estate was held in trust for the intended recipient. I'm the sole inheritor. She knew I was still alive, because she'd—" Mikelos paused. "She'd been watching our family. She met Toria and Kane when they first came to Parisii."

Asaron laughed, devoid of humor. "But the kids met Natalia Della Zanna. Are you trying to tell me your original bond was with the Dowager of Parisii? You're full of surprises today."

"But it saves us a lot of trouble now. I'll run into that restaurant and make a telephone call. David still runs the house. He'll come get us, and we'll have a place to stay and access to funds and other supplies." Without waiting for their assent, Mikelos darted around the corner and onto the sidewalk. He held open the restaurant door for a party to exit, and disappeared inside.

Instinct screamed at Victory to follow her daywalker into unknown territory, but she planted her feet next to Asaron. "This is so weird."

"Now you think something about all of this is weird?" Her sire snorted. "Did you know about this?"

"Mikelos told me when he received all the paperwork. I wasn't about to interfere with anything that came from Connor, even if the fucking Dowager was involved."

The Dowager of Parisii had earned her title by refusing to claim the mantle of Master but still maintaining immense power over the supernatural population of the city. Even becoming involved with the elves who'd set the world spell.

Connections and extrapolations spun through Victory's mind. "Magic." At Asaron's double-take, she continued, "Serena must have had this magic Syri seems to think you have. This vampire magic that allowed her to bring Kane back to life."

They dropped into silence when a cluster of teenagers passed the alleyway, joking about cutting curfew. When the kids departed, Asaron said, "I hate everything about this. Magic. Vampires having power over death itself. It's not natural."

"I know." Victory rested against his shoulder.

Mikelos returned, rounding the corner and joining them in holding up the wall. "Ride will be here in a few."

The three of them lapsed into silence. A million questions raced through Victory's mind, still riding a combat-high, but at the moment, none seemed important. She stood between two of her most beloved people in the world, and she savored it in the midst of the surrounding madness.

The kitchen door swung open again, revealing two servers on break. They propped open the door while they smoked, and the smell of roast beef poured toward the street.

Mikelos pressed his hands to his stomach. "Wow, I am starving."

Asaron grunted in return, the closest Victory's sire would get to admitting his own hunger.

But after all these years, Mikelos knew the other vampire almost as well as he did Victory. "Don't worry," he said. "Everything has been arranged. Just a few more minutes."

As Mikelos promised, a black luxury town-car pulled to a stop in front of the alley not more than ten minutes later. The driver emerged and opened the trunk, where he withdrew a small bundle and two unmarked glass bottles. He peered into the darkness. "Mr. Connor?"

The man wore a plain suit featuring a tie knotted in haste, but the lines of the fabric hid no shoulder holster or other weaponry Victory discerned. After Victory's sign of approval, Mikelos exited the alleyway and approached the man.

Awkwardness followed. Finally, Mikelos took the bottles and they exchanged pleasantries. She overheard their low conversation even over the bustle of the diners. "Nice to finally meet you in person, David."

"And you, sir. Your call was unexpected." David followed Mikelos into the alley. He didn't flinch at the two vampires standing in the darkness and instead offered the cloth bundle to Asaron. "I believe this is for you, sir. I apologize if the shirt is tight in the shoulders."

Asaron accepted the bundle, which fell unfolded in his hands. "Thank you." With the slightest grunt of pain, he removed his tattered, blood-blackened shirt and pulled on the replacement. It did strain at the width of Asaron's bulk, but no more than any shirt designed to show off a man's physique might.

Once Asaron dressed, Mikelos passed over the two bottles. Victory inspected the chilled glass. Dark, viscous liquid shifted within the opaque green glass in the dim light. Though the bottle style differed from the type Toria preferred, they seemed like the same sort her daughter enchanted for her mother and grandfather to maintain an emergency blood supply. "May I ask where these came from?"

David's neck bobbed in a nervous swallow, but Mikelos rescued him. "David maintained Serena's household in Parisii, and I asked him to stay on. He never canceled the regular exchange for her emergency stock."

Because even magic bottles couldn't maintain blood indefinitely. Satisfied Parisii's vampire population had a professional system in place that Serena would have participated in, Victory popped the cap.

No matter how high the quality of blood when bottled, something about the preservation sucked all life out of the liquid. It might still provide the necessary nutrients and keep her going for a few more days, but it paled in comparison to the fresh blood acquired from her usual supply, coordinated with Limani's hospital.

It was a mere shadow of blood straight from the source, but her daywalker's blood was a rare treat.

This would do for now. She drained the bottle in one shot. By the time she finished, Asaron had already recapped his bottle and returned it to David with his thanks. Already, her muscles relaxed, and the injury on her arm flared with the heat of accelerated healing. "It's all a little weird, but I can't complain."

"Indeed," Asaron said. "Your foresight may have saved us much trouble."

Mikelos gestured toward the waiting town-car. "Shall we?"

David darted forward to open the car's rear door for Mikelos and Victory to slide in, while Asaron claimed the front seat. Victory rubbed her hands on the smooth leather seats.

David must have made some sort of expression when he climbed into the driver's seat, and Victory's sire laughed. "Not about to wait for a door to open when I can open it myself."

"Sorry, David," Mikelos said. "We're not going to be what you're used to."

"I'm sure I will have no problem adjusting, sir." David pulled away from the curb, and the town-car moved through the Parisii streets. "Barring any unseen accidents or road delays, we will arrive in approximately five minutes."

Mikelos thanked him, then settled into his seat and grasped Victory's hand again. He tapped her hand three times with his thumb, a silent question. *Everything okay?*

She tapped back once. *Yes.* They'd talk more at their destination, but for now she turned her attention to the city outside the town-car's windows. She had not traveled to Parisii in decades, and familiar styles of buildings on the city blocks fronted by lines of parked modern town-cars disconcerted her, when she expected the larger, gas-guzzling vehicles of her memory. She'd had a similar experience when visiting Roma a few years ago, reminding her that while Limani had aged around her the rest of the world had done the same whether she witnessed it or not.

Though the neighborhood they'd arrived in was far from a slum, the buildings around the town-car grew grander, switching from townhouses and apartments above commercial spaces to single-residence homes surrounded by fenced-off gardens. David pulled into the circular drive of one such house, stopping in front of the entrance. The pale blue double doors shimmered in the porch lights.

They followed David out of the town-car. He pushed open the front door and waved them in. He winked at Victory when she passed, and a small portion of the tension she carried eased from her shoulders. Evidence of the manservant's personality beneath his professional demeanor made her a lot more comfortable in the home of Mikelos' former vampire.

The foyer they stepped into might have been a near-cousin to Victory's own manor house—the original owners had built her home to mimic the Parisiian style. Even the blackout curtains that could be lowered to protect the circular stained-glass window over the entrance seemed familiar. But where Victory's house carried the warmth of a lived-in home, even when only she and Mikelos were in residence, this house smelled of cleaning supplies and sterility.

They had no coats for David to take, so he gestured for them to follow him upstairs. "I maintain this residence alone, but I never lost the habit of keeping two of the suites habitable at all times, Mr. Connor. I live in an apartment on the third floor and keep to that space."

"Call me Mikelos, please." They clustered in the hall at the top of the stairs. "I might be the technical owner, but I'm not the master of this house."

David flushed. "The first suite is here, where I you and Master, er, Victory will be comfortable." He pointed to another door along the hallway. "The second set of rooms is right there for you, sir." He directed this last bit toward Asaron.

"Thank you." Mikelos cracked open the door. "We'll get washed up and meet downstairs to figure out where we go from here."

"Where we go from here is a meeting with Parisii's Master of the City," Victory said, and Asaron hummed his agreement. "We would value your input, David."

If the request surprised the manservant, he masked the emotion well. "I will endeavor to be of service. May I prepare something to eat for you, sir?" He directed the question to Mikelos.

"That would be amazing. Whatever you have on hand is fine." As if summoned by the idea of food, Mikelos' stomach rumbled loud enough for even human hearing.

"I shall bring a tray to the sitting room at the bottom of the stairs," David said. Instead of going downstairs, he followed the hallway toward the rear of the house, presumably toward a servant staircase from which he accessed his own living space. If he'd closed up the main portions of the house, any foodstuffs on hand would be in his own rooms.

Asaron disappeared into his own suite, and she followed Mikelos into the one designated for their use. A space once again almost lifted from her own home, filled with antique furniture. Even the mismatched chair and writing desk between the curtained windows was a familiar sort of idiosyncrasy. Mikelos bee-lined toward a chaise lounge in the corner of the room but drew to a halt a foot away. "I'm filthy."

Victory found the energy to laugh even through her exhaustion. "We could split the shower?" She spied a welcome beacon of shining tile through a doorway in the far corner of the elegant room. The enormous four-poster bed, topped with a luxurious quilt, also called her name, but where a layer of gray grime covered Mikelos, she had both grime and her own dried blood.

Mikelos dipped his face to hers for a kiss. "Brilliant, as always."

Their water conservation effort had more to do with saving time than any desire to express passion. Though they both exchanged more kisses and soft touches in the modern shower stall large enough for two, Mikelos' willingness to scrub Victory's back was a higher priority. The emergency blood supplied by David in the alleyway had healed Victory's wounds, so they emerged from the bathroom clean and refreshed. Mikelos found terrycloth bathrobes and cotton pajama sets in the bathroom's linen closet, which Victory donned with a groan of pleasure. She hadn't fancied a return to clothing stiff with dirt and blood.

They found Asaron in the front sitting room David had directed them to, wearing a robe over pajama bottoms. The pale skin of his bare feet contrasted with the plush burgundies and browns of the rug, and he perched on the edge of an ornate cream sofa. He peeked at the covered food arranged on the wooden coffee table. The aroma of savory pastries stuffed with beef and vegetables swirled through the room.

Mikelos dropped onto the sofa next to Asaron and batted the vampire's hand away from the tray. "Get your own dinner." He tugged the tray closer and skipped the utensils in favor of draping a cloth napkin over his lap and scooping up the pastry with his hands to tear into the flaky crust.

Asaron raised his hands in innocence. "Just checking."

Victory inspected the curio cabinet displaying a collection of blue and white Wanli plates. "Why would anything be wrong with it?"

"We don't know where we are. We don't know how we arrived here. We need to be on our guard."

Mikelos swallowed and nudged Asaron with his elbow. "Stop being paranoid. We're in Parisii. Magic transported us here. It's strange and complicated, but it's the truth."

"And you conveniently own a house here?"

Though she'd been about to sniff the amber liquid in a crystal decanter, Victory returned the stopper and whirled on Asaron. "You don't get to be a jerk about this." Asaron had not lived so long without absorbing all possible information like a sponge, and it must grate on her sire that, through Victory, he had no knowledge about this part of Mikelos' life. But Victory had never subscribed to the idea that her daywalker was anything more or less than his own man. They were partners first and foremost.

To be honest, she preferred to know little about Mikelos' life before her. This was the sort of lifestyle he'd been accustomed to before he moved to Limani, and while they lived well, it didn't hold a candle to the luxury he'd once treated as his due. She checked the rest of the decanters and found two glasses in the cupboard beneath.

Except Mikelos had begun life on the streets, before Connor heard his singing voice and snatched him up. After Connor's death, he'd left his life in Europa and moved to Limani of his own free will, where he'd rented a small set of rooms and seemed determined to live a life opposite from the glitz and glamour afforded to a famous musician. Victory shoved a snifter of cognac at Asaron and settled in a nearby armchair with her own glass of port.

Asaron toasted her. "What could I have to be jealous of? I'm merely commenting on the potential issues."

"You'd prefer we be stuck on the streets of Parisii with nothing at all?" When Asaron didn't respond, Victory sipped her port. Ruby instead of tawny, and a bit too strong for her taste. "Relax."

Footsteps came down the hallway and a knuckle rapped the door frame at the sitting room entrance. David lurked in the doorway, clutching a pen and notepad in his hands. "Am I interrupting?"

Mikelos wiped his hands and waved him in. "No, please join us."

The manservant parked himself next to the empty armchair, then sat when Mikelos pointed to it. The man's nervousness did not surprise Victory. At the least, she and Asaron had to be different from the sort of vampires he might be used to, such as his former employer. She hoped it wasn't too much of a shock to his system. "David, what day is it?"

"Very early morning on Thursday the fifth, ma'am."

A weight lifted from Victory's shoulders, and Mikelos let his head fall back on the couch. She thanked David, and turned to Mikelos and Asaron. "We've been gone for one day, essentially. We have to let the kids know we're okay."

David lifted the pad and pen. "I thought you might want to do that. I'm happy to record a telegram message for Masters Connor and Nalamas and get it to the office when it opens."

Victory stiffened, before she remembered David knew those names because the kids had stayed at this house the first time they visited Parisii. But that was the past, and she wasn't keen on dwelling on how Mikelos' former vampire had stalked her family for years, so she accepted the notepad from David with a thank you. What to tell them that wouldn't sound insane? Except after the last few weeks—months, in Toria's case—nothing seemed so crazy anymore. With a steady hand, she jotted a short message that shouldn't raise too many unnecessary eyebrows on its way through the lines to Limani.

Safe in Parisii with M and A. Stop. More research into artifact needed. Stop. Do not destroy. Stop. Much love. Stop.

After presenting it to Mikelos and Asaron and receiving their approval, she handed the message to David. He ripped the top page from the notepad and tucked it inside his suit jacket. "There, one thing taken care of. What's next?"

"Clothing. Weapons. Meeting with Parisii's Master." Asaron paused and plucked at his pajama pants. "Not necessarily in that order."

"Clothing can be arranged, sir," David said. He seemed unsurprised by any of Asaron's requests. "Unfortunately, weaponry might be more difficult for me to acquire. You might perhaps have better resources in that regard."

"I do," Asaron said.

Victory hid amusement behind her hand. While most of his work since she'd adopted Toria had been limited to the Roman colonies of the New Continent, he'd ranged farther afield since Toria and Kane launched their own mercenary careers. They'd even worked a few jobs together. How Asaron seemed to find work in the Roman territories of Europa more often these days, especially when the kids were in Britannia, was no coincidence. It did not surprise her in the slightest that he had quickly found the connections a merc needed in the field, and that he and David would have different resources in this city.

"Well, we have forty-eight hours from our time of arrival to present ourselves to the Master of the City." Mikelos paused. "It occurs to me that I have no idea who the current Master is."

"Madam Stefania, sir," David said.

"Stefania." Victory perused her memory. "No last name?"

"No, ma'am."

Victory's heart sank. Yet another wrinkle in their plans. "Which one? The former senator, or the poet from Chora?" She crossed mental fingers that he referred to the poet, though she doubted anything could ever drag Stefania away from her dedication to her art.

"The former senator," Asaron said. "She passed her seat to her progeny and moved here about sixty years ago."

Trust Asaron to be aware of such details, despite his frequent protests that he had no time for Roman drama. "Damn." Victory downed her final sip of port. "Neither of them like me, but the senator likes me even less." She set the empty glass on the floor next to her armchair and slouched.

"I wasn't aware you two even knew each other," Asaron said.

"It was a long time ago. Maybe she doesn't remember me."

"Victory." Mikelos braced his elbows on his knees. "What did you do?"

"I did nothing." She'd prefer to leave it at that, but the matching disbelief on Mikelos and Asaron's faces, two men who never seemed to agree on anything, spurred her to explain. "She thinks I manipulated a duchess I was contracted to bodyguard in Rus into offering an inferior trade deal to the Senate."

"Well, did you?" Mikelos asked.

"Of course not. I used my information sources to verify that the Senate placed a higher value on access to the duchess' mineral rights than they had let on," Victory said. "Galina figured out the rest for herself."

"How much could she hate you now, if this was a long time ago?"

David made a sort of strangled noise, choking on his laughter. "I'm sorry, pardon the interruption."

"No, please do share," Victory said, amused. "Because I'm sure it's exactly what I was going to say."

"Well—" He turned to Mikelos. "—Have you met vampires?"

Asaron's laughter boomed through the room, and he slapped his knee. "From the mouths of babes."

Victory followed suit when Asaron stood and stretched. "It's late. Let's get some rest and tackle our problems tonight." She pulled Mikelos to his feet. They thanked David again, and he stayed to collect Mikelos' tray while they climbed the stairs to their suites.

Tangled together in the privacy of their bed, Victory tucked her face against Mikelos' shoulder. "I never thought I'd be back in this city. Limani is my responsibility."

Mikelos pressed a kiss to her temple. "We'll make it home soon. Somehow."

Mikelos woke Victory at sundown. He and David had spent the late afternoon shopping for replacement clothing, including garb suitable to wear for a meeting with Parisii's Master of the City, and David had even cleaned her boots. After a quick shower, Victory wandered downstairs in fresh, brand-new clothes. She found Asaron lurking in the formal dining room, also clad in new jeans and a better-fitting shirt. "What are you looking at?"

Asaron backed away from a large portrait, featuring a statuesque blonde. "I did meet her once, on a job. I recall that she wasn't polite to me. I have a hard time imagining a woman so close to Mikelos trying to kill the kids."

Victory joined him in front of the oil painting. The subject's pose was demure, with hands crossed on a lap draped with the velvet of her skirt. But the way she faced the viewer, with chin lifted high and upswept blond curls, exuded confidence and power. The broach at her lace collar depicted a stringed instrument, but it seemed odd to Victory, used to the silhouette of Mikelos' violins. Because it wasn't a violin—it was a cello.

Victory turned in place. On the opposite side of the room hung another portrait. The small details of the suit the man wore matched the time period of the woman's dress, though the high collar that brushed his chin did not flatter. Hazel eyes stared above chiseled cheekbones, and his hands seemed to caress the bow he held in his lap. "I never met Serena. But I saw Connor, once. On stage with Mikelos."

Steps approached, and Mikelos slouched against the entrance to the dining room, hands stuffed in his pockets. "I'm glad Connor wasn't around to see whatever Serena became. I'm glad I wasn't, either." He studied Serena's portrait, ignoring the one of Connor. "I always knew she wasn't a very good person, but she was good to us. Connor adored her."

"The emotions get complicated." Victory drew Asaron away from Serena's portrait before he did something rash, like vandalize an innocent painting. "I could be the evilest creature on the face of the planet, and you'd still love me because you're my sire."

"I'd stop you from being evil," Asaron said. "But you're right. I'd still love you. Not sure I could forgive her, though."

Mikelos led them out of the dining room toward the front of the house. "You don't have to. I'm not sure I will, either. But she's dead anyway, so it doesn't matter."

According to Toria and Archer's description of events, Serena had killed Kane in the Catacombs of Parisii when the kids stormed the place to rescue Syri and stop her sacrifice to feed the world spell. Syri had died in the crossfire anyway, her body never recovered. In a final moment of something—compassion, maybe—for the adopted daughter of her former daywalker, Serena traded her own life for Kane's, in a bit of magic Victory had never heard of and never expected to see again.

Except if the Syri in the shadow plane was to be believed, vampiric magic was real.

In the parlor, Victory followed her nose to the coffee service and poured herself a drink, chasing the black liquid with a healthy dose of cream until it swirled tan. Asaron and Mikelos helped themselves, and the three found seats. "I heard you two speaking while I was in the shower, but I didn't listen. Care to fill me in?" Victory asked.

"We were discussing potential routes to make it home after we meet with Stefania tomorrow night," Asaron said.

Victory set her cup down so hard the coffee almost sloshed out. "Is that the best idea?"

"How is going home not the best idea?" Mikelos lifted his hands in dismay.

"The shadows Asaron and I have been seeing are a direct result of the world spell," Victory said. "Which we know was maintained here, by the elves of Parisii, with the help of the vampires. We need to figure out what's going on."

"You can't storm into a meeting with Stefania and accuse her of murdering baby elves," Asaron said. "She likely already hates that you're here, hates that she has to meet you as an equal. You sling that at her, and I can't guarantee your safety."

"You're not my protector, and I'm not an idiot. We can't return to Limani without finding out what we can here. When I came to you about the shadows, I never expected your response to be, well, 'We can't do anything about it so we might as well hide our heads in the sand.'" Victory's voice rose in pitch until Mikelos touched her shoulder in warning. "We're here. We have to take advantage of it."

Her sire might act the part of disaffected mercenary who couldn't be bothered with the bigger picture, but in the past, his mercenary role had included leading armies. She reached for him, and he accepted her hand without hesitation. He sat so still, staring past Victory to something unseen, that he might have turned to stone. With a movement too quick for her to register, his eyes bore into hers, the gray-green of his irises like being buried in soft moss. He held her gaze long enough to say, "I will always be your protector," then released her before she drowned in his power.

"Thank you," Victory said. His faith in her, his willingness to let her take the lead, was a precious gift. "We'll see how the meeting with Stefania goes first."

Mikelos, often silent through these tense exchanges between the two vampires in his life, expressed his opinion here with a mere nod. The three agreed.

Releasing her sire's hand, Victory settled in her seat. Time for a safer topic. "Do we have a lead on weapons?"

Asaron's entire face transformed, delight wiping away his previous consternation. "I made some calls. We have swords lined up through a friend of a friend. We have to swing by Parisii's Mercenary Guildhall."

"I'm sure that can be arranged," Mikelos said. "Want a late dinner after? Or to at least watch me eat a late dinner? Because I'm not visiting in Parisii and missing out on the food."

"That can be arranged," Victory said, "because I'm not visiting Parisii and missing out on the wine."

They stayed out later than David may have liked, first asking the manservant to recommend a restaurant and then convincing him to join them. The location he proposed shouldn't have let them in dressed in such casual attire, despite David's suit, but the name Mikelos Connor opened doors in Parisii even a hundred years later. Mikelos had his confit de canard and Victory had her wine.

But the next night, show time.

Mikelos dressed before Victory, leaving their suite while she finished styling her hair. Once she placed the final pin and set the style with a healthy dose of holding spray, she admired her reflection. The braids evoked an actual crown. She might not presume to control Limani beyond her seat on the city-state's governing council, but as the Master of the City, Limani was hers. Best not to let Stefania forget.

She unzipped the garment bag hanging on the outside of the wardrobe and considered the contents.

The outfit was not her. Hard to believe Mikelos had picked out something so outré.

At the same time, the blood-red halter top, with its delicate collar decorated with intricate bead work, was everything she needed to be tonight. Butter-soft black leather leggings hugged her hips. The delicate silk top draped from the collar to flow over her torso like a waterfall of blood, leaving the pale expanse of her shoulders and arms free. The asymmetrical hemline allowed her to belt a sword around her waist without ruining the drape of the garment.

There. She settled the worn belt over her hips and rested her hand on the hilt of the nondescript short sword, and something in her reflection shifted. Though nothing changed, the woman who stood before her transformed from a model displaying couture fashion to Victory. The vampire who'd had eight centuries to become comfortable in her own skin, no matter what she wore.

The outfit screamed for a pair of red stilettos, but even Mikelos wouldn't dare suggest such a thing. Instead, she slipped on black suede flats that cradled her feet like a second skin, reminding her of the slippers common to Qin highborn ladies. But where the silk of their shoes disintegrated at more than a gentle stroll, she'd be able to fight in these shoes if necessary.

Victory hoped for no combat tonight. She preferred boots, since her tactics leaned toward kicking opponents when using a blade shorter than her favored bastard sword.

After ducking into the bathroom to apply mascara and a touch of lipstick, a shade darker than her top, she headed downstairs. Her bustier forced her torso straighter, and by the way Mikelos' lips parted as he watched her approach from the bottom of the stairs, it did other things to her physique as well.

Asaron stood behind Mikelos in the foyer. "You clean up nice." Her sire cut a sharp figure in a black-on-black pinstripe suit over a crisp white shirt, left unbuttoned at the top. The pocket square at his chest was the same blood-red as her shirt.

Like Asaron's, Mikelos' suit appeared bespoke instead of tailored to fit. The coolness of his navy-blue undershirt contrasted with the vampire's. "You look amazing," he said as she descended the final steps. He pressed a kiss to the side of her bare neck.

"Hey, now," Asaron said. "Keep it clean for the kids."

Victory checked over her shoulder and waved at David, who waited farther down the hall. After the shared meal the night before, he'd relaxed in their presence. "Good evening, David. Thank you for finding the hair stuff I needed."

"You use it to good effect, ma'am." The way David inspected her reminded Victory of the way she once checked what a much younger Toria wore to school, to be sure she was presentable. "Something is missing, though. Wait here." He vanished into a room off the hall. She caught the unmistakable clatter of muffled tumblers when David unlocked a safe hidden somewhere in the room.

When he reappeared, the manservant presented Victory with a jewelry box crafted from wood polished to a high gloss. She accepted the offering and snapped it open to reveal a pair of teardrop rubies that dangled from thin links of white gold.

Mikelos touched a tentative finger to one of the rubies. "Everything is still there? I never thought to ask."

"I transferred it all to the safe, but yes, I kept it all," David said. "You never specified what you wanted done with her personal belongings, so I erred on the side of caution."

"Thank you. I'll make sure to go through everything while we're here." Mikelos lifted one of the earrings from the box.

Victory drew away before he raised it to her ear. "Really?" She wasn't keen on wearing her daywalker's dead vampire's jewels.

Asaron's voice rumbled behind her. "Perfect."

"It's another sign you're worthy of what you claim to be," Mikelos said. "I don't imagine Stefania will be without her own signs of wealth."

This time, when Mikelos lifted the earring, Victory held herself still. He didn't want her to wear the jewels in honor of Serena. He wanted her to present the best possible face to Stefania, and if the earrings helped, so be it. The ruby brushed her neck when she turned to allow Mikelos to place its twin.

David pulled a set of keys from his trousers and passed them to Mikelos. "The town-car is parked out front, and I left the directions on the dash. I'm still more than happy to drive."

"And I appreciate that, but we're not sure what we're up against tonight." Mikelos slipped two of his fingers through the keyring and offered his elbow to Victory. "Your carriage awaits, your ladyship."

The earrings brushed her neck in a way she wasn't used to, and the slippers offered no support compared to her customary boots, but Victory held herself high as Mikelos escorted her to the town-car. Asaron held open a rear door, and she didn't protest when he joined Mikelos in the front. He might be her sire, but tonight he was her honor guard. A proper Europan Master of the City traveled with a number of vampires who had sworn allegiance to her, whether progeny or not, and at least the same number or more of human aides, even if none were a daywalker. One of the many marks against Limani's Master was how she "controlled" only one other vampire. The Masters of the Roman colonies on the New Continent had gotten over it decades ago, usually once they met either Victory or Asaron, but she was well aware of her status in Europa.

Neither man spoke during the trip, and Victory used the quiet to her advantage as she attempted to shift to the mindset of a true rather than titular Master of the City. Victory's seat on Limani's governing body, voting on city bylaws regarding taxes and construction permits, put her on equal footing with the local werewolf and werepanther alphas, the dean of Jarimis University, the city's elven representative, and even worse: a whole passel of humans. Limani's political debates involved raucous laughter, queries to pass the coffee, and arguments about whose turn it was to host the next poker game. Limani's other city councilmembers didn't see her as a vampire—they saw her as Victory, the city's living history and recent staunch defender of its sovereignty.

Tonight, however, Victory needed to be a queen. To emulate the sense of superiority that elevated Roman vampires above the humans who shared their space. Though the vampires respected humanity and saw the benefit of a symbiotic relationship in everything from politics to economics to culture, age still brought them the experience of the long view humans would never be able to achieve.

Well, Victory had the long view. Time to play the part.

Mikelos turned a final corner and drove the town-car along a wide avenue that ended at the foot of a building dotted with spotlights, shining like a beacon among the duller apartment buildings. Parisii's opera house towered above them, decorated with multicolored columns and adorned with friezes and statuary that symbolized immense culture to all who passed by. It had been designed to evoke Grecian architecture from a time before the Roman Empire absorbed each of the city-states. The name was a misnomer, since it staged productions of all types, but the original title had stuck.

To Victory, it was gaudy and extravagant enough to match everything she remembered about Stefania.

Asaron peered out the front window. "Interesting place to hold an official audience." He glanced at Mikelos. "You've been here, I imagine."

"Yeah, once or twice." Sarcasm oozed from Mikelos as he pulled the town-car to the front of the building and rolled down the window. A human man peered inside the vehicle. "I'm Mikelos Connor. We have an appointment to see Madame Stefania, Parisii's Master of the City."

The guard checked his clipboard. "Yes, you're expected. Your appointment is in twenty minutes." He pointed to the side, where men in black pants and plain white shirts chatted around a podium. "You can valet your vehicle there."

Mikelos pulled toward the valets, exiting the town-car and conversing with them in low tones. Victory forced herself to stay seated until Asaron opened her door for her, then allowed him to help her out. She arranged the way the sword fell at her hip, setting her stance and drawing her shoulders back. Asaron had decided against a sword of his own for the meeting, but he'd acquired more knives to secret away within his fashionable suit.

A human woman in sensible heels descended the opera house steps toward them. Severe braids gathered the woman's graying hair tight against her scalp, but her teeth flashed against her dark skin in the light of the spotlights. "Master Victory? Master Stefania has set your appointment for ten o'clock. If you'll follow me, I'll show you to where you can wait with your staff."

Mikelos stepped forward, the public face of Victory's entourage, and thanked her. As the woman escorted the group through a back hall, Asaron gestured to a particular poster out of the many framed historical adverts lining the walls. It featured Mikelos and Connor in stark black and white. The camera caught both men with fierce stares, clutching their instruments in a staged pose that bore no resemblance to how the violin or cello were played. Victory did not acknowledge Asaron's gesture. She'd already spent too much mental energy on Serena. She couldn't afford to be distracted by Connor as well.

Their guide escorted them to a vacant green room, an interior space within the opera house with no windows. Though the floral wallpaper was a few decades out of style, the furniture had been updated within the past few years. Victory perched on the stool in front of a mirrored vanity while their guide pointed out the small refrigerator tucked into a cupboard if they needed refreshments and the controls for raising the volume on the screen in the corner showing a view of the main stage. Mikelos sank into the plush cushions of the couch, while Asaron prowled the room.

The guide hovered in the doorway. "Will you require anything else until Master Stefania is ready for you?"

Victory preferred to wait in this out-of-the-way room without a babysitter. "That will be all, thank you."

The guide exited, pulling the door closed. Mikelos' attention was lost to the screen, where he tracked the ghost-like dancers who cavorted across a silent stage. Asaron checked inside the refrigerator but seemed to find the contents lacking. He closed it again without offering anyone else a beverage. He parked in front of an empty spot of wall, as if unwilling to relax in an environment over which he had no control.

Victory echoed his discomfort, hence her seat on this stiff wooden stool instead of her natural inclination to curl on the couch next to Mikelos. Best not to wrinkle her top, anyway.

Mikelos studied the dancers, but before Victory offered to turn the volume up, he dragged himself away from the screen. "We won't be seeing Stefania at ten. This ballet is running a few minutes late. Maybe an intermission ran long. With the bows and applause, and getting herself to whatever room she's meeting us in, we're looking at about twenty after."

Asaron broke the stunned silence first. "How can you possibly know that?"

"I recognize the show."

"From watching a few minutes of silent dancing?" Victory asked. From the dancers' costumes, she could maybe identify it as a classic Parisiian ballet instead of, say, a modern dance from the former lands of Aragon or Castille. Certainly not the actual production, or where they might be in the schedule. And she'd seen a lot of productions in her years as a high-class bodyguard.

Mikelos laughed. "You both forget, sometimes. There's the mystique that I was a famous musician. But fame came after a lot of work. And a lot of that work is boring. So yeah, picking out such details was literally my job." He paused, drawn back to the dancers. A single woman spun in the center of the stage, the corps posed around her. "The hours it took to pick up on those details I don't miss. But the dancing was always nice."

"It's a power play," Victory said. "She wants us to be irritated and impatient when we're summoned." This was gleaned from hours upon hours of watching the powerful women she protected manipulate those around them.

Asaron twisted the volume control. The orchestra's low strains filled the room, and the three settled in to enjoy the rest of the show. The tension in their guide's shoulders when she knocked on the door and cracked it open closer to thirty minutes after the planned appointment time proved Victory's point. But if she expected a frustrated Master of the City or belligerent companions, her mood improved at once when Victory instead thanked her for the opportunity to watch the end of the ballet.

They followed their guide through the private halls of the opera house, which now teemed with performers and stage hands. A brief elevator ride shared with a costumer, who shoved herself into the corner of the car and pretended not to stare at the vampires, brought them to a higher floor of the building. The costumer fled into a nearby office, and Victory followed their guide down an opulent hallway toward closed double doors bracketed by two vampires.

The pair drew to attention at their approach. One kept his eyes forward, but the woman captured Victory's gaze for the briefest of seconds before she opened a door and waved them through.

What might function as a sort of executive boardroom during the day served well as a meeting space for Parisii's Master of the City. Stefania sat at the opposite end of the long table as if her chair doubled as a throne, a human woman at her right-hand side. A second vampire stood behind them, arms crossed over a chest bulkier than Asaron's. The trio represented a microcosm of the Roman Empire. Thick black hair that absorbed the overhead lights topped the man's olive-toned face, whereas the human woman's skin was a rich carnelian. Next to them, Stefania's unblemished skin reminded Victory of the unadorned marble statues of Roma, before they received their technicolor paint jobs. To top it off, her diamond choker and platinum blond hair glowed like a beacon to capture the attention of anyone who approached.

Victory had no difficulty reconciling the modern woman, hair trimmed chin-length, with the overdressed noblewoman who lived in her memory, who'd never step foot in public without her hair curled and styled and adorned with unnecessary ornaments. She paused at the end of the long table, Mikelos and Asaron a comforting presence at each shoulder. "Stefania. How lovely to see you again."

The male vampire stiffened, hands dropping to his side. Victory caught a flash of pistol when the movement shifted his suit jacket. "You will address the Master of the City with respect."

Stefania lifted a manicured hand, the sculpted nails glinting with a sheen of silver. Throwing a proper punch would be difficult with Stefania's talons. "Quite all right, Pietrov. We're old acquaintances." She studied Victory in return. "Nice shirt. I bought the white one for my daywalker last year." The human woman at Stefania's side smirked as she lifted a glass of champagne to her full lips.

Victory ignored the dig as she sat at the other end of the long table without invitation. "I'm here to request temporary residency in Parisii. My sire Asaron, my daywalker Mikelos Connor, and I will be staying at the former home of Lady Natalia Della Zanna. Our departure date is uncertain at this point."

"Request granted. On one condition."

"I'm happy to fulfill your condition if at all possible," Victory said. With their luck, Stefania might intend to take advantage of the skilled mercenaries suddenly at her disposal, and Victory didn't look forward to doing the canny vampire's dirty work.

"I was alerted to your presence in my city when your daywalker went on his extended shopping trip. But my sources in the city have been unable to ascertain how you slipped through their fingers with your arrival." Stefania exchanged a quick glance with her daywalker, who dipped her chin in confirmation. "I need to know whether you took advantage of any holes in my security, so I can rectify the error as soon as possible."

Oh, hell. Only one real way existed in and out of Limani—the ferry system to Calverton in the north or to the Roman colonies in the south. The alternative was an over-ground route skirting the edges of the Wasteland, and only one person crossed it without significant backup—the crazy vampire merc who stood behind her. The customs master at Limani's dock notified Victory of incoming vampires, rare though they were, as a matter of mingled courtesy and self-preservation.

She put herself in Stefania's shoes. The idea of random vampires appearing in Limani freaked Victory out, too. One problem, though.

Victory donned her politest mask. "Magic transported us to Parisii from Limani against our will. You have no security breaches I'm aware of."

Stefania's fingers jittered. "I wasn't an idiot however many years ago we met, Victory. Don't play me for one now."

Victory hadn't figured that would fly either. "I wish I wasn't lying to you. My city currently has no vampires in residence to act in my name. I might miss Europa on occasion, but I imagine I'd have organized a much better tour to revisit the highlights rather than scrambling to find appropriate garments to seek an audience with you." Victory touched the neckline of her blouse as proof of her claim. "It sounds absurd. That doesn't mean it's not true."

Stefania sat frozen in her seat, and the daywalker placed her empty champagne glass on the table. The way the woman's attention darted between her vampire and the visitors did more to show the extent of Stefania's anger than anything the Master of Parisii might do herself. Some daywalkers could be used as effective measures of their vampire's moods, though Victory knew Mikelos was the image of calm behind her. He only lost his temper when she wasn't around to be a calming influence. Asaron, on the other hand—

"I vouch for it, and you know I'm not an idiot either."

A muscle twitched in Victory's left thumb. But Stefania's gaze had already settled behind Victory, and she didn't like the curve in the woman's painted lips.

"If you vouch for this nonsense, your time in the colonies has rotted your brain, Asaron. I shouldn't be surprised two mercenaries won't give away their secrets, especially if they're planning to use them against me."

Victory did not have time for someone else's paranoia. She threw up her hands. "Don't be ridiculous, Stef. How do you know we didn't drive into town on our own, instead of via train? I gave you the courtesy of telling you the truth. If you don't believe it, you have bigger problems." Pietrov dropped his arms to his side, once again flashing the hilt of the pistol inside his suit jacket. That must be it. If Stefania's hold on this city was tenuous enough for Victory and Asaron to represent a threat, the woman's paranoia might be justified. She relaxed in her seat, lowering shoulders that had tightened in irritation. "I'm sorry. Is there anything we can do to help?"

But the damage was done. Stefania scoffed. "What help could you possibly be? You're the Master of a tiny city in the middle of nowhere. You know nothing of the current state of politics in the empire."

"My tiny city in the middle of nowhere isn't part of the empire because I know exactly as much as I need to." Did no one remember the invasion attempt less than ten years ago? It still shone in Victory's memory. "Limani may not rival Parisii in size or power, but at least I don't answer to those in Roma."

Stefania's daywalker flinched. Victory had struck a nerve. Stefania stood, shoving her chair away from the table where it caught Pietrov in a glancing blow. The man sneered as Stefania braced both hands on the end of the table. "Answering to those in Roma is why I'm more powerful than you'll ever be. You're still a jumped-up mercenary who doesn't know her place."

Victory had forgotten how short Stefania was. She resisted the urge to stand, to show how easy it would be to dominate this encounter. Stefania may have forgotten Roma's loss against Limani, but this was not an argument worth having. "Okay, stop." If Victory had to treat Stefania like a petulant child, she had perfected that tactic during Toria's terrifying pre-teen years.

The woman jerked, as if startled by the exhaustion in Victory's voice instead of the matched anger she might have expected.

Victory plowed on before Stefania responded. "This is ridiculous. I came here out of respect for you and your position, even if we don't have the greatest history together. You don't respect me as a person, as a jumped-up mercenary or whatever, fine. But you should damn well respect me as the Master of Limani. I have no idea what you might be facing in your city, but I can offer our services to you if you need them. Otherwise, let us be on our way. You can give us a deadline to leave or not, but I've done nothing to deserve this rudeness, and I won't stand for it."

Nervous human heartbeats thundered in Victory's ears over the distant sounds of the rest of the opera house. She hadn't given Stefania an ultimatum, but the sword at her side and Asaron at her back comforted her.

Stefania raised her arm, but it wasn't to set Pietrov loose on them. She pointed toward the door. "The day I need anything from you will be the day I have nothing left to my name. Get the hell out of my sight."

No reason to prolong this ridiculousness any longer. Victory stood, inclined her head to Stefania without lowering her eyes, and marched for the exit. With a burst of vampiric speed, Asaron reached the door first and opened it for Victory. She strode through without slowing, Mikelos on her heels, past the two vampires who maintained guard outside. Neither appeared surprised at her presence, since they'd heard every word spoken inside. The way vampires gossiped, the details of this encounter would spread through all of Parisii by the end of the night.

Halfway to the elevator, an unknown feminine voice called from behind. "Mikelos, please wait!" A harsh accent tinged her Loquella.

Victory turned, resisting the urge to grab for the short sword. Asaron made a similar restrained jerk. Stefania's daywalker hurried toward them on her tall heels. With the two vampire guards still at the end of the hall, neither dared make a threatening gesture toward the woman. Instead, Victory twitched her fingers for Mikelos to answer the daywalker.

His face brightened in a way Victory could tell was false through long exposure to the man. "Can I help you?"

She dug in her clutch, causing Victory to tense again, but withdrew a pen and ticket stub. "I know it wasn't your show, but can you please sign this for me?"

Mikelos accepted the items. "My pleasure. To?"

"Amara, please." The daywalker spelled it out while Mikelos wrote, hands clasped in front of her. "Thank you so much! This has made my day."

Mikelos handed the items to the daywalker. "Well, I'm glad I could make somebody's day."

She tucked them away, shooting a furtive glance toward Victory and Asaron but keeping her attention on Mikelos. "Oh gods, don't mind Stefania. It's been a rough few months, with everything going on."

"Oh? What's been going on?" Mikelos turned the charm up a notch, angling his body toward Amara and shifting his hips.

Mikelos wasn't good at subtle, except when he played the part of Mikelos Connor, concert violinist extraordinaire. Victory had seen women who didn't even speak the same language fall over themselves to give her daywalker everything his heart desired. Since her talents lay more in sliding into the background, it never failed to impress.

But the other daywalker bit her lower lip. "I'm sorry, I shouldn't have said anything. It would be rude to involve guests in our issues."

"Is that what we are?" Asaron kept his stance neutral as he drew Amara's attention. "Guests?"

Amara laughed, the tinkling of wind chimes. "Yes. Absolutely. I love the woman. She's my best friend, obviously, but Stefania gets stressed and takes it out on everyone else. Pietrov needs to learn to stand up to her better." She shook

Mikelos' hand and favored Victory and Asaron with a short bow. "Please don't hesitate to give me a call if there's anything you need while in town." With a final dive into her clutch, she presented Mikelos with her card.

Mikelos slipped it inside his suit jacket. "Thank you very much. It was a pleasure to make your acquaintance."

"Yours, too! Have a great rest of your night." Amara waved in the direction of the boardroom. "I'm going to drag Stefania out dancing, try to get her to cool off." With an infectious grin to Mikelos, she returned in the direction she'd come, leaving them to close the remaining distance to the elevator unmolested.

Once inside, Mikelos sagged against the wall. Victory braced her hip against the handrail. "That could have gone better," she said.

Asaron selected the button for the lobby, and the carriage jerked downward. "That could have gone a hell of a lot worse."

"We are intruders on her territory, and it'd bother me not to know how vampires got into Limani," Mikelos said.

"Our isolation gives us the advantage. If the customs house doesn't alert us of travelers by water, the werehyenas would give warning if anyone crossed by land." Victory led the way out of the elevator when it finished its descent. The ballet's audience had all left by now, leaving a bartender cleaning the refreshment stand and a janitor mopping a corner of the empty lobby.

After retrieving the car, they debated going out for a late dinner and drinks. But Victory claimed discomfort in her fancy clothing, and Asaron hesitated at the idea of flaunting their presence in the city further, after their awkward encounter with Stefania. Back to the townhouse it was, where they stripped out of their finery while David ordered in a meal.

Though the efficient manservant had offered to fully open the house for their use, Mikelos had waved him off. Instead, they piled into David's apartment at the top of the building, a much more comfortable and lived-in space. The men shared dinner while Victory and Asaron demolished another bottle of stocked blood.

Asaron did leave the house, in the hours before dawn, for some unknown destination Victory did not ask after. Once Mikelos and David retired, she curled up with a book of poetry chosen at random from the bookshelves in the parlor that appeared more decorative than useful.

After four pages of flowery language, she had no idea what was going on and placed the book on the end table next to her. Still too wired from the meeting with Stefania to relax, she slipped out of the house into the garden. She kicked off her boots and let her bare feet sink into the grass beyond the patio. Bathed in moonlight, accompanied by the nighttime sounds of summer—crickets, the occasional passing town-car, a bird confused by street lamps—she extended her arms and stretched, forcing the anxiety from her body.

Settling herself into a fighting stance, she launched into a series of kicks and punches against an army of invisible enemies: Stefania as Victory remembered her centuries ago, Serena's dining room portrait brought to life, that brooding hulk Pietrov, Rubin in the museum in Nacostina....

The shadows.

She caught movement. A shift of the light spilling across the patio from inside the house. Victory spun, dropping into a crouch. She'd left the short sword inside, and this was the real world, where no weapons could be summoned from thin air.

But this was a normal shadow, a drifting amorphous form that disappeared when she focused on it. Dark laughter escaped her throat. Normal. Since when had this become her life, where magic powerful enough to be seen by a vampire became normal?

That was it. Time to go to bed. She wasn't tired yet, but curling around Mikelos' warmth was better than stressing out here. Things would look better the next night.

Instead, the next night brought an unexpected visitor.

When the door chimed, Mikelos set a hand on Victory's shoulder before she rose from her spot on the parlor's sofa. She'd been keeping Mikelos company while he sorted Serena's enormous collection of jewelry, offering opinions on which pieces she or Toria might like to keep and which to sell or pass on elsewhere. David clattered down the stairs to answer the door, shrugging on his suit jacket as he passed the parlor entrance, despite Mikelos' assurances that he didn't need to dress up to serve them.

Out of sight, he opened the door. "Can I help you, sir?"

"I hope so. I heard rumor Victory was in town. Is she perhaps here?" The low bass contained a hint of accent, that of an elf who'd spoken Loquella for years but had spent even longer with the elven tongue.

Victory dropped the bracelet she'd been toying with into the jewelry box. She reached the front door before David finished answering that he would check whether she was accepting callers. "Zerandan!"

The elven man hadn't changed in the handful of years since she'd seen him, but time passed differently for his kind. If an elf could be called elderly, Zerandan approached that description closer than any other she'd encountered over the years. His dull silver hair fell across his shoulders, and laugh lines accented the corners of his eyes and lips. He carried a cane he used for support on the rarest occasion.

"This is a surprise." Victory kept her tone neutral. Mikelos approached behind her, also summoned by the familiar voice. He made no move of welcome toward the man either.

Zerandan coughed, clearing his throat. "I realize this is not a pleasant surprise. But I must speak with you. I know how you came to be in Parisii."

Mikelos' sucked air through his teeth, echoing Victory's own sense of surprise. She wanted nothing to do with the old man. But if he truly knew how they'd found themselves in Parisii, traveling via the strange world where they had found Syri, Victory couldn't afford to turn away this potential source of information. Through gritted teeth, she said, "Come in."

To his credit, the elf seemed to recognize the thin ice on which he thread. With careful movements that belied his spryness, he allowed Victory to escort him into the parlor and settled himself into an armchair.

Victory and Mikelos resumed their previous positions, and David absented himself with a quiet word about fetching tea. "Speak your piece," she said.

Ignoring Victory's demand, Zerandan peered at the array of jewelry scattered on the low table between them. "What a fascinating collection. Your inheritance, Mikelos?"

A pained expression, between embarrassment and pride, crossed her daywalker's face. "They belonged to my previous vampire. The house, too."

"Yes, yes." Zerandan selected a choker, letting the pearl strands run through his fingers and rubbing the amber centerpiece with the ball of his thumb. "Much here in Parisii is still relevant to your interests."

"I thought I'd left it all behind, but here we are." Mikelos accepted the choker from Zerandan and placed it in the "sell" pile. "I might as well take care of things while I'm in residence, despite the unplanned trip. You were going to tell us what you knew about it?"

Zerandan caught Victory's gaze. "I heard about your confrontation with Stefania last night."

Victory picked up the bracelet she'd been playing with before, caressing the cool white gold that would never warm beneath her fingers. "I'm not surprised the story spread, but I wonder what state it's in."

Mikelos spun his pen. "How could it be more ridiculous than what we told Stefania herself?"

Asaron followed on David's heels into the parlor, throwing himself into the second armchair while David arranged the tea service. "It can't. The gods-damned shadow creatures controlled a rock that had already thrown Victory and Toria back in time."

The blood drained from Zerandan's face with an audible rush in Victory's ears, and she feared the ancient elf verged on a heart attack. "It appears there is more to the story than I suspected. I'd assumed that artifact was destroyed in the Last War. Its last known location was Nacostina."

"That's where we found it earlier this summer." Victory paused, allowing David to serve tea and exit the parlor. He must have sensed the delicate nature of their conversation, because instead of waiting in the kitchen, he returned to his rooms upstairs. Part of her wanted to tell Zerandan the entire story. That she and Toria had visited Nacostina as it was almost a hundred years ago. Instead, she shared the bare minimum: "It was during an attempt to investigate the artifact further that it snatched us again."

"And deposited you here? In Parisii?" Zerandan clutched his seat's armrests.

Victory glanced between Mikelos and Asaron, waiting for agreement from both men before she elaborated further. "Yes. But not before we were in another world." She paused, but Asaron's touch to her elbow prodded her onward. "Zerandan, we saw Syri there. She's trapped in some sort of shadow realm. She helped us escape."

But her revelation did not have the effect on Zerandan she had expected. "Yes, when Toria said there was no body to be recovered in the Catacombs, I expected she'd found her way home."

The quiet fury simmering in Victory since Zerandan appeared on their doorstep uncoiled in her chest. But before she could demand more of an explanation, Zerandan continued, "You three, however, must count yourselves lucky. We have no record of anyone ever leaving that place. Your arrival here was a surprise, but your timing was fortuitous."

To cover her fizzled anger, Victory sipped her tea. It wasn't sweet enough.

Asaron took over the interrogation. "We're trying to figure out what's going on, so we can go home."

"Then my visit here will require much less explanation than I had expected. We have work to do." With a total shift in attention, Zerandan switched his gaze to Asaron. "Have you discovered your magic yet?"

Asaron gave no sign of displeasure other than a subtle twitch of his sword hand, indicating the greatest distress Victory had seen from her sire in days. "This is ridiculous. I have no magic. It's hereditary, but Toria's not actually my granddaughter."

"No need to be an ass to a fellow old man, Asaron," Zerandan said. "What do you three know about the world spell?"

A knot of tension built behind Victory's left temple. "It suppresses technological capability in the world beyond a certain level. The elves established it after the Last War, then sacrificed their own young to maintain its power. Toria, Kane, and Archer disrupted it here in Parisii." Too bad Zerandan had disappeared from Limani afterward, unable to give anyone further explanation. Victory gestured between herself and Asaron. "Which is when we first saw the shadows."

Zerandan lifted a finger, which meant he might arrive at a point soon. "Yes, but it was never just the elves. There's a detail everyone likes to leave out. Why Serena was in the Catacombs for the sacrifice."

How did Zerandan know anything about this story? Perhaps Archer had relayed his version of events a few years ago, but Zerandan acted like he'd been there. "Kane died, and Serena brought him back," Victory said, drawing out the words. "I always assumed Serena was there as... a sort of representative. That the vampires were in on the plot of the world spell, because they'd taken the long view like the elves." The shorter-lived werewolves and the slightly longer-lived weredragons had led the humans on either side of the Last War after all. Even the weredragons never lived beyond three centuries, whereas the combined age of the people in this room topped five millennia.

Zerandan remained silent for a handful of Mikelos' heartbeats, which rang in Victory's ears and underscored the tension in the room. "What I'm about to tell you is one of the most closely guarded secrets of the last hundred years."

"Be out with it," Asaron said, "and spare us the melodrama."

"The elves took public responsibility for the world spell because the vampires did not want to risk accusation that Roman powers were making some sort of world domination attempt."

"Makes sense," Mikelos said, tapping his chin. "But the Romans, military and civilian alike, are hindered by the world spell like everyone else. We'd all have known pretty quickly otherwise. That sort of advantage doesn't stay hidden for decades."

"They were equally affected, but that's not the point." Zerandan quieted again and set his empty teacup on the table. "The elves never had the power to create the world spell on their own. It's not elven magic, not alone, especially once the world spell started to fail less than twenty years in. By then, we'd realized newborn elves were—different. Not genetically or biologically, but magically. The magical ability of vampires allowed us to harness the power of the sacrificed elven children. That's what Serena was doing in the Catacombs. She meant to channel the energy released from Syri's death to the elves present, who would have powered the world spell."

Syri's kidnapping in New Angouleme and the race to save her in Parisii from this fate wasn't news to anyone present, but hearing it jolted adrenaline through Victory. "So, the vampires are involved. Is Stefania one of them?"

"Stefania rose to power in Parisii because she had the political acumen to wrangle much older vampires. Like Serena, who had the power necessary to help the elves maintain the world spell." Zerandan spread his arms. "But with Serena's death, the vampires have been hesitant to maintain their end of the bargain. Now, Stefania is under pressure from the elves to control her people, but also under pressure from the vampires to ensure their protection."

"Protection from whom?" Asaron asked. "Only one vampire has died so far. And the kids haven't continued to threaten the world spell. They've been living their lives, doing mercenary work. Not hunting elves or vampires."

"It is only a matter of time before Stefania finds another vampire willing to work with the elves," Zerandan said. "Despite my best efforts, another sacrifice has been arranged."

"And by another sacrifice, you mean another young elf?" asked Mikelos.

"Yes," Zerandan said. "I apologize for sugar-coating a horrific reality."

"As long as we're clear that we're discussing the murder of children," Asaron said.

"Zerandan," Victory said, "I appreciate you explaining all of this. But why are you here, other than to tell us these things? What do you need from us?"

The old elf seemed to expect the question. "I need the three of you to help me stop the sacrifice, to stop this attempted repair of the world spell. You traveled through the shadow plane and came out the other side."

"What does that have to do with stopping the ritual?" Victory asked. "And what would you be doing if we weren't here? It's not like we planned to drop by Parisii like this."

"I'm not one to miss an opportunity," Zerandan said. "There were backup plans in place, to rescue the sacri—to rescue Doyl. But why put another patch on the problem when a potential solution has dropped into my lap?"

"You want us to go there." Terror dawned on Victory like a sunrise. "Back to the shadow plane."

"We barely made it out of there in one piece," Asaron said, his voice growing louder with his anger.

Victory dug her fingernails into her palms as she clenched her fists. "You want the same thing Syri wanted. Asaron's magic."

Asaron slammed his hand on his knee. "It was ridiculous even when we were in another damned dimension, and it's even more ridiculous now. I don't have magic. I've lived by the sword my entire life, and I'm not about to give it up now."

Zerandan held his peace through Asaron's outburst. "Embracing your power does not require you to change who you are as a person. Think of it as a sort of added bonus. Do not Toria and Kane fight with sword and magic together?"

"Because they're warrior-mages," Asaron said, a touch of snarl entering his voice. "It's what they were born for."

"And it's what you've lived a long time for," Zerandan said. "Your fate, even."

"I create my own fate."

"Asaron." Victory's voice drew her sire away from the edge.

He switched his glare to her, then closed his eyes. A human might have heaved a sigh, but Asaron counted to three or prayed for patience to an unknown deity. Or both. When he brought himself back to the present, he jabbed a finger at Zerandan. "I'll give your craziness a shot, but we're going to rescue that kid, you hear me? That seems a hell of a lot more important than whether I have vampire magic, or whatever you want to call it."

"Mikelos, is there a place that might be suitable for such practice in this house?" Zerandan asked.

"I'm not sure what you're even thinking of," Mikelos said. "This isn't like the mage schools, where there are rooms designed for magic works."

"An open space where we won't be disturbed." Zerandan used his cane to lever himself out of his chair. "We won't spend too long working tonight. It is like muscles that must be toned."

"I suppose you could move the furniture in the dining room."

"Perfect," Zerandan said. "Lead the way."

"I'll take them," Victory said.

They left Mikelos to sorting jewelry. Zerandan trailed after Asaron and Victory toward the dining room. Whispering, Victory said, "Thank you for humoring him. We need him for this."

"I'm willing to waste an hour of my life to show the old man he doesn't know anything about me," Asaron said. Once in the dining room, he grabbed the first chair. But instead of crushing it into kindling, he carried it to the wall and set it down with the gentlest scrape against the wood floor.

Reassured that her sire wouldn't vent his aggression on the innocent furniture, she helped him line the walls with the ten chairs. Together, they hefted either end of the table and also hauled it to the side, creating a wide space free in the center of the room. Leaving the portraits of Serena and Connor to supervise the two men, she drew the double doors closed behind her.

Asaron was over twice her age, and she planned to make it to his age or beyond. She had already seen much of the world and had no intention of leaving it anytime soon.

One day, this supposed vampire magic might be hers as well.

For now, she'd leave Asaron to his destiny. She walked to the parlor toward hers.

When she returned, Mikelos glanced from his writing when she dropped next to him on the sofa. "They okay?"

Victory pressed her shoulder against his. The low rumble of male voices carried from the dining room, but the tones remained civil. "I'll hear if they're not. It's all very strange."

"You're telling me." Mikelos dropped the notepad and pen on top of a precarious stack of ring boxes, ignoring the pile when it collapsed. "If Serena had magic when I was with her, I never knew about it. For all the time I spent with them, I always belonged with Connor first. There was a lot I didn't know about her. She was the money, and she took care of us. Connor was devoted to her, of course. But looking back, there's so much I never knew, which seemed normal until my life with you."

Enough drama had invaded the house for one night. Victory nudged the edge of the coffee table with one bare foot, setting another ring box toppling. "Like how much jewelry the woman had?"

Mikelos' chest rose in laughter. "Oh, I was well aware of how much jewelry she possessed. All genuine, of course. Not like Serena would wear paste. Too bad you and Toria don't wear rings."

"Interferes with grip," Victory said. "You don't have to feel like all of this should become ours."

Mikelos stilled beneath her. "I'm sorry. This must be awkward for you. I hope I'm not shoving the jewelry at you too hard."

"I appreciate how your first inclination is to shower you partner and daughter with sparkly things," Victory said. "As long as you're aware your partner and daughter have never been those types of girls." At least this conversation distracted her from Zerandan's presence in the house. Despite her long friendship with the man, she'd had to evaluate everything after his manipulations put the kids in such danger.

Mikelos stacked the boxes again. "Here, make yourself useful."

"I'm always useful," Victory said. She accepted the pen and notepad from Mikelos to record notes while he sorted through the rings, marking the unique features of each piece of jewelry so he'd have a full list to work from when he and David coordinated the best way to dispose of the pieces they wouldn't be keeping. It wasn't as if they could exchange them at a pawn shop for a wad of cash. From what Mikelos knew of Serena, many of these might be works of art from famous designers, and everything required professional appraisal—an investment itself.

As Mikelos returned a stack of plain silver bands to their box, the dining room doors banged open. Victory dropped her writing supplies into Mikelos' lap and leapt from the sofa, skidding into the hallway. "What's going on? Are you okay?"

Asaron stormed past her, though the carpet muffled his harsh steps. He picked up Victory's boots, discarded by the entrance, and tossed them to her. "We're going out."

Victory clutched the boots to her chest. Mikelos lurked behind her. "I need socks first."

Mikelos touched Victory's elbow. "I'll get them." He ascended the stairs two at a time, leaving Victory between the two men glaring daggers at each other.

"Perhaps it would be best if you considered our discussion and I returned tomorrow night?" Zerandan was the epitome of serenity, except for the way he clutched at the top of his cane.

Asaron checked the placement of two knives on his person, one at his ankle and the other tucked at his waist. "If you must."

"You can't rescue Doyl without my information, and you can't rescue him tonight at all," Zerandan said.

Ah, so that's what this was about. The magic lessons hadn't gone well, so Asaron needed a solid goal to accomplish. Victory caught the pair of socks Mikelos tossed down the stairs and sat on the bottom steps to put them on. "Asaron, I'll go out with you right now, but we're not doing anything ridiculous."

"Nothing we ever do is ridiculous." Once she secured her boots, Asaron hauled Victory to her feet. "Especially not going to a bar."

Right. When in doubt, find beer.

Though over one hundred years had passed since Victory last swept through Parisii at night with Asaron, some things never changed. Finding a drink turned into finding multiple drinks turned into stopping a mugging and putting the fear of two inebriated vampires into a cadre of trouble-making teenagers— Victory didn't relish the news of that incident getting back to Stefania—then visiting the cousin of one of Asaron's Fort Caroline contacts to acquire more weaponry.

Victory slouched in the doorway. The man brought out blade after blade for Asaron to inspect. "I'm surprised you're not finding something similar to your Schiavona."

Asaron lifted a saber to check its balance. "Not enough room to swing that around where we're going."

To be fair, Victory had already made that determination and decided to settle with the short sword she'd acquired over finding a meatier bastard sword. She hummed low, under the dealer's hearing level, indicating her opinion about each of the weapons. Finally, her sire ordered her to the man's sparse living room. Apparently, he didn't value her backseat sword expertise.

Not trusting the cleanliness of the furniture, Victory parked herself at the apartment's window. The city's skyline of historic palaces-turned-museums and monuments to Parisii's string of conquerors gave no indication of what existed below. The stone for the palaces and monuments had come from somewhere, and that meant abandoned quarries had transitioned to a darker purpose in the city's history. While vampires might define part of the Roman Empire's ruling class, not every vampire held such political or social power. And the city had not always respected members of other supernatural races, leading to the eventual decision that all deceased nonhumans must be interred below ground rather than in traditional graveyards or cemeteries.

The old quarries had been joined with smuggler's tunnels and abandoned construction projects to form the Catacombs, where the deceased were laid to rest.

As Asaron's criticisms of another potential sword drifted into the room, it occurred to Victory that if her sire met his end while in Parisii, he'd be added to the faceless, nameless collection of bones underground. She had once known people—vampires, elves, werecreatures—in repose below her even now.

If she died in the Catacombs during this crazy mission to rescue an innocent elf, they could leave her where she fell.

Except the Catacombs were a respectful place, not a discarded collection of bodies left to rot. Even if the elves and, apparently, vampires had perverted that purpose to use it as a base of operations to cast and maintain the world spell.

Perhaps this supposed vampiric death magic meant the Catacombs were where this power was strongest, and that was the reason Asaron had no luck in Serena's townhouse. She made a mental note to suggest it to Zerandan when he arrived the next night.

More questions about this magic she'd never heard of turned over and over in her mind, keeping her quiet while Asaron paid the dealer for his two new blades and they settled in the car. She waved off his concern, blaming her silence on tiredness.

They passed a cemetery littered with faded tombstones dating back two or three centuries. If she died in the Catacombs, what would be Mikelos' fate? He would live out a human life without her, like he'd been prepared to do after losing Connor and Serena. But that was his old life, and not her partner now.

Now, he'd do something idiotic like try to avenge her death. He'd die trying. Would they bury him in the Catacombs with her? Or separate them forever, on opposite sides of the planet?

She had no idea who this nebulous "they" might be, but the idea of such permanent separation chilled her to the core. Once at the house, she wished Asaron a brisk good night and climbed the steps to the suite she shared with her daywalker. He'd already passed out, sprawled across the bed and mouth half open as if he didn't possess a care in the world. Victory stripped, leaving a trail of clothing between the door and bed, and slipped next to him.

Mikelos turned in his sleep, wrapping Victory in a cocoon of lanky limbs burning with human heat. She nestled against his skin and pressed her face into one of the soft pillows that didn't smell like home.

If Kane's death in the Catacombs had been permanent, he might still be there, too.

Victory expected her morbidity to keep her awake into the daylight hours, as the thin slice of light around the thick curtains lightened with the dawn, but she opened her eyes into pure darkness. The empty spot next to her no longer retained Mikelos' warmth.

The doorbell had woken her. She strained her ears in time to catch David thanking an unknown voice for a delivery. She expected it to be a meal for him and Mikelos, and she contemplated going back to sleep and avoiding everything to come.

Mikelos burst into the bedroom. He threw himself across the bed, propping himself on his elbows with his face inches from hers. His fond expression promised mischief, and Victory didn't have the energy, despite her hours of sleep. She groaned and buried her face into the pillows, but Mikelos stopped her with a kiss.

"Good news," he said. "Special delivery from Pietrov."

Pietrov? Her muddled brain needed a second to catch up, until she remembered Stefania's bulky second, standing over her in the conference like a grim shadow. "What could he have for us?"

Before he answered, Asaron's voice boomed through the house. "Victory! Food!"

The words woke her faster than a double-shot of espresso. Mikelos laughed at the speed with which she untangled herself from the bedclothes and threw on a robe. She paid him no mind, dashing downstairs. She brushed past David lurking in the parlor's entrance, and Asaron gestured toward a bottle on the coffee table. A second bottle already tilted to his lips prevented any comment. She dropped next to him on the sofa, bottle in hand. She toasted David, pulled the cork, and drank.

Thick, coppery liquid coated her tongue before it slid down her throat. Where the blood David had provided from Serena's emergency store was stale water, this was a bold wine, full-bodied and heavy with the taste of life. Fresh, too, not more than a few hours free of whoever had donated it. Victory drained a third of the bottle in one go. "Wow," she said, pulling it from her mouth.

"Right?" Asaron had already finished his bottle. "I hate to owe the man, but Parisii's second has access to the good stuff."

"If I may," David said, "you owe him nothing. Pietrov's assistant said it was with the compliments of his master, who felt Master Victory deserved a more proper welcome to Parisii than Stefania provided."

Drinking again, Victory raised her eyebrows. Next to her, Asaron laughed.

When Mikelos descended the stairs, he asked, "What?"

"Trouble in paradise, it seems." Asaron rolled his empty bottle between his hands. "Otherwise Pietrov would have delivered it on Stefania's behalf, not presented the gift from himself."

Mikelos served himself tea from the service on the buffet, gesturing for David to pour some for himself. "I'm getting tired of feeling like we're pawns in someone else's game." The two men sat across from the vampires.

The doorbell rang again, and Mikelos gestured toward the front door as if it proved his point for him. David made to set down his tea, but Asaron waved him off. "It's for me anyway," he said, and he heaved himself off the sofa.

Victory caught Asaron's low murmur—"I'd prefer bullshit vampire politics over this ridiculous magic nonsense any day"—and almost choked on the dregs of her bottled blood. He opened the front door with a terse greeting for Zerandan.

Asaron led Zerandan into the parlor. Opposite the hand gripping his cane, the elf carried a house plant in the crook of one elbow. "Best we get straight to work," he said.

Victory stood. "I'd like to watch this time."

Her sire's entire face twitched. But if Asaron was willing to put up with this for two nights in a row, perhaps there was something to this vampiric magic. And if this destiny might be hers one day, all the information she gathered now was worth its weight in gold.

"Of course, my dear," Zerandan said, as if he didn't recognize the tension his presence had brought to the group. "Better you learn as much as possible now, so you're not in Asaron's straits in a few centuries."

Victory's first instinct would always be to defend her sire, regardless of the truth in her statement. "I'm sure it's not that bad."

Asaron snorted.

She requested a moment to run upstairs and throw real clothing on, and when she returned to the main floor, Asaron held open the dining room doors for them.

Zerandan settled himself in a chair, facing one of its fellows in the center of the cleared room, and Asaron claimed the opposite. "Let's start fresh tonight, shall we?" Zerandan asked. He placed the plant between them.

Victory perched in one of the seats pushed to the edge of the room. Something about the imperious painted gaze of the vampire Serena made her want to be on her best manners, to sit with perfect posture. In a silent "fuck you" to Mikelos' former vampire, she spun the chair around and straddled it, bracing her forearms on the seat's backrest.

"We'll begin with the meditation again. Concentrate on the plant. Feel its life force. Feel my own."

Following the same instructions Zerandan provided to Asaron, Victory did her best to block out the outside world. To narrow her heightened abilities to this room alone and sense the living beings within. Block the scent of tea that had followed them from the parlor to the dining room. Tune out Mikelos and David's discussion of what should be done with various objets d'art scattered about the public areas of the house, which Serena had collected over the years to impress guests.

Before long, Victory settled into her own mind. After cutting out all smells from beyond her immediate vicinity, the lemon tang of furniture polish from the chair she sat in dominated her palate. Refreshing after the richness of the blood she'd drank, like a crisp glass of lemonade in the heat of a humid summer night. Beneath that, the soothing solidity of the oak from which the chair was crafted brought to mind a stroll through a dense forest.

A place as far from the rocky, barren shadow plane as Victory could imagine.

Zerandan spoke again, his voice a gentle counterpoint to Victory's calm. "Have you centered yourself? Found the space at the heart of your being where nothing else matters, where the external world is but a distraction?"

Victory opened her eyes in time for Asaron's jerky nod.

"Now," Zerandan said, "cup your hands before you. Imagine your own center in that very space. Your own being. Your power. Your intention."

Zerandan and Victory stared at Asaron's hands, lifted above the plant.

Perhaps Toria or Kane, using their magesight, might have experienced Asaron's supposed power swirling between his palms. Victory, magical dud that she was, saw nothing out of the ordinary.

She wasn't sure what she'd expected of Zerandan's training, but it wasn't this. Now she had a sense of Asaron's frustration, and a notion niggled at the back of her mind that this vampire magic might be a giant hoax.

Except Serena had brought Kane back from the dead. Victory shifted in her seat under the silent gaze of the portrait behind her.

Asaron grunted. "Still nothing. This is absurd." He crossed his arms in a sulk worthy of Kane at fourteen.

Zerandan blew a short burst through thin lips. "I'm not sure you gave it enough time."

"I gave it plenty of time. My power, or whatever it is you think I have inside me, stays inside me. It doesn't move between my hands."

Yep, a proper sulk. Asaron's foot twitched. He was seconds away from storming out of the room. Victory spoke from her corner, hoping a distraction would calm her sire enough for a second attempt. "What do the shadows even want? We never asked."

Zerandan crossed his arms too, but in contemplation. He drummed his fingers against his shirt. "Honestly, we have no idea."

"Not much of an answer." A growl tinged Asaron's voice.

"It has something to do with the world spell," Zerandan said. "Something about the way the spell limits the ability and development of certain technologies seems to also affect the barrier between worlds."

"Have the murders of your children been to continue to limit technology, or to strengthen this barrier?"

Zerandan flinched at Asaron's artlessness. "I'm not sure about that, either."

Asaron glanced to the side, meeting Victory's eyes with a clenched jaw. She'd been able to read his tells within a few decades of becoming his progeny. After centuries, he was an open book. "What do you know, then?" she asked. She left her seat to stand at Asaron's shoulder.

"Nothing more than legends," Zerandan said. "That once upon a time, another world existed alongside this one. This was the mortal plane—for various definitions of mortal." He motioned between himself and Asaron. "And theirs was the immortal. Filled with creatures of spirit, of darkness and light."

"Darkness?" Victory asked. "Like the shadows?"

"Exactly like the shadows. The story goes that they overwhelmed the balance between darkness and light in their own world. Now, I theorize the cracks the world spell created in the barriers between our planes have allowed the shadows through. And they will overwhelm our world in darkness the way they have their own."

Tension radiated from Asaron's core, even when Victory rested a warning hand against the nape of his neck. "Stories and theories," he said.

The doorbell rang again, chiming through the house.

Asaron met Victory's gaze. "The daywalker is right. Let's find out the next move in this chess game."

They emerged from the dining room as David opened the front door. Victory caught his words of greeting but did not recognize the exuberant tenor who replied with a request to speak with Victory or Mikelos.

She called down the hallway. "I'm here, David."

David moved aside to reveal an unassuming gentleman of middling height, dressed in a suit a few years out of fashion even by Limani's standards. It was in desperate need of a press, and even the man's shaggy hair, caught in a shade between blond and brown, was long past time for a trim.

But the man—vampire, from the lack of heartbeat and distinctive pallor under his pale skin—was clean-shaven, and he beamed at the sight of her. He juggled a satchel to one arm and thrust his free hand forward.

"Victory! Such a pleasure to meet you. I never expected you'd make your way to Parisii again, and my commitments here haven't given me occasion to travel to the New Continent since the Last War."

With Asaron's steadying presence at her back and Mikelos lurking in the entrance to the front parlor, Victory stepped past David to accept the man's hand and return his enthusiastic shake. "Good evening. I believe you have me at a disadvantage."

"Oh, I'm sorry." He caught his satchel before it tilted out of his hands. The corner of two worn hardcovers poked out of the top. "Professor Felix Bergman, currently of the University of Raetia. I was an associate of your progeny Jarimis. My belated condolences."

A month ago, Victory could have accepted the platitude with grace. "Thank you," she said through clenched teeth. She suppressed the urge to follow up with unnecessary sarcasm, but what the hell was the man doing here?

The professor abandoned the fight with his bag and pulled three books out before they came loose. "I'm sure you're wondering why I'm here."

Victory snatched one of the books when it fell from his hands. "If this is a social call, I'm afraid we're otherwise occupied this evening, Professor." The book she rescued featured a simple fabric and board binding. The stamped title had almost worn away with age: *Ancient Mythologies of the Elves of the Britannic Highlands: An Analysis and Modern Commentary.*

"Oh, it's just Felix. You're not one of my students." He clutched the satchel and displaced books to his chest, peering past Victory's shoulder into the house. "Zerandan! What a fortuitous surprise. How have you been?"

Zerandan approached the doorway, and the muscle in Victory's temple twitched in counterpoint to the click of his cane on the hallway floor. "I am well, Professor Bergman. What has pried you from your libraries in Raetia at this time of year?"

Another bout of book juggling began, until Victory took pity on the man and accepted the two other tomes—*The Role of Religion in a Post-Technological Society* and an unlabeled leather-bound text—while David rescued the bulging satchel. With free hands, Felix checked two pockets until he withdrew a crumpled telegram. "I received word from a mutual friend that my expertise might be of assistance in light of your current dilemma."

Victory ignored Asaron's low growl of concern behind her. She passed her stack of books to Mikelos and accepted the slip of paper.

Find Victory or Mikelos Connor at former residence of Natalia Della Zanna in Parisii ASAP. Stop. Your expertise is needed. Stop.

The telegram listed the sender as Liamacorin. She held it out for Mikelos to read. Though she'd never heard of Felix, his reference was excellent. Until a more terrifying idea struck her. "Jarimis wasn't your—"

"No." Felix's interruption was quick, and his demeanor sobered. "He'd have told you. Though we've been told the resemblance in attitude is uncanny."

True. But the man's unexpected appearance had thrown her for a loop. "Well, come in. I'm curious as to what expertise you have that Liam thinks we need."

Mikelos ushered everyone into the parlor, where David deposited Felix's bag onto the coffee table, murmured something about fresh tea, and disappeared. Felix dropped into an armchair to sort his books while the rest jockeyed for seating. Zerandan claimed the other armchair, leaving Mikelos and Victory to the couch. Asaron, maintaining his silence, positioned himself along the wall behind Felix's chair.

The professor paused in his stacking. "Oh! You must be Asaron. I've heard only good things, sir." He returned to his books, shuffling another older, untitled text to one pile.

Victory hid a smile behind one hand at Felix's lack of fear. Mikelos selected the book nearest to hand and flipped through the pages.

"Wait—no, go ahead, we won't need that one yet," Felix said. He dug a final batch of notes from the bottom of his satchel and placed the empty bag on the floor. "Since I seem to have been unexpected, I suppose a more formal introduction is in order. I'm a professor of history, religion, and philosophy at the University of Raetia."

"All of those?" Mikelos asked, snaking an arm behind Victory's shoulders.

"Yes. Being well-versed is a benefit to a long life," Felix said. "Jarimis and I met through our work, and I corresponded with Liam when searching for a particular book, oh, years ago at this point. Is he teaching at the university in Limani again? I haven't felt right bothering him since his leave of absence."

Mikelos suppressed a snort of laughter, so Victory responded. "I'm not sure what he's planning these days." Other than dating her daughter. "So, what can your history, religion, and philosophy tell us about the shadows?"

Felix froze at her question.

Zerandan gestured to the stacks of books spread before him. "The area of expertise Liam referred to, Felix. I suppose you know more about them at this point than anyone outside of elves older than me."

"Ah, I see." Felix twisted a lock of short hair. "You're among those seeing them?"

At Asaron's slight gesture, Victory responded with the truth. "Asaron and I both."

"Fascinating. I'm fairly certain I've only seen them twice, myself, but I recorded both instances in my journals. Not enough of a sample size to make adequate judgement, and it's been difficult getting information from the few other vampires in Raetia. I'd love to hear about your experiences in detail." Felix patted the pockets of his jacket. "I seem to have lost my pen."

David retrieved one from inside his suit and handed it to Felix with his tea. "Do you also require paper, sir?"

"Yes, I suppose that would be helpful."

No wonder people assumed Felix was Jarimis' progeny. Victory accepted her tea from David with quiet thanks. "I'll be happy to give you whatever information I can provide, but perhaps it would be helpful for you to fill in some details, first. You know what the shadows are?"

"Well, I'm familiar with the myths and legends featuring the shadows." Felix touched the capped end of the pen to one stack of books, then another. "They are featured heavily in the creation mythos of some groups of elves, particularly those from various regions in Europa and Rus."

Zerandan cleared his throat. "That's not to say the elven populations in the rest of the world might not have similar legends or aspects of their religion. For example, the elves of Dongqu have been reluctant to participate in cultural exchanges."

"I imagine the way the Qin conquered large swaths of their territory during major colonial expansion didn't endear them to strangers," Mikelos said.

"Quite." Felix dug through one stack for a slim volume and handed it to him. "This would be a good source for basic information. I wrote this for one of my higher-level lecture series, to give my students additional background into how heavily the concept of balance features in many religions."

Asaron left his spot behind Felix. He plucked Victory's cup and sipped, then pursed his lips, as if he wasn't well aware how sweet she drank her tea. "What does all this have to do with sealing the breach once we stop the sacrifice?"

Felix stared at Asaron before switching his focus to Zerandan, but the elf had schooled his face into blankness while he perused one of Felix's books. "Zerandan."

"Hmm?" He shut the book and set it in his lap.

Felix's lightheartedness leached from his body, and a familiar vampiric intensity crept into his voice. "You promised me those were rumors."

"I did, because at the time, it was none of your business." Zerandan stroked the book cover. "Now, however, everything you've studied as theory will soon be put to practice."

Felix placed his pen parallel to the edge of the coffee table and cupped his tea between both hands. "I see I have some catching up to do."

Between Zerandan and Victory, with occasional input from Mikelos and sarcastic commentary from Asaron, they informed the professor of their current dilemma. Victory counted them lucky that the news of time travel did not strike Felix as surprising—he already had a passing familiarity with the artifact that sent them to Parisii from his working relationship with Liam.

For his part, Felix filled in some of the blanks left by Zerandan's grand pronouncements of the past two days. References to beings of light and shadow littered the elven mythological record, unknown to most members of other races. Werecreatures had their own mythologies, vampires didn't have the same sort of collective memory for such things, and most human legends could be traced to supernatural or magical incidences.

Mikelos refilled his tea. "Couldn't it be said that these light and shadow creatures are elves and vampires?" he asked.

"That was my first working hypothesis," Felix said, fiddling with his pen. "It took me years of field work to gain the trust of certain elven populations. And the conclusions I came to never upheld the theory."

Instead, legends told of a brutal war fought between the light and the dark. Eventually, the shadows were forced from this world into their own, but the beings of light sacrificed themselves to keep the borders between the worlds sealed.

According to Felix, creation myths by disparate groups of elves supported the story that this alternate plane existed. No one knew the current state of that world, but if the shadows were spilling into their own realm of existence, Felix suggested that perhaps the shadows had beaten their opposites back and claimed supremacy. Though he admitted to a lack of knowledge of magical theory, he agreed the power of the world spell could have cracked a breach between the two worlds, giving the shadows an opening to return.

Along the way, they'd switched from tea to beer, and David supplied a late-night snack of sandwiches and fruit. Asaron toyed with the cap of his beer bottle, flipping it between his fingers. "We need to get our priorities straight. Sounds like a shame that the shadows have overrun this other world. But we need to rescue the sacrifice and repair the breach so they can't do the same here. Not solve the problems of a race of magical light beings who, from what he says, are a hell of a lot more powerful than we can even comprehend."

"Even if it means destroying the world spell?" Felix asked. "We all lived through the Last War. You might be a mercenary, but do you want a return to that?"

"It's a risk we need to take if we're to prevent the shadows from destroying our world as thoroughly as unchecked nuclear war," Zerandan said. "Either way, rescuing Doyl will be the final straw. Without his death, the spell will fracture, and lack of power will cause a collapse. But we will have to fight or evade the elves and vampires who roam the Catacombs and protect the ritual space."

"There's our plan," Asaron said. "We interrupt the sacrifice and close the breach. No more shadows."

"Except for the ones already here." Even now, their potential presence itched at Victory, and she tried not to look into the darkened corners of the parlor.

"We'll figure out how to deal with those once we know no more are coming." Asaron rubbed his hands together. "A proper hunt."

"But what about that other world?" Mikelos asked. "Where the shadows are destroying these light beings. Syri and the others helped us. Can we leave them to be overwhelmed and destroyed?"

The room descended into silence, and Zerandan shifted in his seat. "Leave it to the youngest of us to be our conscience."

"Young is relative," Mikelos said. "Maybe if we hadn't seen them and experienced this place, I'd feel differently. But knowing Syri is there, and walking away? I'm not sure I can do that."

Victory sought Asaron's gaze and held it. "Would you be able to look Toria in the face if we abandoned her friend?"

The weight of Asaron's gaze threatened to overwhelm Victory, but he ducked away first. "When you're right, you're right." He surveyed the room. "Looks like we have two rescues to plan."

Felix rubbed his hands together. "I can help you get into the Catacombs. I didn't bring them with me, but I have access to the most comprehensive maps created within the past few years." He checked his watch. "I can never remember whether there's a time difference between Raetia and Parisii."

"There's not," Zerandan said.

"Still, for me to get the information tonight?" Felix paused. "I don't mean to presume, but—"

"Yes, we have plenty of room for you here if you return before dawn," Victory said. She clapped her hands. "So. Rescue Doyl. Open a breach between two worlds. Defeat the shadows. Come home."

Asaron laughed, a dark sound with a touch of eagerness. "Sounds so easy when you put it that way."

Felix dug through his piles and selected a thick volume. "Keep in mind that all we know about this other world is based on myth and legend, which contain multiple discrepancies based on the sources and time periods. But one thing all of them share about details regarding the 'darkness' or 'shadows' is that they are ruled or connected by a sort of collective hive mind."

"Well, that's terrifying," Mikelos said.

Unbidden, a voice rose from the depths of Victory's memories. *We will return one to whence one came. We will wait for one.* The creeping hands touching every part of her, within and without. "But possibly better than the prospect of cutting them down one by one on another bloody planet."

True to his word, Felix returned before first light with a detailed map of a little-known entrance to the Catacombs and the tunnels around it. Zerandan established that he would be able to get them from the entrance to the ceremonial space where the sacrifice was performed.

Studying the intricate drawing, Victory asked, "Is it the place where Syri… died?" A difficult question to ask, when she'd seen the young woman and fought by her side mere days ago. It already seemed like months since she'd been in Nacostina, when little more than a week had passed.

"Yes," Zerandan said. "Which makes the next sacrifice all the more integral to maintaining the world spell. The area was out of commission for a time after young Archer flooded out the caverns and destroyed the sculptures used to channel power. Perhaps that sort of external focus is what we have been missing in attempting to access your powers."

Asaron ignored Zerandan's contemplative stare. "What you see is what you get. I'm still pretty handy with a sword."

Mikelos leaned into the parlor. "Felix has settled in. David has agreed to drive us to the drop-off point, and he'll act as if the house still contains all of us for at least the next few nights."

"You think we're being surveilled?" Zerandan asked.

"Of course," Victory said. "We're in Stefania's territory under sufferance."

Zerandan heaved himself from his seat and searched for his cane. "I'm much too old for all of these conspiracies and secrets."

Victory led him to the front door. "Which is why you're helping us destroy them, right?"

"Precisely, my dear." He moved as if to embrace her, but Victory backed away. That level of their friendship had long passed. Instead, he said, "I'll see you tonight. Rest."

"You, too."

Once he'd disappeared down the street, toward wherever Zerandan was staying in Parisii, Victory closed the door behind him and fell into Mikelos' warm embrace. She tucked her face into the crook of his neck and soaked in his familiar, reassuring scent. "I'm sorry I dragged you into all this."

"Do you see me complaining? I'm worried I won't be more help. At the least, a liability in the Catacombs. This is your old world, not mine."

"And we thought we'd be done with my world after Jiang Yi Yue, which is why I'm apologizing." She squirmed out of his grip but caught one of his hands to lead him upstairs.

"Well, once we get to the shadow plane, I can summon more impossible weapons and make up for it." Mikelos paused in the doorway to their room. "Which sounds ridiculous, but I kind of love it."

"Do you think this is what life is like for the kids, with their magic we don't understand?" Victory stripped off her clothing, arranging it on the foot of the bed.

Mikelos tugged his shirt off. "I'm sure they'd be the first to reassure us that they don't do the impossible every day."

Once he'd dropped his shirt, Victory pressed in close. "This might be our last sane day for the foreseeable future. Shall we do something incredibly ordinary?"

Instead of answering, Mikelos caught her mouth with his, nipping at her bottom lip as he pulled her toward the bed.

"We're getting into Parisii's underworld—where the bones of elves, vampires, and werecreatures are kept—through the back of a bakery?" Asaron glared at those clustered behind him.

Victory repressed her laughter at his consternation. "Felix?"

The professor appeared almost a different man today, in jeans under an untucked button-up, the sleeves rolled to his elbows. Now, the rumpled hair struck her as dashing instead of unkempt. He peered at his notes in the dim light of the street lamp. "A patisserie that used to be a coffee shop. According to Mathieu's records, Parisii's resistance forces used it the last time this territory swapped hands between the British and Romans. There's a hidden entrance in the rear of the kitchen."

"How cloak and dagger," Mikelos said, peeking around the corner. "Hey, at least I'll get my macarons."

A growl touched Asaron's voice. "Priorities, daywalker."

Victory patted her sire's chest. "Like you don't have a soft spot for the coffee ones."

Felix perked up. "Oh, I do like those. And the raspberry."

Mikelos raised a hand. "Strawberry, here."

"Not that this discussion isn't relevant," Zerandan said, "but how are we supposed to get through the bakery into the tunnels?" He'd traded his familiar cane for a thicker walking stick. Two long knives hung from either side of his waist, similar to those Syri wielded.

Perhaps he'd been the one to train Syri in her chosen weapons, so many years ago. Now, however, they formed an incongruous group on an even stranger mission. Victory moved past Asaron for her own peek around the corner. The bakery cast a welcoming glow along the street, where in the evening hours, it appeared to be a quiet spot for a snack and drink instead of a bustling purveyor of baked goods. Within hours, the real work would begin when ovens fired up overnight in the summer heat. "Mikelos has the right idea."

Asaron groaned but waved them past. "Just give us a signal. Try to be subtle."

"Subtle is what we do best," Mikelos said. He followed Victory away from the group.

They paused at the sidewalk for a town-car to pass, and crossed the street. Once on the other side, Victory tucked her arm into the crook of Mikelos' elbow. An anonymous couple out for an evening stroll. With the short sword belted at her hip, but Parisii was a civilized city that hosted an active Mercenary Guild. No one would think twice.

They stepped inside the bakery accompanied by the tinkle of a bell at the top of the doorway. With a glance, Victory noted two students studying at adjoining tables. A young professional couple, flirting over espresso. A trio of teenage girls, paging through glossy magazines and exchanging the latest gossip. Behind the counter, another teenager with a sad attempt at a goatee called out, "Good evening, welcome to Georgina's. Would you like to try one of the drink specials?"

Mikelos radiated his trademark charm. "Young man, I hope you can help me. This is the seventh bakery we've visited tonight, and I'm at my wit's end."

Rafael, by this nametag, straightened at Mikelos' feigned urgency. "Um, what can I do to help?"

"Our boss is considering a formal visit from Veneti, but he's adamant his suite be stocked with the best macarons, like those he remembers from his youth." Mikelos waved Victory forward. "If your kitchen is amiable, we'd like to inspect the premises for quality. If the baking technique is suitable, we'll be ordering a significant sampler for final approval, which might lead to a large contract."

"Um, one moment, sir." Throat bobbing in nervousness, Rafael backed away from the register and ducked into the rear of the bakery, past a partial wall separating the commercial area of the business.

"Go call them over." Mikelos nudged Victory with an elbow.

"I have no idea where you're going with this." But she followed his request, opening the front door and murmuring Asaron's name into the breeze. The three men left their waiting spot and crossed the street.

"Mikelos already got us in?" Felix asked when they neared.

"He's working on it." They followed Victory across the shop. Their unique group had caught the attention of the young couple, though the students and teenagers remained oblivious.

Rafael emerged from the rear, followed by a flour-dusted woman wiping her hands with a cloth. She considered Mikelos, then the rest of their party. "It takes all this to sample some macarons?" She cracked the knuckles in her left hand, but it seemed an unconscious habit.

Mikelos ignored the question. "If you'd be so kind, we'll place an order now of a variety." He plucked three bills from his wallet. "Heavy on the raspberry, strawberry, and coffee."

The baker tilted her head from side to side, long neck arching like a crane's, and jerked her chin toward the display case. Rafael accepted the cash and pulled out a cardboard travel box for assembly. "While he's doing that, you might as well come on back." She paused. "Don't touch anything."

They followed her around the counter where Rafael curated a selection of macarons. With a pang, Victory realized they wouldn't be fetching the treats if everything went according to Mikelos' bizarre plan.

A good sign—her brain operating under the assumption that this crazy mission would be a success. She and Asaron lurked in the doorway between the kitchen and front of the shop while Mikelos and Zerandan followed the baker around the working space, murmuring assent at her talk of cooking temperatures and pastry technique. Perhaps Zerandan understood the details, but Mikelos' primary knowledge of baked goods was in the eating of them.

Felix, however, drifted toward the rear of the kitchen. The baker kept half an eye on him, but he kept his hands shoved in his pockets. Until she bent to open an unused oven for Zerandan's inspection. With vampiric speed, Felix crossed the final feet and plucked at a metal sconce protruding from the wall, one of the few historic touches left in the expanse of modern stainless-steel appliances and marble preparation spaces.

The baker whirled, the oven slamming shut. "Hey—what the hell?"

A section of wooden paneling shuddered and jerked to the side, rusted mechanisms fighting their way to life. A sliver of darkness sliced through the brightness of the kitchen, and cool air cut through the sweeter scents of rising dough and fruit preserves.

Zerandan bowed to the baker, who continued to gape at Felix in shock. "Apologies for our deception, madame. If you don't mind, we'll continue our inspection at a later date."

"Whoa." Rafael lurked at Victory's shoulder, clutching a paper bag to his chest. "That always been there?"

The baker rubbed her brow. "I'd heard rumors, but I got this place for a steal." She waved a hand, and another joint in her wrist creaked. "You people doing something illegal?"

"We're on a rescue mission," Mikelos said. "We'd appreciate your discretion in this matter."

The baker brushed past Felix and peered into the darkness. "Looks like you're going to need a flashlight or two."

Felix patted his satchel. "We've come prepared."

The baker braced her hands on her hips. "Guess you're not taking the macarons?"

"Alas, no." Mikelos' longing expression toward the package Rafael clutched amused Victory. "But I'll probably be back, if it's any consolation."

"The consolation is that you're not getting a refund." Her stern demeanor broke at that point, and the baker shooed them away. "Go on your rescue mission. Good luck."

Felix dug the flashlights from his bag, handing them to Mikelos and Zerandan. Asaron sidled sideways to fit his broad shoulders through the thin opening. Felix, Mikelos, and Zerandan followed, and Victory touched the baker's hand on her way past. "Thank you."

"I like stories. Come back and tell me a good one."

"I will." Victory slid into the entrance to the Catacombs. The entryway creaked shut behind her, plunging her into the cool depths. She'd expected dampness in her mental image of the Catacombs, moldy ichor dripping from hand-carved corridors entrenched with the scent of death.

Instead, brick that matched the bakery's far wall surrounded her, its mortar crumbling in places from lack of maintenance. The air was cool and dry, but not stale as she'd expected, which meant air flow from elsewhere in these passageways. She caught up to the men over slate pavers worn smooth by the passage of feet and time.

"Shouldn't we be going down at some point?" Mikelos asked.

"Phrasing." Victory tossed off the quip out of habit, but her daywalker was right. By her sense of distance and direction, they'd traveled further into the depths of the interconnected buildings on this city block.

Felix consulted the note sheet he clutched. "No, we should be about... there." He pointed, and each flashlight aimed to illuminate an apparent dead end.

Asaron scratched his nose. "How useful."

Victory suppressed a scathing comment, and said "If this is a bust, going back to the bakery is going to be embarrassing."

"No, no. These were Resistance tunnels first, remember?" Felix hurried ahead, shoving his notes in a pocket. He ran his hands over the brick at shoulder height, testing each one and counting to himself. "Hmm. A bit of help here, please."

He directed Mikelos to one brick and Zerandan to another. With his own hands pressed to a third brick, he counted down. Victory shifted her balance to the balls of her feet, adrenaline surging. With simultaneous crunches, the men forced the bricks into their settings, and a section of slate pavers dropped away.

Asaron checked inside the revealed space. "Clear."

Victory edged next to him. The flashlights pierced the inky blackness like daggers, illuminating pieces of a corkscrew stairwell. "Anything?" Nothing but silence sounded beyond Mikelos and Zerandan's heartbeats, but Asaron might hear something she missed.

"Nope."

Victory backed away, allowing him to descend first. Rear guard suited her. Let the veritable tank encounter any potential obstacles first.

They proceeded along their course for close to an hour, but they found architectural obstacles instead of the combatants prowling the Catacombs whom Zerandan had warned them of. Twice more, the group encountered a blocked passageway. Felix consulted his notes, and lead them through a complicated pattern of hidden latches and mechanisms.

Victory lost all sense of depth or direction. Each secret doorway led to a section sealed long ago.

At least she wasn't claustrophobic. She had no idea how Toria had managed a similar journey. The weight of the earth would be a comfortable burrow for Toria's earth-mage partner, but torture for her storm-aligned daughter. Well, she did know how. If Toria had a job to do, she'd do it. Come hell or high water. Or buried depths.

The building materials around them shifted from sturdy hardwood to brick, then to the minerals of the old quarries. Through it all, they found occasional rodent traces—and once more than a trace, as Felix trod on a large rat that scurried away with an aggrieved shriek—but neither whiff nor whisper of another sentient being.

The group halted when Asaron raised a fist. He stooped over to snag something off the ground. Turning, he extended a palm. "We're close."

Victory peered around Mikelos. Asaron cupped a single vertebra in his broad hand. No blood stained the bone, nor was there any other sign of viscera. Time and exposure had worn it smooth, until it was almost indistinguishable from the other random rocks tucked against the base of the surrounding walls.

Zerandan hovered his hand above the bone but did not take it from Asaron. He closed his eyes in quiet contemplation. "A werecreature, once upon a time," he said. "But I'm unable to determine further. We're getting close, at least."

"Um, yes." Felix consulted his notes. "Close to one of the outer stretches of corridor where reliquaries are kept."

Asaron replaced the bone against the base of the wall, tucked against another rock and away from unobservant footsteps. "Be on guard."

The group descended into silence, Asaron's order putting a stop to the previous quiet conversation. Trusting Asaron to keep watch for anything they might stumble across, Victory listened for movement behind them as branching corridors and air shafts intersected this main pathway at regular intervals.

She followed on Mikelos' heels around a curve, where their hall joined with an even larger corridor. The Catacombs lacked the aura of death she had assumed would permeate such a massive collection of remains, but the arranged piles of bones spread along the opposite wall stopped her short. She slipped her hand into Mikelos'.

He returned her firm grip. "I used to think I would end up down here one day."

Uncanny how he echoed her thoughts of the previous evening. "I'm not sure I ever thought I would. And now I suppose I'd like to stay in Limani if—if anything ever happens."

"But a hundred years ago," Mikelos said, "or five hundred years ago, could you have imagined that? Where might we be years from now?"

Asaron, leading Felix and Zerandan farther along the passageway, called out behind him. "Dying of old age if you two don't get a move on."

Mikelos drew away from her. Because he stepped to the side, rather than forward, the slim dart passed his neck and clattered against the bones lining the wall.

Victory slammed against the empty side of the hall, flattening herself to provide a smaller target. She'd heard no heartbeat behind them, no breathing, not even footsteps, which meant—

A vampire sped toward them, pale hair streaming behind. Her fingers gripped another slim dart in a hand cocked to release. Victory cried out and drew her sword, but the arc of the blade was too slow to block the second dart. It flew by her. Her momentum knocked her shoulder into the side of the vampire as she sped past, killing the other woman's velocity and sending them both crashing to the ground.

The vampire clawed at Victory, trying to scramble out from under her weight. Victory dropped her sword in favor of hand-to-hand combat. She managed to pin one of the flailing arms but the woman's fingers caught her thick braid. The vampire wrenched Victory's head to the side.

Dull metal flashed, and in an instant, the woman beneath her stilled. A human would have heaved for air past the adrenaline, but it was as if Victory sprawled over a statue.

"I've got her," Mikelos said, the blade of his multi-tool pressed to the vampire's throat.

Victory eased herself off the tense woman. Her terror was rational—recovery time for throat wounds was a bitch. Victory loomed over the prone woman, slipping into her fierce Master of the City persona. Her people had been attacked, and she wouldn't stand for it. "Who the hell are you?"

Asaron stepped next to her with daggers held in each hand as Mikelos eased away from the vampire. Felix and Zerandan muttered to each other in low tones behind her, but Victory kept her attention on their attacker.

The woman surveyed them with an aura of disdain. "I'm a chosen guardian of this sacred space, where you trespass." She telegraphed deliberate movement, easing herself to her elbows and shifting forward to her knees. Even in this subservient position, she radiated attitude. A blouse showing her curves to good effect topped artfully ripped jeans and scuffed boots. And because the vampire was Parisiian, her blond curls had survived their scuffle intact, flowing over her shoulders.

Victory's own hair tickled her neck where it straggled out of her braid. "Unfortunately, we're here on a mission." Mikelos retrieved Victory's fallen sword and pressed it into her hand. She shifted her grip on the hilt but kept it lowered at her side.

"The younger vampires and elves of Parisii patrol these passages," Zerandan said. "It started as an honor guard for the dead but transitioned to protecting the magical spaces where the sacrifices are performed." He paused, unruffled. "They do not generally travel alone."

As if his words had summoned them, dual sets of heartbeats and footsteps coursed through the faintest edges of Victory's hearing and grew louder, like the rumble of thunder across an open plain. She brought up her sword. Asaron looped his arm around the vampire's neck and hauled her to her feet, keeping her immobile by placing the flat of a dagger against her throat.

Victory preferred him at her side, but none of the others had the combined strength and skills necessary to incapacitate a vampire. At least the heartbeats indicated elves who approached. Still strong and fast as hell, but not to vampiric levels. She half-heard Asaron's instructions for Mikelos to guard Felix.

Her daywalker dropped back. Zerandan moved to her shoulder, gripping his walking stick between both hands like a short staff, as if affirming his commitment to their cause even if it meant fighting his own kind.

With a skitter of old gravel, two men burst around the corner.

One hesitated at the tableau before them, but the vampire in Asaron's grip called out. "Kill them!" Asaron choked off whatever else she might have ordered.

The second elf never slowed. Victory blocked one knife with her short sword, then side-stepped to deflect the second jab by crossing her forearm against his. The elf grunted when Zerandan slammed his stick into the man's ribcage, washing Victory with a wave of sour breath. In his distraction, she punched him in the side of the skull. But with the odd angle, and her nondominant arm, the blow only staggered him.

Zerandan blocked the second elf from making it past them. With a flick of her wrist, she reversed her grip on the short sword. This time, her punch slammed the pommel of the sword into the elf's temple. The slight crack could have been skull, or another kicked rock. No matter, the man crumpled to the ground. His knives fell from limp fingers.

Zerandan forced the second elf away, stick brandished before him. Victory didn't recognize the language Zerandan spoke, but his harsh, urgent tone translated clearly.

As did the other man's response. "Fuck off, old man." He ducked under Zerandan's defense and knocked him to the side. Two steps beyond Zerandan, his torso slid to a halt against the cross guard of Victory's short sword. Pain jerked his head back, and Victory withdrew the sword from his body. Red liquid coated the blade, the savory scent of elven lifeblood, and burbled out of the wound in his chest. He dropped his knives and clapped his hands over the wound, collapsing to his knees, then to the ground.

"Shit! You little—"

Victory whirled at Asaron's curse, ignoring the fallen elves at her feet. The heady scent of their blood filled the passageway. She caught the tail end of the female vampire writhing out of Asaron's grip. The woman slid past Mikelos, snatching the knife from his hand.

Toward Felix.

He should have run.

He should have been anywhere except in the Catacombs with them.

Instead, he met the woman head-on. Unable to block, the knife she wielded knocked the flashlight from his hands. In the wild beam of light, she buried the knife in his throat, slicing to the side.

Asaron grabbed her shirt to drag her away, but she pulled a second throwing dagger from her belt. With a smooth motion, she stabbed it in Felix's eye, far enough to penetrate brain.

Victory didn't remember reaching them. The world didn't always slow down when she acted, and on occasion, her brain made decisions for her body at lightning speed, without conscious input. And now two vampires littered the ground.

The woman's head rolled to a halt next to Mikelos' boot. He stared at Victory. Not in horror, but absolute surprise.

Asaron knelt next to Felix, checking his wounds. "We could have used her."

"She killed Felix."

"Is she dead?" Zerandan asked, moving next to Mikelos. "The other two are."

"She's dead." Asaron stood, brushing dust from his knees. "We can survive a lot, but a double wound to brain and throat? All the blood in the world can't fix that."

Victory wiped her blade clean on the dead woman's shirt. Death didn't come easy to her, except in defense of her people. Felix had been one of them, and already his loss weighed heavy on her shoulders. The man might not have been Jarimis' progeny, but he was of the same ilk. A link to the man she'd left behind in the past. She forced down a growl at a death that should not mean this much to her. Would not, except as she stared at the man's bloodied visage, it was too easy to overlay Jarimis' olive skin over Felix's face. An unstaring black eye instead of gray.

She should have been faster. Asaron should have been faster.

If her sire experienced the same guilt, however, he showed none of it. "What the hell do we do now? Felix could read the damned map."

Mikelos balked at leaving the bodies—Felix's body—abandoned in the passageway. But they had a mission to complete, and they were close enough to the main sacrificial chamber for Zerandan to lead them the rest of the way.

While Zerandan and Mikelos kept watch, Victory and Asaron arranged Felix along the edge of the passageway lined with bones, beneath the empty eye sockets of vampire, elven, and werecreature skulls. They pulled the dead elves and unknown dead vampire to the opposite side. Victory tugged the knife from Felix's eye socket and returned it to the woman's belt. The weapon was well forged, but she wasn't in the business of collecting trophies.

They followed Zerandan away, leaving behind the fallen to be consumed by darkness. If they failed in this mission, they would join Felix. They'd join all of the dead in the Catacombs, forever buried beneath Parisii.

The group moved along corridors lined with bones in silence. Zerandan traced an unknown mental map, though he did pause at one doorway in a hallway lined with empty cells. "We are close. This is where they kept Doyl."

No one questioned the elf. The organization of bones in the hallways became more elaborate the farther they trekked. An alcove with a detailed carving—the side of a castle and aqueduct brought to life in stone—broke the macabre.

"Huh," Asaron said. Even his low grunt seemed loud in the rarified Catacombs air.

"Hmm?" Victory kept her voice low.

"I've been there. That's the palace on Balearic Minor."

Zerandan silenced them with a hiss. "We're close to the main chamber."

She did not respond, either to Asaron's comment or Zerandaon's order. Professionalism had never defined Victory's working relationship with Asaron, since she'd gone from new vampire who only knew the pointy end of the sword went into the other guy to the partner in a well-oiled mercenary machine. But soon she would need her Master of the City persona again. Better to draw it close now, enveloping her like a robe of state, than scramble for the correct attitude when needed.

A warm glow emerged at the end of the passageway. Zerandan flicked off his flashlight and collected the other from Mikelos to stow in the satchel spattered with vampire blood he'd retrieved from Felix's corpse. The group paused a second time once they drew closer. Victory tuned out the two heartbeats in her own group and stretched her hearing into the cavern beyond.

The air had turned musty, a touch of dampness where there had been none before. The stacked bones nearby showed significant color striations, as if the delicate stacks had collapsed and been restored in a different pattern. She peered toward the clear side of the pathway in the low light and found a water-level mark two hand spans above the floor.

Signs of floodwater. An unnatural flood, summoned by a terrified water mage, doing his best to help his companions in an impossible situation.

The cavern they approached was where Syri had died. Where Kane had died, until Serena traded her life for his.

Zerandan's aura of calm disclosed none of the emotions that might roil beneath his placid surface. After all, his machinations had led to Syri's kidnapping and eventual death. Did he feel anything of that? For all the similarities between elves and vampires due to their long lifespans, the two species were as alien as possible from each other.

The old elf led them onward, toward the voices spilling from the cavern. His footsteps grew heavier and his walking stick scuffed at the pathway in a clumsiness he hadn't shown before.

Which meant that when they stepped out of the darkness, entering the wide cavern below a soaring ceiling, an expectant audience awaited them.

The vampires clashed with their surroundings, their formal evening wear out of place among the floor tiled with patterns meant to enhance magical power. It was as if they visited the delicate bone sculptures that decorated the room to drink evening cocktails at an art gallery rather than a scene of death.

Stefania spoke first, Pietrov at her back. "I should have known you wouldn't be able to stay out of my business while you were here." Her daywalker was nowhere to be seen, but across from her stood three elves. Two glared in Zerandan's direction. The third, a young boy barely out of his teens, knelt on the floor in an almost catatonic state. Doyl's dirty T-shirt and bare feet contrasted with the immaculate, jewel-toned ceremonial robes of his elders.

Showtime. Victory lifted her empty hands, though she itched to draw her sword against the rage that flashed across Stefania's face. "I apologize for presenting us under false pretenses earlier, but the situation is out of my control."

"Don't you see you're being manipulated?" Stefania thrust a finger toward Zerandan, who maintained his unflappable calm. "You wouldn't be here if it weren't for him."

"We're here to prevent another in a series of unnecessary deaths." Victory gestured toward Doyl, who had yet to even look in their direction. "Zerandan doesn't manipulate us because I agree with his cause. Killing elves to maintain the world spell is opening this world to further attack."

"If an attack is coming, I know exactly where from." Stefania placed one hand against a cocked hip. "Is that what this has come to? A formal challenge for my territory in return for the hospitality I've shown you?" The Master of Parisii shifted her attention from Victory to Pietrov. "Isn't this adorable? The vampire mercs think they can trade their little city for mine."

Her second did not return her humor, keeping a posture and tone in studied neutrality. "I do not presume to know Victory and Asaron's true intentions here."

But when Stefania spun to confront the intruders again, he slid two steps away from her.

"What will it be, Victory?" Stefania strode through the open space, stepping across the magical circles as if they were nothing more than colorful floor tiles. "How are you and Asaron going to stop what we are doing here, when we have the full backing of the Senate in Roma? With the help of a musician and an elf who needs to remember his proper place?"

Dread collected in the pit of Victory's stomach. Stefania had confirmed Zerandan's words, that the Senate supported the world spell despite their silence. This wasn't a fight against a collective of rogue elves and the vampires of Parisii. This was a fight on a global scale.

Asaron collected his wits first. "We have no interest in Parisii. We're here to rescue the boy."

At his words, the young elf who cowered at the feet of his robed elders trembled harder. Doyl's shaggy hair and long limbs had fooled Victory at first glance. This wasn't an elf on the verge of true adulthood. Syri had nearly achieved her first century before her murder. This boy had not passed the stage when elven aging slowed in comparison to human. He appeared in his mid-teens because he was. His obvious terror firmed Victory's resolve. "Come here, kid. We won't hurt you."

Doyl scrambled to his feet, dodging the outstretched hands of his guards, and raced to Victory's side. She exchanged a wordless glance with Mikelos, who tucked the boy under his arm.

"Master Stefania!" One of the elves fluttered his hands, his voice anxious. "The success of the ritual requires strict adherence to the agreed-upon schedule. We have no time for your petty politics."

"And I intend to dismiss this temporary setback. I won't let outsiders distract me from my duty, unlike the moment of weakness that led to my predecessor's death." Stefania inspected her manicure, and turned to Pietrov as if they discussed nothing more important than the weather. "The lives of more dumb mercs are not worth the effort we've needed to restore the damage to the world spell after the last pair."

Mikelos beat Pietrov to responding. "You speak of my children, there."

Stefania's peal of false laughter echoed in the chamber. "Even worse! It's as if, after Connor and Serena, the world is telling you your family doesn't deserve to be alive, and you're too stupid to listen."

"You have no right to comment on my family in such a way." Rage seethed in Mikelos' voice.

"And you have no right to be in my presence, daywalker." Stefania spat the title. "Hell, you have no right to be alive, considering Connor disappeared almost a hundred years ago." Of course, Stefania subscribed to the traditional belief that a daywalker not outlive his vampire.

They couldn't risk losing what little control of this situation they wielded because Stefania goaded Mikelos' temper into explosion instead. But before Victory could respond, help arrived from an unexpected source.

"Enough!" Pietrov's baritone rang out, and vampires and elves alike froze. He grabbed Stefania's shoulder.

She gaped at his breach of protocol. "How dare you interrupt me."

"No, Stefania." With his solid bulk of muscle, Pietrov didn't budge when Stefania attempted to wriggle loose. He ignored her sputters of indignation. "Master Victory, will you pledge your support to my claim of Parisii and its surrounding territory?"

Stefania's outraged shriek almost rattled the delicate sculptures of bone. The robed elves burst into their own aggrieved protestations, but Zerandan stepped forward, snarling at them in the elven tongue until they fell into wounded silence.

Victory caught Pietrov's dark eyes. He returned the gaze with stoic calm, showing neither deference nor an attempt to dominate her. "How long has this been in the works?"

"Since I connected the blasted shadows I keep seeing with the world spell's power and influence. You lot arriving in Parisii, and now here, only moved my time-table forward."

"I imagine this isn't how you planned to stage your coup. I'd have a lot more muscle with me."

"Which is why I hoped I could count on you. Though my compatriots will be irritated to miss the fun."

"You bastard." Stefania wrenched herself away, or Pietrov let her go. "Who else is part of this conspiracy? I'll kill them after I rid myself of you."

Pietrov ignored her. "Do I have Limani's support?"

This decision was well within Victory's right to make, but Limani had never had a typical Master of the City. She checked over her shoulder, where Asaron kept a white-knuckle grip on Mikelos' wrist. Doyl had retreated behind Zerandan, who brandished his walking stick.

Her sire jerked his chin once.

She turned to Pietrov. "You have Limani's support."

Stefania lunged at Pietrov with clawed fingers, a wordless growl on her lips. Unarmed except for his suit, the new claimant to Parisii's metaphorical throne dodged her raked nails. His dapper shoes lost their grip on the tiled flooring.

Victory maneuvered herself between the vampires, sword drawn. But the weapon did nothing to deter Stefania, who turned her rage to the foreign intruder.

The robed elves broke rank at this breakdown in civility, and Asaron ordered Zerandan to protect the boy.

Victory covered Pietrov while he regained his footing. "Give it up, Stefania," she said as Stefania flinched away from the exposed blade.

"How dare you break the law of hospitality. You should be defending me."

Accurate. Victory hadn't gone far in her lone attempt at Roman respectability, because she valued pragmatism over tradition. But some actions were sacrosanct, and Victory had no desire to claim Parisii herself. "Don't worry. Pietrov will still be the one to kill you."

Her words goaded Stefania, who lunged at Victory. The woman might not be a professional fighter, but no one lived centuries without learning a few tricks. Stefania dodged at the last moment, sacrificing a slice to her forearm to slip into close range where the sword became useless. Victory tilted away, and the woman's nails raked her neck, opening lines of fire along the side of her throat. Instead of raising her free arm in defense, Victory shoved her shoulder at Stefania, forcing her back. But Stefania snatched at Victory's arm, tugging her off-balance.

Victory swung her sword, and this time the blade struck a solid blow. Steel grated against bone in a spray of black blood that stained Stefania's silk dress and the interlocking ritual circles beneath their feet.

They broke apart. Stefania clutched her wounded arm to her side. She opened her mouth, but no words came out. She doubled over in pain, dropping to her knees.

"Victory!" Asaron's call rang across the space. He restrained one of the elves, a dagger braced across his throat. A trickle of red stood out against the man's pale neck. The other elf sprawled at their feet, unmoving. Zerandan still guarded Doyle, but Mikelos pointed with an arm outstretched, horror stretching his face gaunt. Pietrov stared at a far corner, unmoving.

Toward the gathering shadows.

A high-pitched keening reverberated through Victory's skull. It came from Stefania, still curled at her feet. Right now, the shadows seemed content to writhe in a static pattern rather than coalesce to attack the way they had in the shadow plane. Or perhaps, even in this place saturated with death magic, they did not have that ability in this more mortal realm.

"Please don't let them have me. Please. I never did anything. I just want to go home."

Doyl's begging penetrated Victory's shock. The kid gripped Zerandan's sleeve, though it was unclear to whom he directed his pleas.

The elf captured in Asaron's grip answered first. "Your death will serve a far greater purpose than your life ever has." He struggled against Asaron, heedless of the blade at his throat. "You will die for the greater good, broken one."

Asaron withdrew the knife, but not to release the man. Instead, he reversed his grip on the weapon and slammed the end of the hilt into the man's temple. He crumpled to the ground, silenced. "We don't threaten kids," Asaron said

Zerandan wrapped an arm around Doyl's shivering shoulders. "Have no fear, child. I'll make sure you're kept safe." He didn't promise he'd send Doyl home. After all, it might have been his own blood who'd sent him to be the next sacrifice. Perhaps Zerandan's miscalculation, risking Syri's life for the greater good, haunted him more than Victory knew.

"I've seen this before," Pietrov said. "The shadows still need a sacrifice. Some sort of death. Or they'll keep coming." He glanced over his shoulder, where Mikelos stood rigid. "And it won't just be the vampires who see them. Right, daywalker?"

Mikelos remained silent, but Zerandan said, "It is why Serena sacrificed herself when the warrior-mages disrupted the ceremony."

But it wasn't any death that the shadows needed. Or else Kane's death would have banished them to whence they came. They needed—

"Give me the sword, Victory." Pietrov stretched out his hand, as if requesting a spare pen. "Tradition requires a death."

This spurred Stefania from her near-catatonia, and she moaned at their feet. "No, Petey. I trusted you."

"And I trusted you, until I learned the truth of what I supported." Pietrov accepted Victory's weapon. The short sword fit in his hand like a toy. He placed the tip of the blade under Stefania's chin, urging her to a kneeling position.

Her hand gripped the gaping wound on her opposite arm, though blood no longer seeped from it. Her demeanor changed yet again, trying another tack.

"You'll regret this. The others will never follow you. Amara will avenge me."

"Apparently, your daywalker will be too busy committing suicide to come after me." Pietrov lifted the sword, prepared to swing.

Victory grabbed his raised elbow. "Killing her will close the portal."

"I bloody well intend to, before those things figure out which way is up and come for us all."

"We're here to stop that. We didn't just come to rescue the boy. We're going to close the breaches once and for all." Victory cocked a thumb in Zerandan and Doyl's direction. "Make sure they make it out of here, okay?"

Pietrov's brow furled. "You're insane."

Asaron and Mikelos approached, skirting the blood-stained ritual circles. "Maybe," Asaron said. "But it sounds like you're ready to be rid of these shadows, and my progeny has a plan."

"A bare-bones plan," Victory said. "But we have to get through that portal first."

"Go." Pietrov gestured in the shadows' direction. "I'll handle the elves."

Victory didn't wait for him to change his mind. She sprinted across the cavern, weaving around the bone sculptures, with Mikelos and Asaron on her heels.

The shadows loomed, a swirling mass of darkness upon more darkness. Everything in her, every iota of self-preservation that had kept her alive for centuries, screamed at her to stop. To back off and find a way to combat these shadows from the safety of her own world.

Lifting crossed arms before her face, she sped through the maelstrom.

The worn cavern floor beneath her boot treads turned gritty, but she did not slam face-first into the bones that lined the walls. The shadows enveloped her body, sweeping like a lover's caress over her bare skin. Victory screamed, but never heard the sound.

And then it all stopped.

She slid to a halt and dropped her arms. The eerie touch fell away, and the air around her was still. Pale, diffuse light cascaded through the flat landscape of gray hues, almost blinding after the dim cavern of bone.

Footsteps crunched behind her, and she turned. But Asaron and Mikelos had already transferred between worlds, and she missed any glimpse of the portal behind them. Either Pietrov hadn't wasted any time removing Stefania's head from her body or the portal simply wasn't visible on this side.

Mikelos turned in place. "This doesn't look anything like where we left."

Dread pooled in Victory's stomach. He was right, and she hadn't realized. Or hadn't wanted to face it. Gone were the towering pillars of gray rock where they had stood their ground against the shadows before. This might be the exact spot where the artifact had first transported them to the shadow plane from the mage school in Limani, or somewhere else in this other world entirely, without features to distinguish the two.

SHADOW

"About time you guys showed up again."

Victory's hand spasmed for a sword no longer there, until the familiarity of Syri's voice penetrated.

This time, the elven girl ducked when Asaron lashed out. "Too slow, old man."

"Have respect for your elders."

Unbidden, Syri approached Victory and hugged her. "It's good to see you all again. I mean, not good, I guess," she said, her voice muffled in Victory's shoulder. "You know what I mean."

The girl should have seemed frail, ghostly, the way the strange light of this world washed her out. But she was strong and firm in Victory's arms, reassuring in a place where nothing seemed right.

When they broke apart, Syri turned to Mikelos for the same. When they too stepped away from each other, she seemed to be checking the area around them. "Hmm, the others should have tracked me here."

They all tensed. "Who?" Asaron asked, demand and fear warring in his voice. "Them."

Three figures appeared nearby, with no sense of transport or movement, as if they'd always stood there.

A short woman with close-cropped black hair, corded with muscle. Age lines creased her bronze complexion, and her dark eyes flashed beneath hooded lids that softened the edges of her square jaw. She carried the weight of her leather armor, the likes of which Victory had never seen, as if born to it. Next to her stood a dashing young man. An exact match to the painting of Connor in the Parisii townhouse. And by his side—

Victory sprinted forward and threw herself into Jarimis' arms. Her momentum spun them around, both laughing. After their goodbye in Nacostina, she'd assumed that had been it. But then she'd caught the glimpse of him before they were hurtled between space once again, and she hadn't dare let herself hope.

"I thought that was you," she said, her face mushed against his broad shoulder. He'd lost the drab suit he'd worn in Nacostina, exchanged for jeans and a colorless shirt like Syri's.

"It was me. I'm sorry our forces didn't arrive quick enough for me to greet you." He released Victory from his embrace but kept one arm clasped around her, as if he didn't want to let her go any more than she did. "Is it bad that I'm glad you're here?"

"Well, I'm pissed." A strident tone interrupted their reunion. The other man had a vice grip on Mikelos' wrist, shaking it while he ranted. "How the hell could you let this happen? You lot are supposed to protect your daywalker, not let him follow you into danger!"

"Connor."

At Mikelos' reproach, the vampire released his grip and stalked away in a huff. He paced three or four strides before turning on his heel and returning, catching Mikelos in a back-pounding hug. "Damn it, it's good to see you." He seemed comically short next to Mikelos, except Mikelos stood so tall.

It was easy to pretend Jarimis had returned to her, healthy and hale. And Syri was, well, whatever Syri was. But Connor's appearance jarred her equilibrium. The dead had risen in this strange place. Or had they ever been dead at all?

One anomaly remained. Past Jarimis' shoulder, Asaron stood near the mysterious woman. Though they didn't touch, he dipped his ear toward her low tones in an unknown language. The woman touched Asaron's hand in wonderment.

Mikelos cleared his throat, capturing their attention.

Asaron presented the woman as if making a formal court introduction, but words seemed to fail him. "This is Ahn." The woman touched his arm again, firmer this time. "My sire."

Victory's mind whirled, and moments in time surfaced from the deep recesses of her memory. Asaron training her in combat, a brand-new vampire learning everything about death and life at the same time. His muttered comments about how someone would be so disappointed in her, or perhaps in him. But she'd improved, and the comments had stopped. Or perhaps time had stolen Asaron's memories as well.

She could never imagine forgetting Asaron, but he'd been her stalwart companion for centuries. If he'd died long ago, would he still be such a dominating figure in her life?

Mikelos, ever the gentleman, presented a short bow. "An honor to meet you, Ahn."

Her brow furrowed while she inspected the daywalker. Did she not speak Loquella? Asaron's original people hailed from the northern expanse of Europa, where land touched ice instead of sea. But this woman's dark features originated from a different source. Victory tried Qin, instead. *"A pleasure to make your acquaintance, honored elder."*

Ahn snorted. "I understand you, girl. But I appreciate the effort. I might still be in shock."

"Aren't we all," Connor said. "We're minding our business when Syri swoops in and says we have to go. And then you lot show up. Which I'm still mad about, by the way."

"But where have you been all this time?" Victory asked. Jarimis felt solid beneath her touch. As solid as he'd been in Nacostina. "You're not… dead?"

Jarimis looked away, his familiar tell for words he'd prefer not to speak. Ahn's placidness contrasted with the stubborn jut of Connor's jaw. Syri sucked her cheeks in. "They're not dead any more than I'm really an elf, in the grand scheme of things. It's complicated."

"It's all been damned complicated, from the beginning." Asaron jabbed his finger into the empty distance. "Do we start walking again, or what?"

"We start walking again," Mikelos said. "We follow Felix's instructions. We have to find the center. Find this hive mind of the shadows and do what we can from this end to cut them off."

"Cut them off from what?" But Jarimis' eagle-eyed gaze settled on Syri this time. "Your kind has never been forthright with us. What's going on?"

"The shadows are invading," Mikelos said. "And we have to stop them before they destroy our world like they did this one. Oh, and magic will die if we don't succeed."

The three memories of the past rounded on Syri. It seemed they were already familiar with who held all the cards in the situation. Syri let her hair fall in front of her face like a shield. "Yeah. And you guys have never been to the protected lands, so we can't transport you there. We're walking."

Syri's explanation filled in some of Felix's blanks. Where Felix's information had come from millennia-old oral histories, Syri spoke of the here and now. In the same manner that the walls crumbled between this world and the "real" one, the borders the creatures of light had erected to contain the shadows here also shrank. Now, Syri led them to one of the last strongholds of the light in a world either consumed by shadows or abandoned to this in-between territory known as the badlands.

Syri trudged next to Victory, the two of them leading the train of the displaced. "No one has been able to figure out how the intelligence behind the shadows, what your friend called the hive mind, lost control so thoroughly," Syri said. "It's not like we can speak to it."

"Has anyone ever tried?" Mikelos asked.

Jarimis laughed, a harsh tone devoid of humor. "Don't ask that in the stronghold. The inability of Syri's people to communicate with the shadows is a sore point."

"Sore is an understatement," Connor said. "It's the sort of question all newcomers to this world tend to ask, and we get shut down right quick."

"Leaving aside the how for now, why are you here, though?" Victory walked backward a handful of paces, until Syri tugged her around to avoid tripping. Over her shoulder, she called, "Other than Syri, who apparently belongs here. Except that doesn't explain how she was in our world, first."

"When the world spell tapped into the power of the shadows for fuel, my people knew it was a bad idea," Syri said. "The elders used the breach to send some of us to be born as young elves. We didn't anticipate the divisiveness it would cause when the elves realized we were more fuel for the spell."

This created far more questions than it answered. Victory dug at one sticking point. "How did the death of my Syri create you?"

But the strange yet familiar young woman next to them was still the Syri she'd known, and that Syri could give a master-class in topic avoidance.

"Death isn't the word you should be using, I guess. Not for any of us."

"Are we dead?" Victory asked, swaying on her feet. "Me, Asaron, Mikelos?"

Syri could also give a master-class in sarcasm. "You were okay in Parisii, right? You're not dead."

Connor contributed the snark from behind them. "We're vampires, honey. What's the difference?"

Victory's hands curled, but she forced them to relax when the prick of fingernails dug into her palms. The man wasn't like anything Victory had ever imagined, and she had no time for his casual mockery. Outside of Connor's biting humor, the original source of Mikelos' charm was evident, but she'd expected—

Well, a shorter, older version of Mikelos. Not this man who rough-housed and used five words where one might do.

Mikelos laughed, and Connor smacked his arm. Mikelos smacked him right back. Victory swallowed the odd lump in her throat. Mikelos was her love, but Connor had been his best friend for far longer than she'd been with him. A different sort of friendship, but a true bond. No less significant than her love for Jarimis.

She had no damned good reason to be jealous of Connor.

Or of Ahn, who paced with Asaron at the end of their line, keeping the rear guard. Jarimis had ranged out to the side, as if he knew Victory's current equilibrium depended on keeping him in eyesight. Mikelos hadn't batted an eye when she'd clung to Jarimis' hand for so long. She should take comfort in her daywalker's faith and offer hers in return.

Like last time, the rocks at their feet turned from pebbles to stones to boulders while they traveled. Connor flagged at the unrelenting pace first.

He threw himself on a stone at convenient sitting height and refused to budge. "I'm a man of art, not physical labor. These muscles are better put to more pleasurable activities, not walking through this endless waste of space." He winked at Victory in staged flirtation.

Mikelos settled next to him, shoulders sagging in exhaustion, and her own irritation turned to guilt. Connor had noticed Mikelos' state, where she had been too busy prying information from Syri.

Mikelos' expression of pleasure lightened their dull surroundings. He patted the semi-flat stone on his other side. "How are you doing?"

"I should be asking you that." His hand was dry but warm when she captured it as she settled next to him. At least this strange place maintained a steady temperature, neither too hot nor too cold. No wind ruffled Mikelos' hair or pulled at her braid.

Was it even air they breathed? Or was it all a simulated manifestation created from light and darkness? Pure magic, even if a different sort of magic than her children manipulated. After all, she'd been able to perform magic of a sort here, summoning weaponry from otherwise still air.

Which reminded her. Her sire didn't sit, instead standing watch a short distance away. Ahn stood next to him, a matched pair even if he stood head and shoulders above her. Oh, he would hate her for this. "Asaron. Perhaps Zerandan's lessons will have more effect here, within the place you were reaching for."

His shoulders stiffened, but Syri's bright laughter beat his response. "Oh man, Zerandan tried to teach you vampiric magic? The old man's been up to a lot while I've been gone."

"Only within the last few days," Asaron said. "And his attempts proved I have neither the inclination nor the skill." Any other man might balk at admitting weakness, but Asaron was too much the professional to claim abilities he did not possess.

"That's because he was talking out of his ass." Syri hopped off her rocky perch to approach Asaron.

Mikelos poked her arm when she passed. "Speaking of respect for one's elders."

She spun on her heel, and for a split second, her face contorted in rage before smoothing into her standard amusement. "I love the man like a father, but he got me killed. I'll say whatever the fuck I want about him." Returning to Asaron, she spread her arms. "What seems to be the problem, sir?"

Victory pulled her feet onto the rock, cross-legged, to study the proceedings. Specifically, to watch Ahn. Because if Asaron had never heard of vampiric magic, what knowledge might a vampire thousands of years older than him possess?

It was as if Asaron read her mind. Rounding on his sire, he asked, "Had you ever heard of this? Vampires, using magic?"

She wasn't quick to respond, and in her reaction, Victory found hints of Asaron's deliberateness, and of her own. They might not be related by genetics, but they were, after all, related by blood. "I am not personally familiar with ever using what you call magic, but I imagine I come from what you would think of as a very different time. Remember, even when you were young, we did not associate much with others of our kind." To the rest of them, she continued, "In my time, it was common for an unmarried, unwanted older woman of the household to be handed over to the religious orders. I thought the path of a monk was for me, but after I was turned, restlessness took hold. The path I wandered led me far from my homeland, and I realized in time that the politicians in Roma had no respect for a vampire not bred to be one of theirs. I was always a woman caught between two worlds."

Her gaze settled on Victory, who managed to return it for a mere second before being forced away. Ahn's power thrummed through Victory's skull, but the older woman's expression was kind. "I see my legacy has continued in that regard."

"But, that." Jarimis waved his arms, as if trying to encompass the physicality of their momentary connection. "How is that, what vampires do, not a form of

105

magic? Victory once stared me down hard enough to cause a migraine. Hell, I never considered myself all that powerful in the grand scheme of things, but I can still put a human to sleep with a bit of mental twist and half a thought. That's magic."

"That's who we are." Connor jumped from his rock in a return to his previous semi-manic state. "Those are skills we evolved to be predators. Not magic." He spat the last word.

"And what would you know about being a predator?" Mikelos laughed, a sound that warmed Victory in this pale land. "Stalking cute courtesans doesn't count."

"It's not my fault I was born into a more civilized age." Connor waved in Asaron and Ahn's general direction. "I'm talking about vampires like them."

Asaron might have been offended, but Ahn's wry cackle lightened the tone. "It is true I once hunted humans to feed. If that is no longer the case, the world has grown indeed."

"We're getting off-track," Jarimis said. "If what vampires already do is magic, what is preventing Asaron from doing more magic?"

He spoke with his professorial voice, and a sharp pain of mourning struck her. Would she get used to being with her progeny again, and lose him for a third time? She shoved the fear away. No time for laters when they had to worry about right now.

Syri offered Mikelos a canteen she hadn't carried before. "You good?"

Victory snatched the canteen before Mikelos accepted it. "The last time we did what looked like magic here, those shadows attacked us."

Ahn touched a hand to Victory's elbow. "Summoning necessities is not magic. It is a function of the way this realm operates."

"Yeah," Syri said. "The shadows were attracted to what Asaron attempted to do. On the plus side, it meant you did something."

Victory unscrewed the canteen's lid and smelled the contents—fresh, if oddly sterile, water. She handed it off to Mikelos. "Why would you encourage Asaron to attempt magic again, if it will call enemies?"

"Because this time we're going to try something different." Syri prodded them into moving but didn't let Asaron drop to the rear again. "You and I have work to do."

"And what would you have me do? I can't meditate while we travel."

"Meditation wasn't what you needed," Syri said. "You need to get your brain used to the idea it can do the impossible."

"I could break you like a twig."

Syri paused. "Yeah, but that's not something impossible."

"Your double-negatives hurt my brain," Jarimis said, trailing behind them.

Victory held out her empty hands. Already, their previous trip through the shadow plane felt like a distant memory, a sort of odd dream that had no bearing on reality. But she didn't need long to convince herself she once again held her trusty bastard sword. The heft of its solid, reassuring weight. The leather-wrapped hilt conformed to her grip as if the weapon had been created for her—which it had been, years ago.

The sword appeared in her hands. She'd prepared this time, and the sword wore its sheath, already attached to a belt.

Mikelos snatched at the belt before it slid to the ground. The movement caught Syri's attention, and she jerked a thumb over her shoulder. "Yeah. Like that."

When Asaron checked behind himself, Victory indulged her inner child and stuck her tongue out while she belted the sword around her hips. It seemed a waste, but she left the empty sheath for the short sword acquired in Parisii on a nearby stone. When she joined the group, Mikelos tucked her hand in the crook of his arm, as if they strolled through downtown Limani on date night instead of through a maze of rocks growing taller with every league they traveled.

They formed a traveling audience while Asaron summoned item after item, a replica of his own sword and a collection of other weapons he hid about his person. His rests to concentrate grew shorter and shorter, and Syri challenged him now, branching out into the less familiar and outside of his comfort level. A weapon he didn't own. A firearm from before the Last War. An article of clothing from before the Last War.

Asaron handed Syri a black silk girdle embroidered with red roses. The entire procession ground to a halt to howl with laughter. Victory had almost recovered when Ahn confessed to not recognizing what about the garment the others found so amusing, leaving her to explain to the ancient vampire about modern supportive garments for the female frame.

Like with the other items, Syri dropped the girdle on a random rock. Mikelos poked at it when he passed, saying, "The next person who comes by this way is going to be confused."

"Not really," Connor said. "This is a place of light and darkness, or pure thought and intention. Without that intention, the created items fade into nothingness." He plucked at the hem of his shirt. "I'm not thinking about what I'm wearing every moment, but the intention to remain clothed keeps me so."

"I intend to summon this hive brain and destroy the shadows creeping into our world." Asaron stopped, but nothing around them changed.

Syri patted his shoulder. "Close, but not quite. Let's try something a little different, since now you're sassing me." She planted herself in front of a giant boulder that towered feet above. "Put me on the other side of this rock."

The rest of them took another rest to watch the show. Asaron studied the scene, circling the stone. "Am I moving you? Or am I moving the rock?"

"That's up to you."

In a smooth motion, Asaron settled cross-legged where he'd stood, shifting the sword belted at his waist. He rested the tips of his fingers upon his knees, and his body stilled.

His eyes drifted closed, proving he'd paid to Zerandan after all. Victory and the others froze in place, as if sensing the magnitude of what Asaron attempted.

A ripple, felt more than heard, echoed against Victory's skin. At first, she was sure she had imagined it in the tenseness of the situation.

Then, it happened again. A physical shimmer pressed against her body.

A third time. The same way the shadows had caressed her between points in time. Victory drew her sword. "They're coming!"

Asaron needed no other prompting to quit his meditative pose. He bolted to his feet and interlocked his fingers, then called to Ahn in an unfamiliar language. With a running leap, she stepped into his hands and used his added momentum to launch herself onto the tall stone.

She landed and turned in a circle on nimble feet. "Shadows approaching. Could be five, could be twenty-five."

Victory parked herself in front of Mikelos, keeping him between herself and another large rock. She hoped Connor, the other noncombatant in the group, had the good sense to stay by his former daywalker. Jarimis, brandishing knives with wicked serrations on each blade, positioned himself next to her.

Asaron added to the protective perimeter with Victory and Jarimis, Schiavona in one hand and dagger in the other. "I'm not sure what happened."

Syri climbed another large boulder. "If I'd known they were this close, I'd never have asked. But good news! You can access your magic."

"I have no idea what I did, and I'm not comforted by your accolades," Asaron said. "The shadows overwhelmed us once before. We have any chance against them this time?"

Upon her perch, Ahn nocked a wicked arrow to a recurve bow and tracked the shadows' approach. "Time to find out."

Victory's body vibrated, but it wasn't adrenaline or Asaron's attempts at magic. The ground itself quaked at the shadows' approach. An eerie, wordless howl at the edge of Victory's hearing forced the hair on the back of her neck on end, and it seemed as if the sourceless light suffusing this land dimmed. Victory lifted her sword, prepared to defend Mikelos and Connor against whatever came.

A shotgun racked behind her, followed by Connor's strangled yelp. "What the hell is that?"

"Worked last time," Mikelos said.

Victory risked a glance over her shoulder. Her daywalker once again wielded a hybrid weapon of his own imagination. She opened her mouth to comment, but—

Syri limbered her wrists by twisting the long silver knives in each hand. "Here they come!"

The world went white, and Victory blinked stars from vision. When it cleared, she braced to defend against attack. Instead, a team of armed elves in mottled gray camouflage arrayed itself throughout their position, directed by terse commands from their leader—the same man who had come to their defense previously.

"Fall back, Syrisinia!" Brawleyn shoved her behind him and Victory. "You should have called us sooner." He didn't carry a bow this time, but instead wielded a pair of elven long knives. They seemed incongruous paired with his modern military gear, but if they worked against the shadow creatures, Victory wouldn't quibble.

"I didn't know—" Another rumble, louder this time, cut off Syri's protestations.

A single shadow lurched around Ahn's perch, then exploded in a silent whoosh when she released an arrow through it from straight above. It left the arrow sunk halfway into the ground, quivering from the force of impact. Another shadow poured in, followed by another and another. A fierce cry rose from the gathered elves, and the battle joined.

An eternity passed, in the way combat stretched every second into hours of mingled anticipation and aggression.

It couldn't have been more than minutes, with the roar of Mikelos' bastardized shotgun echoing among the stone pillars. A few of the militaristic elves also carried firearms, precision weaponry that popped in counterpoint. More shadows poured in, and they had evolved. Instead of brute cudgels, Victory crossed literal swords formed of their own substance with a nondescript being who broke through the elven ranks.

A clash of sparks might have been more dramatic, instead of the dull clank of steel against whatever the shadow's variation of the metal might be. The figure stood taller than Victory, with a longer reach. Despite the blade, it handled the sword like a bashing weapon. It voided any advantage by telegraphing every move, a neat trick for a creature with no face.

Victory managed to disengage, to give herself a second to consider combat options. At the looming creature's freedom, shifting in the odd half-light, Mikelos' shotgun rang out. The creature dissolved in a wordless cry, consumed by the surrounding chaos.

Her ears rang with a dull roar from her proximity to the blast. "Bloody hell!"

"You tag 'em, I'll bag 'em." His voice seemed to come from a distance.

She ignored his quip, already angling to entice the attention of another shadow before Syri attracted it. It exploded before she neared it, revealing another of Ahn's arrows embedded in the gravel. Victory searched for the next enemy.

There weren't any. Brawleyn wiped his gleaming face with a gloved hand. "That's the last of them."

Asaron lowered his sword and dagger. "This seemed easier."

"It was easier." Brawleyn sheathed his knives and gestured for Ahn to come down from her vantage point. "They were testing us. Testing you. You're an unknown factor, the first in a long time."

Ahn landed light on her feet, with a small explosion of dust. She collected a nearby arrow and returned it to the quiver now at her hip. "Those in this group were trained by my hand. Why would the shadows need to use these sorties against us to gather information if they already have a foothold into the other world?"

Brawleyn didn't answer her. He gazed unseeing into the distance, as if listening to an unseen voice. "Acknowledged." He raised a fist, calling, "Move out!" In the space between one moment and the next, each member of the elven militia vanished.

"Rude," Connor said. "We could have hitched a ride."

Syri summoned a set of sheaths for her knives. "You know it doesn't work that way. Asaron, Victory, and Mikelos have never been to the enclave, so we have to make it there by foot, first."

"Can we manage to make it there without provoking another attack?" Victory asked. Exhaustion tugged at her, and Mikelos' skin paled even in this colorless landscape. With half a thought, a bottle of water appeared in her hand and she passed it over. He downed half of it, then offered it to Syri.

She considered the bottle but waved it off. "It's complicated. I guess we do need to hold off on Asaron's training until we get to the enclave."

"I have a question," Mikelos said. "Are you and Brawleyn and the others… deities? Some sort of demi-gods? You're from this strange world, too, and like the shadows, seem to have these almost limitless powers—"

Jarimis stopped wandering their perimeter, cutting Mikelos off with a chopping gesture. "I'm going to stop you right there, buddy. She's not going to answer you anyway." He waved away Mikelos' perturbed expression. "Trust me, I've already tried. And I've been here for, well, time runs funny. But it feels like years."

Victory's traitorous brain supplied the math. Fifty-seven years since Jarimis disappeared from Limani, leaving her to save his fledgling college from financial ruin and his daywalker from devastating heartbreak. Syri's studied passivity was enough of a hint that no real information would be forthcoming from her quarter, so she interrupted before Mikelos continued his exhaustion- and curiosity-fueled tirade. "Let's move on. Get to this enclave before we attract more unnecessary attention."

While the first part of their journey had featured a sort of tense levity, it turned now to a plodding, circuitous route through a forest of stone pillars. Conversation trailed off.

Despite Syri's assurances the shadows had tracked their location because of Asaron's close brush with his own magic, Victory remained hypervigilant in this unnatural landscape. She scanned and rescanned each pillar they passed—that Mikelos would pass, marching in her footsteps—for signs of movement. The diffuse light cast no normal shadows, so any hint of darker color variation was suspect.

The pattern of footsteps behind her changed, and a hand brushed her shoulder. Ahn squeezed next to her, shoulder to shoulder between the rocky outcroppings. Such close proximity to the ancient vampire, the sire of her sire, should have unnerved Victory. Instead, the shorter woman exuded a contagious calm.

Ahn broke the silence. "You are the Master of your city, and with that you carry much weight. That responsibility cannot be easy right now, in such a strange place. But you cannot exhaust yourself."

"I'm not sure I have much choice." The immediate honesty surprised Victory, but she was terrible at lying to Asaron, as well. "My progeny and my daywalker are under my care. You know the feeling." She waved in Asaron's general direction, where he marched at Syri's heels.

"I do. But this is my land now, as much as such a strange place can be," Ahn said. "Let me carry the weight for a time."

Victory had no reason to trust this woman, but Asaron trusted her. And she had no reason to trust Connor, yet she let the unfamiliar vampire walk with Mikelos and Jarimis. But Ahn was right—mental and physical and emotional exhaustion wore on Victory. Despite the few nights home in Limani, she'd been running on all cylinders since the unplanned trip to Nacostina's past. And if that had been a shock to the system, this overwhelmed her to the core.

"Thank you." She meant it. Already, the compulsion to check every corner and cranny lifted.

Ahn dropped to the rear of the group. She exchanged low words with Jarimis, indicating he should go on alert. Victory's progeny stopped his soft exchange of gossip with Mikelos, and the entire group descended into quiet purpose during the hike.

Victory made a conscious effort to focus on the expanse of Asaron's back. How the muscles shifted beneath the fabric of his shirt. The pattern of gray dust that broke the solid black cotton. She put one foot in front of the other, weaving between stone pillars, and softened her gaze. The steady pace, in this world without the sounds of nature she was accustomed to, lulled her into a soft trance.

And then, she found herself someplace else entirely.

She clutched the edge of her seat as the carriage jerked and swayed over ruts in the dirt road. Despite the caravan master's reassurance, she'd never adapted to the motion of the awkward conveyance. Her stomach might have an easier time of it if she had the seat facing forward, but that position was reserved for—

Her mind blanked. She peered through the darkness of the carriage's interior, made more difficult by the approaching dusk. She had no idea why the woman across from her deserved the better seat.

She had no idea who the woman who sat across from her was. They both wore long gowns in dark, respectable colors. Perhaps the other woman had a bit more lace at her collar, but otherwise nothing distinguished them. They were of a similar age, as far as she could tell in the low light.

The other woman spoke. "Why do you stare at me so? Like you're seeing me for the first time."

She froze. How to explain to her companion that she had no idea how she'd gotten there. That she had no idea where she was.

That she had no idea *who* she was.

The darkness shifted around them, a sinuous shadow blacking out what little light they had. Her grip on the seat tightened. She had to be careful, else she'd crack the wood—

How ridiculous. Her small fingers did not carry such strength.

She opened her mouth to answer the other woman, hoping she'd manage an appropriate response, when the carriage lurched to a halt. Outside, the driver screamed. On impulse, she scrambled for the latch.

The other woman slapped her hand away. "No, it might be dangerous."

"Sitting in here like ducklings will be more dangerous." She thrust open the carriage door and slid out, staggering on legs cramped from hours of sitting.

Darkness swirled around her. Not the fading light of day, but immense, unnatural shadows curling around the carriage and blotting out any hint of the setting sun. She twirled in a circle, no longer able to find any hint of the carriage.

A horse shrieked, or was it a man? She patted her clothing but found no weapons.

Why would a woman such as herself be armed? She rebelled against these unfamiliar instincts, even as she side-stepped the man who rushed out of the darkness toward her. Blood streaked his face from a scalp wound, and he careened blindly. Distracted, she tripped at the edge of the dirt road.

She cursed the skirts tangling about her legs. The road they'd traveled followed the top of an embankment, and she slid and rolled down into a field. By the time she regained her footing in the fallow ground and hauled herself toward the carriage, the screams had multiplied.

If possible, the darkness pressed closer when she neared the carriage. Sounds grew muffled, as if wax plugged her ears. She dug her fingers into the ground to pull herself upward, heedless of the rocks and nettles pricking her unprotected skin. She peered over the embankment, squinting to make out the carriage's outline and the ominous figures who pounded on the carriage door.

The woman inside—Friend? Sister? Mistress?—cried out, but did not deter the men. They smashed through the paneling and hauled the woman free. Three men wrangled her while she lashed and kicked, but their tone had turned mocking.

Where was the driver of the carriage? Where were the men, the protectors, that should have traveled with them?

The men kicked aside what she'd presumed to be discarded luggage, fallen from the carriage, but lifeless limbs skewed akimbo in the dirt.

She should stay hidden. She should turn and run across the field, out of this unnatural darkness. She did not know this woman. She did not owe her anything. She had her own safety and virtue to think of. Both might be at risk if she fled, but she was sure to be ruined if she stayed.

But that was wrong.

The men knelt around the woman now, pinning her into the dirt. Her screams had turned to pleas. One hit her across the face, stunning her into silence, and he flipped up her skirts.

Rage curdled under her skin. She wrapped fingers around a rock and gripped it tight. Gathering her skirts in her other hand, she launched herself over the top of the embankment and hurtled toward the men. One of them, who ground the woman's skull into the dirt, turned to her and laughed. A shadow curled around his face, until only the whites of his eyes shined through the blackness.

She didn't get far before she tripped, her delicate shoes catching on the rough ground. She lost her grip on her skirts and fell to her knees. Her meager weapon spun away, dancing over the dirt clods until it came to rest against the carriage driver's corpse.

The man shrouded in darkness laughed. He kept his thick fingers splayed over the other woman's face but used his free hand to draw a short knife. "You want to play, too, girl?" He handed the knife to the man at the woman's feet, and his friend slit the layers of cloth.

What had she been thinking? She was no match for these men. She tried to reverse course, scrambling in the dirt, but her many-layered garment hampered her movement. Two of the men laughed again, but other entertainment already occupied the third.

The woman below them had ceased her struggles, but it was unclear whether they had cowered her into submission or she had lost consciousness.

Though in no position to help, she prayed for the latter. She pitched up against the edge of the embankment and halted. A man rose to his feet and picked his way toward her. He stooped to retrieve a broken section of carriage paneling.

She had no time to find her way to her feet, even if she could escape unscathed. Instead, she glared at the man who loomed over her, shaping her hands into claws.

Perhaps she could gouge out his eyes when he came for her.

"You should have run, girl." The man swung the broken piece of board into the side of her skull, and the unnatural darkness surrounding them enclosed her.

Fingers wrapped around Victory's lower arm, tightening. She twisted out of the grip with a snap and dropped into a defensive position. This time, a sword hilt met her hand where she expected.

"Whoa!" Mikelos backed away until he bumped into Connor, lifting his hands to show he meant no harm. "It's me, love."

Victory resisted the urge to shake herself all over, as if tendrils of blackness still clung to every inch of her, and shoved the sword into its sheath. She pressed a palm to her face and squinted through the pale light. "I'm sorry. I don't know what happened." After the dulled senses she'd experienced, even the distilled light of this realm was almost too much to bear.

The group had stuttered to a halt. "Where were you just now?" asked Jarimis. "It wasn't here."

Her progeny's voice boomed in her ears. She waited to answer, until she could keep her eyes open without squinting. Mikelos' concern blinded her instead. "I wasn't here. I was walking, and then, I was riding in a carriage? The carriage was attacked." Dare she confess that she'd considered running, even if the scenario hadn't been real? At least she'd returned for the other woman, though the attempted rescue had been fruitless.

"Sounds like—" Everyone looked to Asaron when he cut off. "No. Can't be."

"Can't be what?" Victory asked. "I didn't know where I was. But the carriage was old, from my earliest memories of life with you." Another detail, unnoticed in the craziness of the moment, jumped out at her. "I wore a dark blue gown."

"It matched your eyes." Asaron's voice dropped to a whisper. "That's what I remember. The color of your gown in the light of my campfire matched your eyes when you opened them."

Victory sank onto a nearby rock but missed the ledge and settled onto the ground instead. Until today, her entire life had started when she woke to Asaron over her, telling her she'd be okay. The brigands who attacked her caravan had cracked her skull, locking away her human life forever. "Why now? Why would I see that?"

Connor raised his hand, like a child in class. "Clue in the rest of us?"

Perhaps sensing Victory was too overwhelmed to answer, Asaron said, "I was running courier messages for the Aragonian military when I stumbled over a caravan under attack. I thought I was too late to rescue anyone, so I killed the bandits." He kept his tone matter-of-fact, but if his report of mass murder disturbed Connor, the musician didn't show it. "Except one of the women still lived, barely. So, I turned her."

His deep voice, one of the constants in her long life, settled Victory, enough for her to add, "But I'd been too badly injured, and a limit does exist to vampiric healing. Some sort of head injury. I've never recalled any of my human life."

Mikelos settled onto the ground next to Victory. "But this time, you remembered?"

"Maybe? But even as I was there, I didn't know who I was. I didn't know the woman I was with." The woman Victory failed to save.

Syri rested against another pillar. "The walls can be thin here."

"But why wouldn't she know who she was, if it was a memory?" Jarimis asked.

"Perhaps it was not a memory."

Ahn seemed nonplussed, shifting her weight from one foot to the other as if she itched to be on the move again. Something about the diminutive, ancient woman drew all attention every time she deigned to speak. "If the walls are thin here, perhaps you simply saw what the shadows wanted you to see."

Much as she wished to never revisit the scenario again, Victory pored over her memories. "No, it was real. But the darkness wasn't natural. It wasn't night falling. It was the shadows." She heaved herself to her feet, as if Ahn's restlessness were contagious. "The shadows were there."

"That's impossible." Syri waved a hand, dismissing Victory's statement. "The walls are thin, but they're not that thin. And you're talking about time travel."

Jarimis laughed, a harsh sound without humor. "Except the shadows draw their power from the same source as an artifact that did cause time travel."

"I'm sorry, *time travel*?" Connor's voice rose in pitch. "You expect me to believe—"

"Connor," Mikelos said. "You should be dead, but instead we're in an alternate dimension. Don't get outraged at something else that shouldn't be possible."

Victory suppressed amusement. She was used to Mikelos' unflappable personality handling her. Nice to know he worked with her so well because he'd already had so much practice on another vampire prone to outbursts.

"We have to consider the shadows may have had a hand in the attack that led to my near-death," Victory said. Saying it out loud meant acknowledging the possibility.

Mikelos shifted next to her. "Did you see that?" He pointed, in the distance between two pillars.

Though they all turned, Victory noted nothing out of the ordinary. Until movement registered in her own field of view, far past where Ahn braced against another pillar to the left. "I didn't see that. But I saw something over there." Her hand aimed at a ninety-degree angle from his.

Connor scrambled to his feet. "That, I saw."

Syri grasped Victory and Mikelos by the hands and hauled them up. "It's not another frontal assault, but they're getting closer. We need to keep moving."

The shadows harried them while they marched, tendrils and snippets of darker gray against stone that faded whenever examined straight on. In a way, it was almost like being home, where the shadows had been a strange constant in Victory's life since she returned from Jiang Yi Yue. Always out of sight but never far, and on occasion, expected when they were least wanted.

They didn't appear to her once while in Nacostina, decades in the past. Yet they'd swarmed the scene of the caravan attack. Perhaps there was something to Jarimis' theory that the shadows were responsible for the same energy that powered the time-travel artifact.

After all, the voice that spoke to her in the space between time had seemed part and parcel of that same energy.

Had she already communicated with the hive mind they were here to destroy?

She turned to propose this theory to Jarimis when Syri stepped between two pillars and disappeared.

Asaron pulled two of his knives and halted the procession. Victory had her own sword drawn halfway when Syri's head reappeared, floating above the dusty ground.

"Sorry, I forgot to warn you we were getting close," she said. A single hand emerged from the empty space and gestured them forward. "It's okay, the barrier doesn't even tingle. We're at the enclave." Her head retracted again.

Asaron turned to the group, his expression wild. This extended far beyond his limit, and Victory didn't blame him. Ahn patted Victory's shoulder when she passed, and the ancient vampire approached her progeny with caution.

"Asaron, it is fine." Ahn placed her hands on Asaron's and forced him to lower his weapons. "Safety is near. Come with me." She led him between the pillars, and they vanished.

By now, the others had clustered around Victory. She released her sword and mock-punched Jarimis in the arm. "A little warning would have been nice."

He hunched his shoulders in contrition. "My apologies. Only Syri's ilk can locate the enclave. We've been following her as much as you have."

"The bloody elves can bounce around this place like distance has no meaning," Connor said, breaking away from the group and approaching the barrier. "The rest of us lowly folk have to travel the old-fashioned way. Come on, I'm past due for a drink. I'll show you around the place."

Mikelos took Victory's hand, and Jarimis offered his elbow on her other side. Together, they followed Connor into what appeared to be nothing more than the path between two more of the never-ending stone outcroppings, leaving a depressing world of grays upon grays and emerging into a bright, airy wonderland.

She flinched, at first, a motion born of centuries of habit. But like the pale lifeless air outside, no sun lit this stronghold.

Victory craned her neck to view the shining silver towers piercing the white sky. These structures that defied the laws of physics with soaring archways and pinpoint balance were constructed not by human hands, but by creatures of magic and light. Evocative of flowing elven design, but further study revealed delicate touches alien to anything she'd ever seen.

Lower buildings mimicking the natural flow of the rocky landscape bustled with activity. And for the first time since they'd arrived in this alternate reality, the world was awash in color. She squinted through the light at structures that continued the theme of grays and whites and silvers and at the clothing, burning bright with colors and patterns, adorned by the people who emerged to study the newcomers.

"It's good to be back!" Connor's clothing morphed, shifting from gray trousers and dingy white shirt to a practical day suit in a fetching brown.

Next to Asaron, Ahn's practical armor had also transformed to colorful felted clothing, from a time period long before Victory's memory. The gathered gawkers all wore garments from a variety of eras. The younger elves, like Syri, chose modern jeans and leggings with colorful tops like she'd seen Toria wear while home in Limani. From the ears, not all of the crowd were elves. Other vampires dotted the crowd in spots of stillness, and the musk of werecreatures underlaid the crisp air.

Brawleyn stepped forward. He'd traded his functional body armor for a kilt and homespun shirt. He approached Syri, whose own faded clothing had transformed into a bright silk sheath dress. She'd reacquired a stud in her nose, which glinted sapphire. The first time Victory met her, she'd seen her as a punked-out china doll. The only thing missing now was her battered black leather jacket.

"Good, you've arrived," Brawleyn said.

Mikelos pointed at the pair. "So, you're not elves, and you're not gods."

As if the daywalker's words sounded some sort of alarm, many of the onlookers dispersed, hurrying to seem as though they had more important things to attend to. Brawleyn moved not an inch.

Syri clapped a hand over her face. "We already established that."

"No, hear me out." With a deft touch, Mikelos pulled Syri's hand from her face and lifted her palm to examine it. "There's a brightness to you that wasn't there outside. Outside of whatever protected place you've established here."

Jarimis nudged Victory. "I always knew the guy was smart. He's figured it out faster than you."

The excitement of arriving at the enclave had pushed Victory's own revelation from her mind, but now it came rushing back. Though she and Mikelos had much in common, they often discovered knowledge via different routes. Could his theories about the hive mind have mirrored hers? But what did that have to do with what Syri was?

"Figured what out?" Victory asked.

Asaron cut her off with the slice of his hand, all of his attention on Mikelos. "Let the man speak."

"Yes," Brawleyn said. "I'm curious as to what conclusions you've drawn regarding us."

"None of what we've experienced here is the sort of magic I'm accustomed to," Mikelos said. "The elemental magic Toria and Kane and Archer perform, manipulating the essence of our world. But this isn't our world." He spread his free hand to encompass the shining towers that stretched to the blinding white sky. "This is a place of shadows. But for there to be shadows, there must also be light."

Syri and Brawleyn exchanged a sort of wordless communication. Syri must have drawn the short straw, because she answered first. "It's a duality," she said. "In your world, elemental magic operates the same way. Water and fire, and earth and air. You're right, in a way. Here, it's darkness and light."

But that left out one of the elements. The one Victory had spent the last quarter-century trying to comprehend, because it came as part of the child of her heart. "But what about storm?"

Syri herded them from the enclave's entryway toward one of the low buildings down a street paved with a patterned mosaic. "Let's walk and talk, okay?"

They entered a chamber molded to create niches and comfortable seating nooks softened with cushions and throw blankets in warm tones. A stained-glass lantern with a light source that mimicked candlelight flickered from the ceiling. It should have been claustrophobic without windows, but though Victory noted the three doorways through long habit, it felt more like a comfortable space to converse and relax with friends away from the stark light outside.

She and Jarimis settled on a low bench and accepted the goblets Connor presented from out of nowhere. One cautious sniff told her it contained fresh blood, but like everything in this place, it had appeared from the whims of Connor's mind, not a human source. "Will this sustain us?" she asked. A test sip revealed a warm bouquet that rolled over her tongue, a luscious flavor with the perfect hint of coppery bite. If this was sourced from a human, it had to be a hell of a human, in the prime of their life in perfect physical condition. Asaron watched for her own reaction before drinking from the goblet Ahn handed him.

Jarimis savored his own taste before responding. "Well, it works for the other vampires here in the enclave. Like summoned food and water support the elves, humans, werecreatures, and—" He snapped his mouth shut.

"No, it's okay." Syri sank onto a ledge built into the wall and hugged a cushion to her chest. "It goes back to what Mikelos asked anyway."

"Victory asked about storm," Mikelos said, around a mouthful of food. After producing the blood, Connor had waved a plate of sandwiches into existence, which Mikelos was in the process of demolishing.

"And it all connects," Syri said. "You're used to elemental magic. Consider the other half of it… primal magic. And storm bridges the two, containing elements of both and bringing them together."

"Don't drag it out, Syrisinia," Brawleyn said from his position by the entrance. It was unclear whether he guarded for the newcomers—or against them.

"Yeah, yeah." She toyed with the cushion's corner fringe. "Even the creatures of light reborn in your world aren't really elves. Most of the 'elves' in the enclave aren't. We're beings of light, the way the shadows are beings of darkness. But that's only half the primal magic. Elves, the real elves in your world, are beings of, well, life. And vampires are beings of death."

Asaron clutched his thick goblet with both hands. "How does being connected to death relate to magic?" He drew out the last word as if it pained him to speak it.

"It's never been clear why elves are born with the ability but it comes to vampires when they achieve significant age," Syri said.

"Probably has something to do with the fact that a mage, an elemental mage, that is, can't be transformed into a vampire." Victory used her goblet to encompass herself and Asaron. "Not that Asaron and I didn't do our share of research about the kids."

Mikelos snapped his attention to Victory, and it was as if the room held the two of them alone. "You'd have tried to turn them?"

"They're our kids."

Her daywalker nodded, as if he agreed her explanation was the most logical in the world.

Connor patted his shoulder, and Victory tried to ignore how the other vampire left his hand there. Instead, she turned to Syri. "Will it be easier, here, to unlock Asaron's magic? Zerandan didn't have much luck in Parisii."

"We need all the advantage we can get," Asaron said. "Even if it means me attempting the bloody impossible."

Ahn broke her stillness. "It will work, though," she said. "You are of my blood, and that lineage is a strong one. It will require a bit of effort on your part. I hope you have not grown lazy without me around to put you to work."

"I don't know," Asaron said. "Have I grown lazy, daughter?"

"I'm the one who retired. You're still going strong." They were more matched in ability these days, though Victory had grown into her own martial style over the centuries. Asaron forced her to spar with him on a regular basis even in the peaceful environs of Limani. His insistence that she not let her skills lapse had come in handy more than once over the years, in the defense of her city.

"We must get to work." Ahn prodded Asaron from his seat. "Syrisinia, will you join us?"

With a mild groan, Syri pushed herself up. "Yes, I'm coming." She followed them from the room, brushing through a curtain further into the building.

"What should we do while we wait?" Mikelos seemed unsure of what to do with his empty plate, until Connor accepted it. It vanished between the other vampire's fingers. "Because I'm feeling a nap."

"Rest," Brawleyn said. "Consider these rooms at your disposal." He exchanged a wordless glance with Connor and Jarimis, then left. The brightness outside pierced the space, then the room returned to a comfortable dim.

Connor pushed Mikelos over, until the man stretched flat on the cushioned ledge. "I'll fetch more blankets."

Warring instincts pulsed through Victory. She should follow Asaron, to also learn as much as possible about this supposed vampiric magic. She should sleep, to recover from the long journey. She should stay awake, to protect her daywalker from the unknown vampire who shared their space.

But Jarimis sprawled against cushions next to her, and she trusted him with her daywalker's life, as he had often trusted her with his Allesandra over the years. Her progeny was family, and family protected their own.

Jarimis patted her ankle after she kicked off her boots and curled up on the padded bench. She ensured that Mikelos slept, that Connor sat next to him with a summoned novel, that Jarimis kept watch over them all. She slept.

The earrings slipped from her fingers. She leaned from her seat before the vanity and patted the plush rug until she found the diamond and pearl drop, which had tumbled under the hem of her skirt.

But when Victory straightened, a strange reflection stared from the vanity's mirror. And her hands continued to move without her control.

The blond woman inserted the earring and pressed an errant curl in place. Life was so much easier with a lady's maid, but they had not been in Parisii for long enough for her to hire one, after Pia stayed behind in Roma.

Victory pounded mental fists against an invisible barrier, but the unfamiliar thoughts tumbled through her own mind, threatening to overwhelm her own sense of self. She'd never had a lady's maid. She'd never had blond hair. This unfamiliar body trapped her, moving without her control.

The woman tilted her chin at an angle, to check the rouge on her cheeks, and familiarity rushed through the small corner of brain Victory claimed for her own.

Serena, alias Natalia Della Zanna. Connor's sire. Mikelos' other vampire, long before Victory.

She'd found herself out of time once again, but this time out of place in a way unimaginable. Victory attempted to wrench control of the body away from the other vampire. Instead, Serena finished inspecting her makeup and stood. She brushed hands across the front of a ball gown that showed her attributes to excellent effect. Studied herself in the mirror. It would do. The Master of Parisii would have no reason to suspect a thing.

Suspect what? Victory's mental voice screamed, but Serena gave no internal or external reaction that she suspected an unwelcome guest.

The woman crossed the carpet with careful steps, keeping her balance in delicate heels. A shadow detached itself from the corner of the dressing room and oozed toward Serena.

Victory scrabbled further into the depths of Serena's mind. If anything might recognize her presence, it was one of the beings creating such mischief. But her vision remained pinned to her host's view, giving Victory a front-row seat when the shadow crawled up Serena's silk skirt and curled around her shoulders like a mourning stole at odds with her party dress.

Additional shadows detached from the walls as Serena proceeded along a familiar hallway, despite the outdated wallpaper. The Parisiian townhouse. By the time Serena descended to the first floor, she carried two more shadows—the second had joined the first around her shoulders, and a third twisted around her arm like an evening glove. More shadows drifted around her, flowing against the wall and twisting among the patterns of the carpeting. And amidst Victory's mental panic, music broke through.

Not the fluttery notes of Mikelos' violin, a constant companion in their house for the past decades. This was a lower, drawn-out tone that could have been somber but for the upswept notes of brevity. Serena followed the music through the townhouse, to a room littered with the detritus of half-finished compositions among the various instrument stands.

Connor lowered the bow of his cello when Serena paused in the entryway. "I know, I'm not dressed yet. But you know how it is, when inspiration strikes—"

"The Ashtons won't miss you if you don't appear at this dinner."

Except there had never been a Master of the City in Parisii by the name of Ashton, male or female, in Victory's memory. Why would Serena lie to her progeny? Victory battered at the invisible barrier keeping her from control of Serena's body.

"You won't have an escort. Mikelos is still out. He left a note that he might join the maestro for dinner if their discussion about this season's productions ran long." Connor set his cello aside and placed the bow on his music stand. Plucking the pen from behind his ear, he marked a notation on the music sheets. "Honestly, I'd prefer they get the details hammered out now, so we're not scrambling to learn a new damned symphony because his lordship doesn't want to offend some British earl with a piece celebrating Parisiian independence. Right, it was two years ago and I should get over it—" Connor cut himself off mid-tirade, seeming to see Serena for the first time. His eyes swept across her body, but they widened in fear, not lust.

Serena pressed into the room. Connor lurched away, heedless of the instruments surrounding him. He didn't seem to notice when a second cello crashed to the floor. But the music studio wasn't large, and he soon stumbled to a stop against the wall.

He drew himself to his full height, widening his stance. "What the hell are you playing at, Serena? You said you'd given them up."

"Only a fool surrenders power." Serena lifted the arm bearing one of her pet shadows. It writhed around her wrist, soaking in the room's lamplight like a bottomless well.

All at once, Victory stopped fighting. She sagged against her mental bonds, knowing what was coming. Nacostina all over again. Another senseless, inevitable death she was powerless to stop without rupturing the time line. She would bear witness to her daywalker's worst moment.

"Please don't do this, Serena. They're manipulating you." Connor pressed himself against the wall, as if the paneling would save him.

But Connor's pleas fell on deaf ears that roared with incoherent whispers, tumbling around themselves to create a wash of indistinguishable malevolence.

Serena lifted her arm, hand outstretched to Connor as though in invitation. But she extended this invitation to the shadows, which leapt from her body to join the others in the room and swarm Connor in darkness.

He disappeared under a wall of inky, serpentine forms, and the whispered roar smothered any sounds. Until, as the world darkened, Victory picked out her own name.

"Victory!"

Her name penetrated the terror-stricken molasses of her brain, and when she found sight in the darkness, it wasn't to what the shadows had left of Connor's body. Instead, three men hovered above her in the cozy room where she'd fallen asleep. She might have found the identical expressions of concern on Mikelos, Jarimis, and Connor's faces hilarious at any other time, but shadowy echoes swarmed beyond them.

"Victory," Connor said again, and perhaps that's the voice she'd heard in the vision. Because there was no way he'd known she had been present, a silent prisoner in Serena's brain. His brow furrowed, as if he saw something change in her face.

Before Connor could ask any difficult questions, she pulled Mikelos onto the cushioned surface next to her, wrapping his arms around her torso and sinking into his embrace. "What happened?"

"You tell us," Jarimis said. "You were thrashing in your sleep."

"It was nothing. A nightmare."

Connor paused in the action of pouring tea from a summoned carafe. "A nightmare where you called my name?"

She flinched, and Mikelos' arms tightened around her. "Sounds like more than a nightmare," he said.

Mikelos had come so close to death. If he hadn't been at that late dinner with the symphony director…. "I don't want to talk about it." But the men wouldn't accept such a brush-off, not when she had no reason to be having nightmares about a man she'd just met.

Jarimis wandered to the other side of the room, where he could hear the conversation but not act as part of it. Connor, on the other hand, didn't budge. "What did you see?"

He already knew. Not a nightmare, but another vision. She owed him the truth. "I wish I could spare you."

"Spare me what?" Connor knelt instead of continuing to loom over her. His consideration was in counterpoint to his usual brashness, and for a moment, she saw through to the man who had earned Mikelos' devotion for so long.

"Another vision from the shadows. I saw your disappearance. I saw how you—died, I suppose." The vampires stilled at her words, and at her pause, Mikelos' sharp intake of breath was the only sound. "What do you remember from that day?"

"I don't." The words dragged out of Connor like crushed gravel. "I never thought about it. I suppose I considered it a blessing, that I had no memory of the space between settling in the townhouse in Parisii and arriving here and being found by Brawleyn." His composure broke, and he dragged trembling hands through his hair, ruining the artful styling.

"I never knew what happened," Mikelos said. "I came home from a meeting. Things were out of place in the studio, but the rest of the house was untouched. I thought you and Serena had gone to a dinner. Then that you'd stayed out too late and needed to spend daylight hours at someone's house. But no one sent a message. And no one in the city had heard from either of you. Eventually, I had to face the truth. You were both gone."

Despair wrenched at Connor's face. "You thought we'd abandoned you?"

"Never." Mikelos gripped Connor's forearm. "I thought you'd both been murdered. I pressured the Master of the City to launch an investigation, but he dismissed my concerns as those of a jilted lover, despite... despite what our relationship, our friendship, really was."

Victory might be his lover, but Connor had been his brother. Serena, some sort of doting maternal figure whose goal in life had been to lavish her progeny with whatever he desired. Until her own desires outweighed the power of that bond.

"It was Serena."

Jarimis jerked in surprise at Victory's words, spilling his tea.

Connor regained his voice first. "What's that supposed to mean?"

"My nightmare. It was a vision, like the one I had of my death," Victory said. "But this time, I was caught in Serena's body. I was forced to watch as she killed you."

"Impossible. She was my sire."

"It was the shadows. She let them have you." Victory paused. "There was no body. And Serena must have run afterward."

Mikelos hadn't released his grip on Connor's arm. "And we know from the kids that she had the ability to manipulate the shadows."

"And when the shadows take you, they leave no body behind," Victory said. "Like when Syri disappeared."

"Is that what vampiric magic is?" Jarimis asked. "The ability to control this darkness?"

They turned to Connor for the answer, but the man had retreated in shock. Mikelos jostled his arm with a gentle shake. "She left us for a few years once," Connor said, the words no more than a ragged whisper. "Remember? When we spent that time touring the Germanic estates?"

Mikelos shifted, as if summoning memories he'd kept buried for so long. "I remember it odd how she kept to herself so much more after that."

"She showed me a trick, right after she returned," Connor said. "She sucked all the light out of a room. I laughed it off, thinking she was showing off some elven trinket she'd found in her travels. But I caught her doing other things in the same vein. Always with weird darkness that I would catch glimpses of. I asked her to stop. I didn't like the secrecy. I didn't like how it changed her."

"I never knew any of this." Mikelos had released his grip on Connor's arm, but the two men still sat close. "Why didn't you tell me?"

"I didn't like it, but I didn't want to burden you with it," Connor said. "My job was to protect you."

"I wonder—" Jarimis broke off when they all turned to him. "It's not important. Or it possibly is. Please pardon me while I check something." He set down his tea and exited the room, patting his pockets.

He'd find what he sought and return triumphant, but until then, she was stuck in a room with her daywalker and his—

Best friend? Oldest friend? Closest companion? All the relationships Victory had taken for granted.

Connor needed Mikelos more than she did right now.

The two men bowed their heads together, sending Victory through her own memories. She'd seen them a handful of times across the years, heard them in concert and run across them when employers she'd been body-guarding attended elite soirees. Their partnership had been the stuff of legends, though they came from different sources than her own partnership with Asaron.

No intentional effort on their part shut her out. Their conversation, regarding what Mikelos and Connor had both seen regarding Serena's descent into darkness, did not exclude Victory. She left them anyway, following Jarimis' path out of this cozy hall into the cold light.

Jarimis was nowhere to be seen, and the crowds summoned by their arrival had dispersed. Victory paused a few paces away from the doorway she'd left. All at once, her energy drained away. What had she even been determined to do? They had no place in this alien world. Victory longed for home. She longed for her daughter, abandoned once again even if she was now in her proper time and place.

Hell, she'd prefer a council meeting to discuss Limani's annual budget over all of this.

"Can I help you?"

The woman next to her might have appeared out of thin air. Perhaps she had. Her serene face showed no offense at the yelp of surprise Victory cut off. Her hair hung past her ears, giving no indication whether she was an elf or a stunning human. The long dress she wore could have been from any time period, swathes of ice-blue fabric gathered around her torso to drape to bare feet, falling in smooth lines that followed the length of her arms to her clasped hands.

She bore Victory's inspection with grace. "You seem a bit out of sorts, and I'd like to help if I can."

"You're right, but I'm not sure you can help me."

"The only way to know for sure is to ask."

Victory wanted to ask a million questions of the first person in this place who seemed to demand nothing from her. What was she? What was her explanation for this world of darkness and light? Instead, she settled on an easy one. "Brawleyn advised my group to stay where he left us, but I'd like to be by myself for a while." When the woman did not respond right away, she added, "I promise not to go where I'm not wanted. I just need to meditate for a bit." These folks seemed like the mystical meditating sorts.

"Have no concern. You wouldn't be able to access a place you were not wanted or needed." The woman scanned both ends of the pathway. She lifted one arm, and her skirts followed, attached to the silver cuff at her wrist. "There."

Along the woman's aim, a slender column of light sprang from the low buildings surrounding them. The glow matched the shade of the woman's dress, and along the pathway, lit lanterns shifted from white and gold tones to the same blue. Victory had assumed the lanterns were ornamental, but this was a handy trick.

"You may use the garden behind my villa. No one will disturb you there." She drifted off, back to whatever task she had interrupted to approach Victory.

Or perhaps the woman's task in this place was to help wayward strangers. Best to accept the offer at face value. At least a garden sounded more pleasant than being a third wheel to Mikelos and Connor.

She followed the blue lanterns, which reverted to their original colors when she passed. Whatever architect planned this city seemed allergic to the concept of a straight line. The final lanterns led her down an alleyway alongside a two-story building to an expanse of space. When she arrived at the rear of the so-called villa, the column of light winked out. She had arrived at her destination, but found no garden.

Rock garden perhaps, of the sort she'd seen at monasteries when visiting the highest-ranking vampire within a Qin region, with boulders carved into abstract shapes. A pair of benches faced each other in the garden's center, and without anything better to do, Victory sank onto one. The woman had, after all, provided what Victory requested—a space to be alone.

But moping was not in Victory's nature, and sitting and staring into space soon lost its appeal. She placed her palms flat on the bench to either side of her and stared at a small pebble in the pathway. Drawing on Zerandan's instructions to Asaron in Parisii, she sank her awareness into the space around her, until her sense of self fell away except for her fingertip connections to the cool stone on which she sat. Her vampiric vision picked out every nook and cranny within the pebble, every surface imperfection. It shouldn't be difficult to just—nudge it a little.

"Don't!"

Greater awareness rushed into Victory's being when Syri interrupted her concentration. She lifted her hands from the bench and rubbed feeling into her palms.

The elven girl dropped onto the opposite bench, chest heaving. "Good, I caught you in time. Asaron and Ahn are working in a shielded space. If you'd touched your power here, the shadows could have achieved a foothold in the enclave."

Victory curled her hands around the edge of the bench. "No one has told me a damned thing about this supposed vampiric magic except in the context of Asaron accessing his power. He wants nothing to do with it. I'm the one who has more familiarity with magic. I'm the one who raised two kids with it."

Syri tucked a lock of hair behind one ear and looked beyond Victory, as if admiring the carved stone around them. "Age is a factor in unlocking these abilities, and Asaron is so much older than you."

"I'm no spring chicken." How old had Serena been? Connor was a few decades older than Mikelos, but Victory had never asked about the other woman. A frisson of fear tensed her shoulders. Toria and Kane had confronted such power and lived to tell of it.

Syri had not.

But before Victory answered, Syri asked, "How are they? Toria and Kane, I mean."

So many answers to such a simple question. Victory settled on the easiest. "They're good. Happy, even." She paused. "They miss you."

"I miss them, too. I've missed so much, but it can't have been that long."

"For us, maybe." They shared the wry smile of the long-lived. "For them, it probably feels like lifetimes. They finished out their journeyman training and achieved full mercenary status. A water mage named Archer Sophin—you met him briefly, I think—took over the mage school in Limani. He and Kane have been together ever since."

"Oh, that guy. I remember him. Good. I'm glad for them. What about Toria?"

How much to share about her daughter's life? "She's always lived for the next job. She may have found someone. It's still new." Being together for a few months out of time was no basis for a real relationship, but Liam had valued his connection with Toria enough to orchestrate events almost a century later to ensure the relationship had a chance. Where they went from here was anyone's guess. Victory hoped she made it home to see her daughter live happily ever after.

Syri studied the manicure of one hand. "I never meant to get so close, but I had no real memory of what I was while I was… alive, for lack of a better word. My disappearance caused them pain, which I never intended."

"Your death may have caused them pain, but I promise that the time you spent with them was well worth it. The bond you shared with Toria helped save Kane, remember? They valued your friendship. They have your name tattooed on their wrists in memory." The permanence had traumatized Mikelos, but Victory understood the honor with which it was intended. "Even Archer."

"Crazy kids." The flush that colored Syri's cheeks belied her dismissiveness.

Victory rose from her bench and crossed to Syri's. "I've missed you, too, you know." She settled next to the elven girl, or whatever she was. Victory might not know much about these beings of light and their connection to the elves in her own world, but she knew Syri. She knew the girl who'd risked her life to save her children, and she cared for that girl as much as she cared for the one who'd regularly visited the manor house with Kane and Toria for one of Mikelos' home-cooked meals.

"Aw, I've missed you, too, lady." Syri snaked her arm around Victory's torso.

Victory tucked Syri into her side for a hug, and the world faded.

Home.

The manor house library spread before her, packed with book-filled shelves along each wall and lit by a dim lamp in one far corner. Violin music spilled down the hall from Mikelos' studio, which meant her daywalker was home, too. Sometimes she sat here to listen to him practice. He was less inclined to show off when she wasn't in the same room, watching.

Victory lifted her hands to run them over the surface of the antique wooden desk, but they were frozen in place. Nerves jangled in alarm. This was like being caught in Serena's body. But how could she be trapped in her own?

Even without control of her head, she glimpsed the hands resting on the arms of her desk chair. They weren't hers. Instead, a man's slender fingers tapped along to the tempo of Mikelos' tune.

She'd know those hands anywhere. She hadn't trained them to wield a knife, but she had forced him to the sword. The sword Toria now carried.

This might be Limani, but it wasn't her proper time. And the body she found herself in belonged to Jarimis.

She peered into the darkened corners of the library. Did a shadow move with purpose, extending toward her, or did the breeze outside jostle a tree branch?

As she gathered her mental energies to scream inside Jarimis' mind and try for his attention, Victory entered the library. Seeing herself startled her into mental silence. This was not like facing her doppelganger in Nacostina, confronting her past self for access to secret documents she couriered for the British. The woman in the library might also be a version of Victory from the past, but the Victory tucked away in Jarimis' mind recognized herself this time. This wasn't a confrontation. This was meeting a kindred spirit.

"Why are you sitting alone in the dark?" Victory of the past crossed the library in a handful of long paces and dropped into an armchair across from Jarimis' desk.

Because if Jarimis was still alive, this was Jarimis' desk. The entire library was Jarimis' domain. Victory didn't make it her own office until almost two years after his death.

Jarimis' baritone rumbled through his chest, and he selected a pen. "I have errands to run. But it's cold outside." He spun the pen over and under his fingers, a trick he could perform with a knife with equal deftness.

"You know we don't feel the cold, right?" Other-Victory smirked at her rhetorical question. Jarimis hailed from a tropical clime, and his distaste of anything below sweltering was a constant source of amusement between sire and progeny.

"Yes, you've caught me out. Perhaps I am feeling lazy."

"You just don't want to climb around a construction site in the dark." Victory propped her bare feet on the opposite armchair. Soon, her own free hand tapped along to the beat of Mikelos' playing.

"That is truer. But I need to check on the site for the new dorms. If we want to increase enrollment next year, we need a place to put the students." Jarimis rose and stretched his arms out, working out stiffness.

The Victory trapped within his body spared a moment to ponder that stiffness. Maybe there was something to his aversion to cold after all. Then, the significance of his words to her predecessor caught up to her.

This was the night it stopped being Jarimis' library, Jarimis' desk. This was the night he left the manor house and never returned.

Jarimis stooped to drop a kiss to the top of Victory's head, and she screamed at her past self. Not to let him leave. Not to let him go alone. Not to let him leave without telling him how much she loved him.

Instead, past Victory twitched her fingers in farewell and settled into the armchair, content with Mikelos' music.

Jarimis tossed a wave to Mikelos when he passed the daywalker's studio. The other man didn't even acknowledge the gesture, intent on his practice. Victory had no recollection of what he might have been working on, whether rehearsing a piece or working on an original composition. She'd lost such minute details in the blur of grief infusing the memories of that time period.

Victory retreated to a far corner of her mental entrapment in Jarimis' mind. She wanted no part of this. Becoming a witness to his death might be more than she could bear.

He dragged her along, unknowing, while he shrugged on a wool coat, plucked a set of keys from the hook near the door, and left the manor house. His long legs led him along the path toward his small town-car, then into the vehicle that started with a low electric hum. Away from home, for the last time.

The land Jarimis had purchased from Limani for his college sat along the road between the manor house and the city proper. Farmland and strips of forest surrounded it, and it bordered the Agios River on one side. He'd been so proud of what he built, even if he'd seen less than a handful of classes graduate before his disappearance.

He hummed while he drove, a tuneless melody that bore a casual resemblance to what Mikelos had played earlier. Jarimis sat relaxed, unconcerned. In contrast, Victory's mental presence was strung tighter than a violin. Though she could not contact him, odd bits of Jarimis' thoughts penetrated her corner, much like she'd heard random thoughts from Serena. He expected a quick visit with the representative from the construction firm contracted to build the new dormitory. Then he might swing into town and visit his daywalker Allesandra at the Twilight Mists, the nightclub she managed. Savor a beer, or perhaps indulge Ally by trying one of the fruity cocktails she liked to experiment with.

When he passed under a streetlight, it flickered out.

The steering wheel jerked to the side. Jarimis wrestled for control of the vehicle when the electrical system stuttered out. He managed to steer onto the verge of the road before he lost all forward momentum. Jarimis released his grip on the wheel. Every indicator light on the dash had darkened, and the town-car did not respond when he pushed the ignition button.

"Damn it." He sat in the silent vehicle, gearing himself up for the walk home. His irritation at rescheduling the dormitory inspection and calling for a tow truck overwhelmed even his dislike of the cold.

He placed his hand on the door and every streetlight dimmed, plunging this quiet stretch of road into darkness. Jarimis waited for his eyes to adjust, but they were two days past the new moon, and clouds blacked out the pale light of the stars.

It's not cloud cover, Victory urged from her blocked-off corner. *Stay in the car, Jarimis.* She beat at her mental cage. But her presence had no effect on the events of the past. Perhaps she had always been here, at this point in history, and the end result was the same every time.

Jarimis stepped out of the vehicle.

He peered through the darkness, but nothing appeared out of the ordinary beyond the trees on either side of the road. His adrenaline surged but not from the same fear Victory possessed. Was Limani under attack? An electromagnetic pulse might have killed the streetlights and the car, but that should have been impossible after the Last War spurred the worldwide elven mandate against advanced weapons technology.

And an electromagnetic pulse didn't explain why he couldn't bloody see anything.

After a few paces in the direction of the manor house, the noise rose. He braced himself against the howls of a storm, but gentle wind pressed against his skin and clothing. Instead of icy tendrils of winter air, the caress warmed him. The sensory details clashed, and he froze in place until he could figure out what was happening.

Victory raged in her mental prison, to no avail. How heartless could these shadow bastards be if they forced her to be part of this death?

The darkness swirled around Jarimis, blocking his sight. The roar in his ears dulled to a cascade of whispers. He plucked one phrase out of the darkness.

One will need you.

Then, he heard nothing at all.

Victory grasped at the hands clutching her shoulders. Syri stood above her, pale skin ashen. They were still in the tiny rock garden, surrounded by sculptures. Victory had been lying on one of the benches. "What—?" Her voice rasped. She coughed, tried again. "What happened?"

"You passed out." Syri released Victory's shoulders and sank next to her. "I called for the others, but you woke up."

As if on cue, Jarimis careened between the buildings toward them. Mikelos and Connor sprinted hot on his heels.

"Oh, thank heavens," Jarimis said, dropping onto the opposite bench. "I'd feared the worst." He caught Victory when she hurled herself across the space between them. He let her hold him close, and wrapped his arms around her like it was any other hug. "Hey, what's this?"

"What is it this time?" Connor let out an *oof* of surprise when one of the others cut him off.

Victory might have liked to see the other vampire put in his place, but she'd buried her face in Jarimis' neck and couldn't bear to let go. When another hand touched her back, she pulled away to acknowledge Mikelos.

He pressed his hand to her cheek. His palm burned, but she turned into his warmth. "You're freezing," Mikelos said. "Was it another vision?"

"Yes." Victory sought Jarimis' hand and clutched it tight. Even his touch warmed her. Sitting between Mikelos and Jarimis should have been the safest place in the world right now, but the anxiety of newfound revelation overwhelmed any sense of contentment. "And I know what the shadows have been doing. I just had to put the pieces together."

"Explain." A harsh edge tinged Syri's words, but it wasn't directed at Victory.

"We've been manipulated. All of us. And not just now." The shadows had been there for Victory's first death. They'd goaded Serena into feeding Connor to them. Even the snippets of visions from days ago, when Victory traveled through time with Toria fell into place. The shadows had been there for everything, watching, waiting. Changing.

The whisper when they stole Jarimis had been the final piece. *One will need you.*

They'd spoken to her enough, now. She was the "one." And the shadows were right. She did need him. Which is why the shadows had ripped him away from her. Manipulated the events that led to his death. She might not know their reasons, but their motive was clear. Destroy everything she held dear. But she refused to be their pawn. "You didn't die, Jarimis."

"Then how in the world did I get here?"

"The shadows took you." Victory pointed to Connor. "What I assumed was the shadows killing you in my vision with Serena was something different. The shadows were bringing you here. The same way they took Jarimis."

"Who were you in, to witness such a thing for me?" Jarimis asked.

"In you." Victory squeezed his hand. "You drove to the college. You never made it that night. We found your town-car on the side of the road, abandoned. I saw the shadows force you off the road, kill the power, and steal you."

He met her eyes for a beat. She could have drowned in their warm, dark depths, but his gaze slid away before her power overwhelmed him. "If there was no body, how did you know I was dead?"

Mikelos answered first. "We searched. For months. In Limani, and beyond. Victory and I traveled the length of the Roman colonies. Asaron combed the Wasteland around the city. Allesandra searched the British colonies, and even spent months in Europa. There was no sign of you."

"We didn't want to, but we had to assume the worst," Victory said.

"No wonder you were so surprised to see me in Nacostina. Must have been a shock."

"Understatement of the century, Zvi." Victory released her death-grip on Jarimis' hands, but he didn't move away from her on the bench.

"I wasn't able to, because I didn't know about her yet," Jarimis said. "But I can do it now. When you get home this time, you can tell Allesandra how much I love her, and how sorry I am that I wasn't able to say goodbye."

Victory kept her poker face, but Mikelos stiffened behind her and ruined everything.

Jarimis noticed the daywalker's reaction. "What aren't you telling me?"

If Jarimis had been a son to her for centuries, Allesandra had been a daughter, long before Toria. Jarimis had found the woman in a small town after the Last War and fallen head over heels. Victory had objected at first, but she'd come to love the daywalker as much as Jarimis.

Allesandra had even come home, after her searching, to live out the rest of her natural life with Victory and Mikelos. If Asaron was Toria's Grandpa, Allesandra with her regal crown of shock-white hair in her later years had been Grandma.

"It's been years, Jarimis," Victory said. "Allesandra is gone."

Jarimis ripped himself away from Victory, pushing off the bench in a fury of limbs to pace between the sculptures. He avoided Connor's outstretched arm. "You were supposed to protect her, Victory, even from herself."

"Hey now—" Mikelos reacted in outrage, but Victory silenced him with a hand.

Victory itched to stand but forced herself to stay seated, to keep the submissive posture in this confrontation with her progeny. "That's not what happened.

Asaron even offered his own blood for the daywalker bond. She refused him, because he wasn't you, and you were the light of her life. She stayed with us until she died of old age. She had a good life, I promise."

Jarimis staggered away. "I knew enough time had passed for you to adopt and raise a daughter, after I met Toria in Nacostina. But if she died of old age," he said, "it's been decades." He turned on his heel and stormed out of the rock garden.

But he couldn't leave now. The shadows were right. Victory needed him. She needed all of them. She pulled away from Mikelos' comforting touch and stretched her arms toward Jarimis. Power fueled by pure emotion—her love for Jarimis, her pain over Allesandra, even her lingering jealousy of Connor—surged through her. It was the work of a mental twitch, a single swipe of her hand, to topple a sculpture in front of Jarimis.

He froze in place.

Syri moved first, bursting off the bench in a frenzy of energy. "What the fuck, Victory? What did I say earlier?"

"I heard you." Victory lowered her arms. "But the shadows already have a foothold into the enclave. They have me. They've always had me."

"Explain it to me again, please." Brawleyn perched on the edge of the cushioned ledge, as if he'd be more comfortable standing at attention.

They'd left the rock garden after Victory's demonstration of power. Brawleyn waited with Asaron and Ahn in their original space—waiting room, holding facility, gilded cage—when they arrived, summoned by Syri through whatever means these creatures of light had.

Victory recognized a fellow military soul, so she told the story again, as though reporting to Asaron after a scouting trip in their mercenary days. But this was no scouting trip.

When she fell silent, Brawleyn turned to Syri. "Do you agree with this assessment?"

"She toppled a sculpture that weighs over a ton." Syri lifted one shoulder. "And she's been having visions. If that's not a sign, I don't know what is."

"A sign of what?" Mikelos sat with Connor across the room. Her daywalker had stuck with his former vampire since the revelation that Connor's sire had summoned the shadows that took him to this strange place. But the jealousy had faded to a low simmer. Begrudging Connor the comfort of his old friend wasn't in her nature. And she had bigger concerns right now.

"Signs from the old legends had given every indication that the tipping point was coming," Brawleyn said. "That we wouldn't be able to hold back the darkness forever. And since it was power from your world that created this imbalance, we had to wait for a source of power from your world to fix it."

"When you all arrived," Ahn said, "we assumed it would be Asaron, the oldest. By all rights, he should have tapped into his magic centuries ago." Next to Asaron, who fidgeted with an empty teacup, the ancient vampire seemed the picture of serenity.

"Why me?" Victory sagged onto the bench next to Brawleyn. "I'm not old enough to have manifested these powers naturally, but the visions seem to prove the shadows had a hand in it. Are we sure we can trust me? If I am a foothold in your enclave, I put all of you at risk."

"You might be a foothold, but we'd be able to tell if you were under their control," Syri said. "We don't know why you were chosen, though from your visions it seems like it's been centuries in the making."

"Zvi, any thoughts?" Victory asked. The use of his nickname did not capture Jarimis' attention as he scribbled notes from his corner seat. Victory tried again. "Jarimis."

"I have no thoughts on this subject, Mother."

Victory longed for a stiff drink. But none of them could afford to be muddled right now, despite Jarimis' apparent distraction. "If I'm not a risk to the enclave, perhaps I am a risk to the shadows. It seems the time to move on them is now. Attack the hive mind, or whatever controls these beings."

"In a normal situation, we would call a council meeting," Brawleyn said. "Perhaps a vote of the entire enclave residency."

Ahn pushed off the wall. "We don't have time for that. Victory is right. We must move on the shadows, while we have this chance."

"You mean before the shadows can get their hooks into me deeper," Victory said. Asaron's sire might be of Victory's lineage, but the creatures of light in this walled-off enclave were Ahn's people now.

Like they were Syri's people. And Connor's. She had no way to gauge how time passed here, whether Connor had been here nearly a century and Syri a handful of years. But this society claimed both of them. Along with Jarimis, sitting alone in his corner.

Would she lose Mikelos to this world, where he could be with his best friend again? The man who'd raised him, who'd created him into the musician he became?

Would she lose Asaron to this place, now that he'd reunited with his sire? She couldn't imagine centuries without the man, and she'd jump at the chance to be with him if she found him again.

"We can't risk finding out what the shadows plan for you," Brawleyn said. He stood, his movements crisp. He must be relieved to have some semblance of a plan. "We need to leave the enclave and march on them, once and for all. Use the tools we have while they're in our grasp."

"You're right," Victory said. "If I have a power, it should be used. We need to go." If she was a tool to be wielded by these creatures of light, so be it.

Syri acted like this might be the end of this plane of existence, if the shadows managed full control. And Victory didn't want to be alone at the end of the world.

They set off at first light. In a world where light never wavered, first light meant when a single light emanated from a central tower in the enclave. Used to setting off at full dark, preparing for an expedition under such terms rankled Victory's sense of the familiar. Everything about the past few weeks had up-ended her idea of normalcy.

Her clutch of traveling companions was both bigger and smaller than expected, as well. Smaller, because Brawleyn and his military corps would not accompany them.

"You're the strike team," he said, when he stopped by to appraise them of the overall plan. "If the shadows are tied to you, they'll know where you are. But my forces can serve as a distraction—"

"So that the entire might of the shadows doesn't come crashing down on us," Victory said without hesitation.

"I anticipated an argument, not for you to read my mind."

"You might be the commander here, but I have my share of military experience," Victory said. "And I'm a hell of a lot more comfortable with a small team instead of operating as part of a larger force. I appreciate the risk your people are taking on our behalf."

Brawleyn extended a hand, and Victory grasped his wrist in an old-fashioned warrior's grip. "We appreciate your willingness to face the shadows on ours." He departed, without wasting time on goodbyes or offerings of luck.

Syri led them to the enclave's entrance, their group decked out in combat armor similar to Brawleyn's forces. The gear resembled urban assault armor similar to current Roman military wear, but she resisted the urge to ask how beings cut off from her own world mimicked such style.

The group was bigger than Victory expected, however, because Connor and Jarimis accompanied them. Jarimis spoke not a word to Victory as they left the enclave, passing through the shimmering boundary. Though the rocky plain had seemed so bright to Victory beforehand, it paled in comparison to the area of this world carved out by the creatures of light. The off-white sky blended into the rocky horizon, until they marched through a barren land without end.

Which was, upon reflection, exactly what it was. Though she'd been at Syri's side at first, Victory dropped back to join Jarimis. He kept silent. She would have to make the first move. Blunt seemed best. "I'm surprised you joined us."

He didn't respond right away, but since Syri had warned them that she had no idea how long this journey into the center of the darkness' territory would take, Victory could be patient.

Finally, he said, "I have a theory that your ties to us have prevented the shadow hive mind from taking you over. It's taunting you with visions of how it is destroying everything around you, but all you've done is draw strength from it."

"You think what the shadows have done has backfired? Forced me to keep you all closer, instead of separating me from the pack?"

Jarimis scratched the side of his nose. "And as part of your source of strength, joining you on this expedition was the responsible option."

Her progeny never played poker, because his tells were open for the world to see. She did him the favor of changing the subject. "It's strange to see you carrying weapons you swore never to wear again."

Jarimis smoothed his hand along the bandoleer crossing his chest from shoulder to hip. It held a row of needle-like knives he could throw with pinpoint accuracy. "I hope you've kept everything I owned in good condition."

Victory pressed a hand to her heart in mock offense. "And risk Asaron's wrath? Most of your gear is still in use. Toria and Kane do a lot of bodyguard work in Europa, and knives are easier to conceal." She paused, but confessing the next bit no longer risked injury to the time-space continuum. "Toria carries your rapier, too."

"Good," Jarimis said. "I imagine it suits her better than it ever did me."

Before Victory turned the discussion to the way Toria had modified the rapier's blade during her metallurgy studies, a strangled cry ripped itself from a throat behind them. As one, Victory and Jarimis spun on their heels and drew blades.

The group had spread while they marched, wending their own paths around the various-sized boulders and rocky outcroppings that dotted the landscape. Now, Connor froze in place, gripping Mikelos' arm and preventing him from moving another step.

Syri grabbed Connor by the shoulders, forcing his attention to her. "Stop. Whatever it is, it's not fucking real. Stop freaking out."

Connor released Mikelos, transferring his white-knuckle grip to Syri's arms. She didn't flinch, instead rising on her tip-toes and pressing her forehead to Connor's. Breathing exercises were wasted on a vampire, but the calm she exuded washed over him.

"I don't understand. What did he see?" Mikelos asked.

Good question. The landscape had not changed. No enemies encroached, not even the vaguest movement of shadows where they should not be.

"Connor." Though low in volume, the intensity of Syri's voice carried. "Tell us what stopped you."

He stayed frozen in Syri's grip, his eyes shut tight. "A river. A river of pure shadow, running silent. You walked into it, and it swept you away. Victory and Jarimis were about to do the same."

Syri didn't react, as if his report didn't surprise her. "Except it didn't take me, did it? Because I'm right here. It's one of the badlands' tricks."

Connor opened his eyes now, pupils blown in this odd half-light. "How do I know you're not the trick?"

Jarimis placed his hand on Connor's back. "The shadows don't talk. It's Syri."

"Is the river still there?" Syri asked.

After a quick peek, Connor turned his face aside. "Yeah. There's no way to cross."

"Yes, there is," Jarimis said. "Because the river isn't there for the rest of us. So, you have to keep your eyes shut and let us lead you through."

Ahn added her hand to Connor's back. "You are stronger than this. You lasted in the badlands for months before stumbling across the enclave and finding refuge with us. You've experienced worse. You can handle this now."

"I still have nightmares about that time," Connor said. "I thought I was willing to leave the enclave because of Mikelos. But this was a mistake."

"Hey," Mikelos said. "I'm right here. I can lead you through this river. You led me through so much, once. Let me return the favor." He took Connor's hand. "Keep your eyes shut, okay? It'll be like we're playing Blind Man's Bluff in Duchess Lauretta's gardens after too much brandy and wine."

Pleasure cracked through Connor's pain, but he did as instructed. "Those were some good parties."

Mikelos stepped forward, leading Connor. "They were excellent parties. We didn't stick around at the boring ones." He maintained a string of calming patter with reminiscences of parties and holidays across Europa, dropping the names of nobility and celebrities from years past.

Syri led the way again, and to be on the safe side, she did not let Connor open his eyes until they'd traveled at least a quarter of a mile. Finally, the raging river fell far behind him.

Victory dropped back to join Ahn and Asaron. "The badlands?"

Ahn pursed her lips. "It's what some of us call the area far away from the safety of the enclave."

"Like where we are right now?"

"Yes."

Boulders forced them to traverse a rocky passage single-file. Ahn continued when they crossed another stretch of flatter ground. "This world thrives on balance. As the creatures who built the enclave of light lose ground, the shadows overwhelm more and more of the world. But as you just saw, it's not always a lifeless realm of rocks and sand."

"Hallucinations," Asaron said. "Connor's river of shadows." He peered into the distance, lifting a hand to shade his eyes from the light, dim though it was. "Am I the only one who sees the clouds massing in the horizon?"

Victory turned in the direction Asaron pointed. But the sky remained its unceasing shade of flat gray, with no variations to distinguish clouds from sky. "I'm afraid so. No clouds at all."

"How about black thunderheads?" Asaron asked. "And—yes, that is lightning. A lot of lightning."

No accompanying thunder rolled across the landscape, and the air around Victory sat flat and still. Yet wind tugged at Asaron's hair and clothing, and he altered his stance, as if bracing himself. It reminded Victory of the invisible hands that caressed her while she fell through time, and she backed away from her sire.

Ahn called out, summoning the group. "Anyone else see a storm coming?" A resounding negative answered him. "Then things are about to get interesting."

Asaron ducked behind a large stone outcropping, which jutted from the ground like a monstrous windbreak. His movements were jerky, and his hair lashed his face as the tie holding it back lost its fight with the strength of the

141

wind. Victory gave him a mighty push against the weight of the wind as it fought Asaron, until he was behind the rock. He collapsed in the relative calm of its shelter. "I'd feel a lot better if all of you joined me." He raised his voice, calling out over wind unheard by the rest, jarring against the otherworldly silence.

They followed his request, clustering around Asaron. It might have been amusing, until Asaron clapped his hands over his ears and winced in pain. "The thunder won't stop," he shouted into the calm that eluded him.

Ten minutes of fear for Asaron and odd boredom for the rest of them passed in agonizing slowness, until the vampire eased away from the rock and peered into the sky. "It's passed. The clouds are dissipating."

"That was very, very weird," Mikelos said. He produced a hair tie and flicked it at Asaron.

"Safe to move out now?" Ahn asked. She tugged a strap of Asaron's chest plate into place, and he nodded.

The troupe moved on, with no mishaps for another hour or so—until hallucinations struck Jarimis and Mikelos together. Flames from the sky were nothing to sneeze at, but Jarimis dealt with the visions with calm aplomb. Using the same trick that had allowed Connor to cross his river of shadows, Mikelos kept his eyes closed and held tight to Connor until Jarimis reported the streams of fire falling from a blood-red sky had ceased.

When Mikelos marveled it had not affected Jarimis, the vampire said, "Doesn't work to scare a man with half-hearted images of the hell from the religion of his childhood. The shadows forgot the multi-headed demons."

"Or perhaps you're a braver man than I," Mikelos said.

"Just one who prizes curiosity over fear. The shadows might understand the latter, but they don't know physics." Jarimis grinned wide enough to show fang. "I had cause to make a study of meteors, once. These visions were so far from reality as to be comical."

Though desperation had tinged that time, Victory would forever cherish the memory of Jarimis and Toria combining intellects in Nacostina. "It's been a bit of a day, everyone. Perhaps we should take a refresher before the shadows inflict another ridiculous trick on one of us," she said.

Everyone met the suggestion with agreement. Within another few minutes, they found a small clearing surrounded by jagged boulders. Defensible, with two passable exits. Ahn and Syri volunteered to guard the passageways since the hallucinations had not visited them so far. Connor produced a hasty meal from thin air, and Jarimis summoned bedrolls.

Victory meant to keep Ahn and Syri company while the rest of them dropped into the sleep of exhaustion. Until a natural darkness descended between one comforting beat of Mikelos' heart and the next.

These fractured ruins of rubble and shattered masonry were not like the boulders in the shadow realm. These were familiar to Victory, from dozens of decimated cities and towns she'd stumbled through over the centuries. But these were not the sterile, time-swept ruins of the Wasteland, picked over and left to molder for decades. This destruction was recent, reminiscent of cities destroyed during the Last War by bombs dropped from planes that no longer flew the skies.

Victory crept through a path in the rubble, careful not to catch her clothing on exposed nails or turn an ankle wrong on a loose rock. After the comparative brilliance of the shadow realm, she squinted in the nighttime darkness, trying to identify familiar details that might indicate where in place or time the shadows had sent her on this latest vision.

At least she seemed to be in her own body this time, instead of a silent passenger tied to the movements and decisions of someone else.

Cold wind found every nook and cranny of her sturdy combat armor, creating a shivering chill for even one such as her. Victory paused in a stable section of rubble, among the remnants of wooden furniture upon a cracked tile floor, and peered into the night sky. Perhaps the stars might give her some clue as to where in the world she'd found herself.

But what she'd assumed to be the night sky was instead a sheet of glassy darkness. Neither stars nor the light of the moon shone through its cover. Instead, shadows roiled across the empty expanse. What light there was came from fires burning in the distance, smaller ones smoldering in areas of nearby rubble and more distant conflagrations reflecting against the darkness above.

No clues would come from there. Perhaps she was not in her own world after all, but merely in a different section of the shadow realm. This might be the remnants of the enclave, or even another holdout that the creatures of light maintained.

A slow heartbeat rumbled in the distance. She wasn't alone in these ruins. Someone yet lived. Victory forced her way through and around crumbling walls and piles of displaced goods until she trod on a leg, prompting its owner to yelp in pain.

"Hold on." She shoved debris away from the body. "I've got you."

Grime and old blood covered the person's garments, making any familiar garb or uniform impossible to identify, but the large hands and broad shoulders indicated a man's form. Victory maneuvered a final beam off his chest, revealing a face littered with bruises that discolored his olive skin, where it wasn't shiny and raw from burns. Though half his scalp was bare and the rest of the hair was half-charred, Victory would know the man anywhere. After all, she'd adopted him as one of her own brood once Kane established the water mage as a permanent fixture in his life.

She clutched Archer's shoulders, and he groaned again in the darkness. "Archer, it's okay. I'm here." He cast about with one arm, and she released his shoulder to clutch his hand. His grip was weak, his fingers skeletal. Though he'd never been a large man, he'd lost significant weight.

"Vic—Victory? Where have you been?" His voice rasped, his throat dry.

"It's a long story. I'm back." Now that she'd identified Archer, additional nearby details sharpened. The ruins of his office at the mage school scattered around them. His desk was kindling, and the various plants had transformed to desiccated husks. Book pages fluttered in the light breeze. "What happened here? Where are Kane and Toria?"

"You disappeared months ago," Archer said. "And that's when they came." A wracking cough rattled his frame.

The unmistakable sound of fractured ribs creaked in his chest. What other internal injuries did the man have? She needed to find help, but without information, she had no idea where to look. Did the rest of Limani suffer the same desolation? "When who came?"

"The darkness. Portals opened across Limani. I got one message—" Another round of coughing. "—from New Angouleme. Same thing there."

"What came out of the portals?"

"Shadows. All shapes and forms. A wave of destruction no one could fight." Tears gathered in Archer's eyes, but remembered pain strengthened him. "Toria summoned a storm, greater than anything possible. She managed to destroy the larger creatures barricading us. But it destroyed the school, too, and the power burned her out."

Pain seized her chest. She already knew the answer to her next question, but Victory asked it anyway. "And Kane?"

"He held on long enough to help me get the students to safety." Archer's voice grew faint, and blood tinged his lips. Internal bleeding. He didn't have much time. "I couldn't leave the kids."

And Kane wouldn't leave Toria, and with the severing of their bond, the other warrior-mage would soon follow her into death. "I'm sorry I wasn't here."

"You're here now." Ever the optimist. Archer's pulse stuttered to a stop. Though his hand was still warm in hers, he was gone.

The last of her children in this world.

Victory arranged Archer's hands on his chest. Nothing else to be done for him. She pushed to her feet, and now that she recognized her surroundings, the greater picture became clear. The large fires, off in the distance, meant Limani's city proper was in flames.

Left unchecked, this was the world the shadows would create. If the shadows destroyed the final bits of light, they would have the strength to push through to her own plane. Limani, and every other city in the world, would fall. Under this cloud of darkness, survivors would starve as crops failed. Even the hardiest vampires wouldn't last much longer.

If this vision showed the future, she had to find a way to make sure it didn't come to pass.

Time to wake up.

When Victory swam out of unconsciousness, Mikelos gripped her shoulder. Memories of Archer's battered face overlaid that of her daywalker, and she flinched.

Mikelos misinterpreted. "Sorry to wake you, hon. We're getting ready to move out."

Though the light level remained unchanged, Victory did have the sense that a quantity of time had passed. She caught the canteen Asaron tossed her and brought it to her lips. Fresh blood, warm and revitalizing. But fake, like everything else in this strange place. It refreshed her, to a point, but she longed for home. For reality.

She emptied the canteen, and set it against a rock where it would fade away into the landscape.

Though they hadn't been inclined to joke or chatter before, their group was even more subdued now. They followed Syri out of the hollow, marching onward into the badlands.

The number of ragged boulders jutting from the bare ground never decreased, but they appeared in random clumps. Victory remained on alert, and no hallucinations startled any member of the group. Either the shadows' attention was not on them, perhaps distracted by Brawleyn's own assault force, or the hive mind had resigned itself to their eventual arrival.

Between one of the rockier areas, Mikelos came alongside Victory. "You're being quiet."

"Everyone is being quiet. This isn't a pleasure jaunt."

"Of course not."

Their regular habit of walking with Victory's hand tucked into the crook of Mikelos' elbow would be difficult, armored as they were. Victory told herself that's why he didn't reach for her. Instead, she looped her thumbs into the front of her chest piece. The material would stop a bullet and leave a hell of a bruise, but it would also stop a wooden stake. Victory made a mental note to have a similar set created when she returned to Limani.

If she returned to Limani, and it wasn't the wreck her latest vision foretold.

Her silence did not seem to offend Mikelos. "At least we're here together."

Victory snorted. "This isn't like when we helped the kids in the Wasteland. Or even that job in Jiang Yi Yue."

"The Wasteland may have been a camping trip for me, but it was a lot more stressful for you. I'm pretty sure Jiang Yi Yue was stressful for both of us."

"At least there's no one here for you to pick fights with."

Mikelos' mischievous nature came to the fore. "Oh, I'm pretty sure I could goad Asaron or Syri into taking a swing at me."

"Don't you dare," Connor said, joining the conversation. "Victory, does he still let his temper get the best of him?"

"I'd say no, but that would be a lie," Victory said. "At least he's only been hospitalized the one time."

"The one time, she says. Damn it, kid." Connor thumped Mikelos on the shoulder. "Do you never listen?"

"I don't have you around to be a paragon of good behavior anymore," Mikelos said, dodging before Connor whacked him again. "I have resigned myself to a life of conflict and warfare in the company of mercenaries of ill-repute."

Once, Victory would have laughed at Mikelos' quips. Victory and Asaron, vampires of uncertain lineage by the standards of the high families in Roma, had always embraced their miscreant reputation, softened though it was by dedication and loyalty to the job. Even in her so-called retirement, Victory treated her role as Limani's Master of the City and her simultaneous role on the city council with the same air of casualness.

Why did Mikelos' jibe sting? He'd always seemed happy in Limani, enjoying his own retirement from the celebrity life of constant Europan touring. But his life in Limani wasn't high-class. Their house might be large and luxurious, but it didn't come with its own servants, like Serena's townhouse in Parisii. A pair of women came to clean once a week. They did their own laundry. Mikelos cooked for himself, or had meals delivered from town, or they ate out. But no one answered the door for them, or arranged food to be available on a whim.

Connor and Mikelos continued to banter, trading tales of the scuffles Mikelos got into when he'd first joined with Connor, when he'd balked at the life of luxury that came with training as a premiere musician. It seemed Mikelos' temper getting the best of him wasn't a new thing, though he often lost it for the right reasons.

Victory dropped away, slowing her pace until she followed behind the pair. They didn't exclude her on purpose, but perhaps this was better. Safer. If the latest vision was true, she had to be willing to go it alone.

They walked longer and farther than Victory thought possible. She checked on Mikelos and Syri more than once, but they both confessed to a strange supply of energy, allowing them to maintain pace with the vampires. But even the vampires should have been dragging by this point. Had they traveled for a day? Close to two?

The off-white sky that never faded to night played merry hell with Victory's sense of time. It was like the lag in time she remembered from when it was possible to cross from Europa to the New Continent in the span of hours by plane. Jarimis, the only other one in their group who'd had the pleasure, snapped his fingers and agreed with her when she brought it up.

Yet they pressed on. And the landscape shifted once more.

Victory looked once, twice, thrice, sure she'd imagined it. A bush, though it hardly deserved the name. A straggly collection of twigs and brush, dotted with sparse gray leaves hanging on for dear life, emerged from the lee between a boulder and the hard ground. When she paused to examine it further, everyone clustered around to gape at the anomaly.

Mikelos stooped to examine the bit of brush that didn't top his knees. "Is it even alive? Where's Kane when we need him?"

Syri crouched on her heels and poked at a branch. "I have no idea if it's alive. Could this have survived in the badlands all this time?"

"A remnant from the world of the light?" Ahn stood back, surveying the perimeter, as if she had no time for such distractions.

"Or a hallucination we all see," Jarimis said.

Ahn urged them onward, and no one protested. The novelty was a relief from the unrelenting press of boulders and sandy gravel and gray, gray, gray. But it wasn't what they were there for. If they ever found what they were there for.

Until Connor spotted the second sign of life.

Half-life was a better descriptor. This bit of shrub was taller, its spindled branches of a height with Victory's shoulders.

This time, Syri risked a brief touch, poking at a branch with one finger. It bent under her pressure, and sprang back.

"Not a hallucination." Jarimis also caressed a branch.

"No," Syri said. "A remnant, perhaps. Of when the shadows didn't rule this land."

"When the light did?" Mikelos raised his hands, feigning apology, at Syri's sharp glare.

"We never ruled." Syri paused. "I think. There was balance here, once. Things flourished where the light touched, but everything has an end. There's no such thing as true immortality." She marched off, away from the shrub, and they could do nothing but follow.

But more signs of life, or this strange mockery of it, appeared all around them. A whole clutch of battered shrubbery, patches of leaves clinging to thin branches. Boulders bore sections of grayish-green moss, small signs no bigger than Victory's hand but soon large enough to cover entire swathes of stone.

A lone circle of mushrooms straight out of a child's storybook, which they all stepped around. Whether due to respect or fear, everyone kept their own counsel.

Then, a battered building. They sped up, led by Jarimis and his endless curiosity. To Victory, it appeared to be a lone shepherd's hut, designed to keep a person safe from the elements while he or she protected the flock. This one stood in poor repair, the wood bleached by time. Half the roof had caved in, and sections of wall crumbled to the ground.

But it was another sign of life. A sign of sentient life, at that, here where nothing should thrive.

"What the blazes is going on?" Connor asked. He peered through a crack in the wall.

"Don't ask me." Syri circled the structure. "This is so far outside my expertise."

"I have been here many years," Ahn said. "Made multiple excursions to the badlands on various missions. And I have never seen signs of life such as these."

"Are we going the wrong way?" Mikelos asked. "Have we circled around to the enclave?"

Surprise ratcheted through Victory. "No." This felt right. Familiar somehow.

Perhaps her mind played tricks on her. How many abandoned buildings had she seen over the course of her lifetime? From war, from age, from the simple fact that sometimes people up and left. Victory resettled the straps of her armor. "Let's go."

They left behind the small ruins, winding and wending their way through boulders dotted with moss and circled with struggling patches of weeds. At one point, half-dead vines blocked the thin path they followed through a veritable canyon of boulders, and Victory, Asaron, and Ahn traded turns to hack a passage through.

Once free, they stumbled out of the mass of boulders into an open space. A crater of sorts, walls stretching into the distance. Flat land, dotted with gravel, opened before them. And in the center of the expanse sat a giant heap of ruins.

With Victory in the lead, they approached the structural remains cautiously. She scanned the top of the crater, but no shadows poured over the edges toward them. They were alone, save for whatever might lurk in the abandoned ruins.

They picked through the edge of the area, through bits of stone and shards of wood. A few sections of the original structure barely stood. All of the wood had toppled, weathered and gray, in piles that littered the ground. Though the shadow plane had no elements, this area seemed as if it had survived decades exposed to whatever the real world might throw at it. But when Victory placed her hand on an exposed beam, reality shifted once again. It wasn't weathered, but petrified. Even this wood had turned to stone in this world.

In silence, she led the group around the pile. Jarimis also noted the petrified wood, but Victory tuned out his rambled theorizing in favor of inspecting whatever clues this new anomaly might offer. After acres and acres, miles and miles, of stone and boulders and rocky outcroppings, any differences deserved extra inspection.

Victory paused at what she sensed was the front of the ruins. Ahn and Asaron maintained a vigilant watch. Syri seemed to have no interest whatsoever, cleaning under her nails with a knife tip. Connor seemed entranced by Jarimis' theories, which had transitioned into a lecture on the origins and circumstances required to create petrified wood.

Mikelos, however, stood next to Victory to absorb the full scope. "I feel like—" He cut himself off. "Never mind. It's crazy, even for everything else we've experienced so far."

"Which is why we can't dismiss anything out of hand," Victory said. She surveyed the outline of the ruins, searching for any clues.

Mikelos tilted back and forth, as if examining it from every angle like an artist prepared to work. "It seems familiar. Like I should know this place."

His words clicked pieces together in Victory's brain. "We're missing something." She wandered to the right, and he trailed behind her.

Signs of scrappy life emerged here, weeds and brush fighting for survival among the debris. Like this had once been a front garden, but the plants had lost their battle against hardier specimens that choked them out. Shattered tiles trailed through the plants, a walkway that had also seen better days. Victory crouched and ran her fingers across one tile. Through the streaks of grime, a vivid blue emerged, all the more brilliant for being the first new color among the grays and browns of this place.

Perhaps it was Mikelos' words prompting recollections, but Victory swiped the dirt off another tile. This tile featured a lustrous green, a tone more alive than the actual plants around it. Another tile, red as blood. And another, covered with a golden sheen.

"Victory."

She turned at the pain that wracked Mikelos' voice. He lifted another tile, still square and whole among the rubble. Dirt coated his hands where he'd wiped it clean. This one was a brilliant violet, edged in green. Mikelos flipped it over before he passed it to Victory. She accepted the artifact and traced the name etched on the bottom in a childish scrawl. *Torialanthas.*

"This is the mage school." Mikelos barely breathed the revelation.

Victory's hands spasmed, and she fumbled the tile. Mikelos wasn't quick enough, and it slipped between their fingers. The tile shattered on the littered ground, a harsh crack that echoed through the crater.

Mikelos grasped Victory's shoulders, tried to pull her in for a hug. "I'm sorry," he said.

But panic surged through her, and she couldn't find the words through a throat choked with fear. If this was the mage school, had her last vision shown her the past instead of the future? She pulled away from Mikelos and charged into the ruins, ignoring the calls of concern behind her.

If they'd stood in the front garden—once bisected with a winding path of tiles created by the mage apprentices when Toria was one of their number—the director's office was back and to the left. Victory forced a path by heaving rubble aside. She didn't feel the wounds that left streaks of black blood on the bricks and stony wooden beams she tossed from her path. Fear supplemented her vampiric strength.

She vaulted over the toppled remains of the fireplace in Archer's office and stumbled to a halt. The harsh light of the shadow plane instead of fire-lit dimness differed from her vision. No body lay where she'd held Archer while he died.

Victory fell to her knees on that spot and dug through the shards of ruined furniture and scattered bricks, tossing items over her shoulders. She sensed Mikelos to the side, begging her to stop and explain what was going on.

Her hand curled around bone, and she froze. Like the petrified wood, it had weathered with age. She released it, and with a gentler touch, exposed the rest of the skeleton. Mikelos kept the others from interfering until she moved two bricks away from a skull. The bricks had caved in the top of the skull, but the eye sockets stared unseeing, no longer containing Archer's brown eyes that always flashed with humor.

"Who is that, Victory?" Jarimis asked. "How did you know it would be here?"

She rested on her heels. Now that she knew it was here, it was easy to pick out ribs and vertebra among the rubble. "It's Archer Sophin. The director of the mage school in Limani. Kane's—my...." Her voice cracked, and she snapped her teeth shut.

Mikelos dropped next to Victory. "How can you know that?" This time, when he pulled her to his side, she didn't resist, instead tucking herself against his shoulder.

Syri answered first. "You had another vision."

It wasn't a question, and Victory found no reason to lie. "When we were resting, hours ago. I thought it was a dream at first. I was in my own body. But it felt too real, like the others." She described what she'd seen, what Archer said before he died. Limani, shattered by an invasion of the shadows.

"Is all this real?" Jarimis spread his arms, encompassing the ruins of the mage school around them. "Or another trick of the shadows, like the river and storms?"

"Maybe we made it back to the real world," Connor said. "I don't think anything is impossible anymore."

"But the sky hasn't changed." Victory drew away from Mikelos, and they helped each other stand. "If we were in the real world, half of us would have burned by now."

"More than half," Jarimis said.

Victory glared at his pedantry, but her progeny ignored her.

They remained underneath the same slate gray, with no shadows on the ground to indicate where the light might originate, if it came from any sort of direct source. No warning tingled across Victory's bare skin. Her hair crackled with the lack of humidity in the air, not because it was about to alight with flame.

"Or perhaps if the shadows invade, they block out the sun and create the same unceasing half-light on our world, as well," Asaron said.

"But that would mean—" Mikelos furled his brow, considering. "We're in the future?"

"Time moves differently here, but how would that be possible?" Jarimis asked.

"If we're in the future, we're too late to save Limani, much less the rest of the world." Dread colored Syri's voice and her hands twitched.

For a moment, Victory stood in the Wasteland among a different set of ruins in another destroyed city. Right before she followed Toria to a place out of time. "The shadows have the ability to manipulate time," Victory said. "The first time I spoke to them was when I was traveling via one of their artifacts."

"The question remains," Ahn said, "whether we are still in the shadow plane, or in the real world." She spun in a slow circle. "I always thought I'd know if I returned home."

They all spoke at once, a dam of words bursting, offering opinions and evidence for where—and when—they might be. Mikelos shot down Connor's theory that they were so far in the future it no longer mattered, and Victory followed Jarimis' trail of thought regarding how her visions might help them determine the answer.

Syri spread her arms, hushing them all at once with a hiss.

Victory froze. They'd lost all semblance of stealth once they arrived at the mage school, or this simulacrum thereof. Her hand drifted to the hilt of her sword.

Syri drew both of her daggers, prompting Jarimis to do the same. In a smooth motion, Victory unsheathed her bastard sword and dropped into a defensive position. Movement beyond their group caught her attention, and she whirled on the shadowy tendril oozing into the half-cleared area of Archer's former office.

More blades cleared sheaches behind her as Asaron and Ahn drew their own swords. The black tendril reared and struck.

Victory hacked at the sinuous arm. Jarimis shoved Connor and Mikelos behind them. Shadowy figures, humanoid and otherwise, poured out of the rubble. In a dance they'd practiced for decades, Victory and Jarimis kept up a flurry of blades to force the shadows at a distance, protecting the noncombatants behind them. Jarimis had honed his skills as a bodyguard with Victory before abandoning it for the life of an intellectual, but he still moved as though the daggers were an extension of himself.

Beyond the cluster of shadows fighting their way toward Victory, Asaron and Ahn also moved like a matched set. Syri was a whirl of blades behind them, protecting their backs from the shadows creeping over the toppled fireplace. If Victory and Jarimis fought well together, even after years apart, the two ancient vampires could have linked brains the way one always seemed to cover the other, each taking advantage of openings maneuvered by their partner.

Asaron and Victory had been known as the mercenaries Sun and Moon. But Asaron and Ahn were matching suns, two binary stars in perfect balance.

A shadow lashed through Jarimis' defenses and opened a gash on his cheek, and he grunted in pain. Victory twisted her blade, severing the inky tentacle. A scream she felt more than heard emerged from the depths of the attacking blackness. She couldn't tell where one shadow ended and the next began, and since they shattered into thin air whenever Victory managed the equivalent of a death blow, it was impossible to determine how many she defeated. The only thing that mattered was keeping them away from her. Away from Mikelos and Connor, huddled behind her in a corner of the ruins.

But her three other fellow combatants were out in the open, and soon Victory lost sight of them among the swirling shadows.

Jarimis darted forward to stab a body with too many limbs, but this opened his far side to attack. When he cried out and stumbled, she blocked and parried in a flurry of steel, moving more on instinct than conscious thought. But there were too many, and without Jarimis' support, she was reduced to pure defense.

Someone reappeared at her side. Had Jarimis recovered enough to return to the fight? No. Instead, it was Mikelos.

"Get back!" Victory blocked a shadowy blunt weapon with her forearm, a jarring hit that rattled her teeth.

Mikelos wielded an unfamiliar weapon, some sort of rifle. He racked the slide, which shouldn't have been possible from the shape of the gun. He pressed the trigger and a spray of bullets cut down the shadows in front of them. Another of his crazy hybrid weapons. Proof they were in the shadow plane after all, but that knowledge brought no relief from the heat of the fight.

Mikelos destroyed the shadows in the immediate area threatening to overwhelm them. He gestured with the barrel of his weapon. "Come on, let's get to the others!"

Victory checked behind her. Jarimis had one arm thrown over Connor's shoulders, clapping his free hand across his torso to his armpit, the place unprotected by body armor. Black blood, which absorbed the light the same way the shadows did, stained his hand.

"Go," Jarimis said. "We'll get there."

Victory traversed the rubble as fast as possible, though putting a foot wrong and breaking an ankle might doom them all. She smashed her way through the wall of shadows and prayed Mikelos didn't shoot her with his absurd weapon. Connor hauled Jarimis close on her heels. He'd summoned a slim rapier into his free hand. The way he waved it around kept the shadows back, even if it was clear the man had no experience with a blade.

Mikelos' weapons-fire almost drowned out the forceful grunts Asaron and Ahn emitted as they fought. Syri fought in complete silence, wasting not a single iota of energy on noise to accompany her blade strikes. Connor hauled Jarimis between them, and Victory positioned herself next to Mikelos. She tried to ignore his fear.

This was a strange sort of battle, where the dead were never alive and vanished where they fell. No scent of blood and guts and perforated bowels to permeate the battlefield and overwhelm Victory's sense of smell until it was a relief to smell nothing at all. No cries of the wounded, for gods and mothers and sweethearts.

None of this absence lessened the overwhelming need to defeat the foe before her. Nicks and cuts from lucky strikes stung her hands and arms, and thick blood from a scalp wound matted her hair. Though the need to feed seemed inconsequential in this world of darkness and light, they'd have to summon fresh blood when they were out of this scrape.

If they escaped this scrape. Those still standing circled Connor and Jarimis, with no defensible position to fall back to. The shadows had cut off her path, and the toppled fireplace to the side was low enough for shadow-figures to crawl over despite Mikelos' best efforts at picking them off before they touched ground on the other side.

Darkness fell over the scene of combat, and Victory spared a fraction of a second, between a parry and strike, to glance upward. A shadow towered over the field of battle, stepping on tree-like legs through its own compatriots. Like many of the others, no head showed where it might keep its brain, but enormous spiked arms hung toward the ground, swinging with every step.

Asaron caught sight of the monstrous shadow as well. "Incoming!"

Victory blocked a blow from a shadow before skewering another. How the hell were they supposed to defeat that thing? If it had been a fabled giant from ancient times, she might hamstring it, or target tendons in the ankles, or pin the feet to the ground. But traditional biology went out the window within this realm, and her exhausted mind drew a blank.

The smaller shadows, most of whom still towered feet over Victory, kept coming. One with three-pronged knives emerging from the end of too many upper limbs ensnared her sword, almost yanking it from her grip. The shadow shattered into fading black shards when one of Mikelos' gunshots blasted through its center mass.

At some unspoken signal, the shadows converged on Asaron. Victory overcame a shorter shadow, bashing it across the shoulders.

On Asaron's other side, Ahn blocked another blow meant for her progeny at the expense of leaving herself open as the giant whipped a long blade downward. Victory screamed a warning, but vampiric speed couldn't save the elder vampire.

The ebony blade cleaved Ahn through the shoulder, bisecting body armor and bone alike as if no thicker than butter.

The giant shadow cut her through, then withdrew the blade from her stomach. Asaron voiced his own howl of rage, a guttural cry that startled the shadow he fought into withdrawing.

Mikelos fired shot after shot into the maelstrom of shadows converging around them as the giant shadow swung both arms and turned away. Victory stabbed a shadow and pivoted to face her next foe before it finished collapsing into nothingness.

But there were none. By some unheard signal, the shadows fled the section of ruins and disappeared into the ether from whence they came. Even the giant shadow, which should have decimated the rest of them with as little effort as it struck Ahn, shrank to a speck and vanished.

Ahn.

Victory clutched Asaron's shoulder with her free hand, ignoring how her blood seeped into his armor. He had gathered Ahn in his arms, holding her together. Her dark eyes saw nothing.

Mikelos dropped his impossible weapon to the ground, where it vanished in the same manner of the shadows, and slid to his knees on Ahn's other side, already shoving up his sleeve. "Oh gods, hold on. Give me your knife, Syri."

"No." Asaron snarled through gritted teeth.

"We can save her." Mikelos opened and closed his hand. "Syri!"

Syri did not offer her blades. "Asaron's right. You and I could both be drained, but it's too late."

Victory wrapped her fingers around Mikelos' wrist. "She's right. Asaron, I'm so, so sorry."

Asaron pressed his forehead to Ahn's one final time, and they watched in silence. They should have been vigilant for the shadows' return, but Victory knew, somehow, that they were safe for the moment. Her connection to the darkness grew, even as her allies fell around her.

Asaron passed his hand over Ahn's eyes to close them. With great care, he settled her on the ground. "We have to move, before the shadows return."

Victory released Mikelos to extend a hand to her sire. But she hesitated, unsure whether he wanted comfort in front of the others.

He claimed her hand in a fierce grip but did not pull her into a hug. She stood steady, though he ground the bones in her hand together. When he released her, Victory's blood mingled with Ahn's on his palm. Now that she'd met the origin of her bloodline, Victory knew without a doubt that Ahn represented more honor and grace than any privileged Roman elder. Never again would Victory allow anyone to disrespect her lineage because Asaron did not hail from one of the great Roman families.

"The world changed too much," Asaron said, retrieving his sword and sheathing it, then collecting Ahn's blade. "Even if we escaped this place, she knew she was never going home."

"The question is," Jarimis said, Connor helping him to his feet. Blood stained the side of his armor, and an ashy pallor dulled his olive skin. "Will we?"

They had no choice but to leave Ahn's body. As if sensing Victory about to protest, Asaron jabbed a finger at her. "She died a warrior's death. I expect you to do the same, if I'm the next to fall."

She bowed her head, chastened. He was right. They had no time to let sentiment get in the way of their goals. Losing Ahn was a tragedy. Victory hoped losing a combatant did not tip any scales out of their favor.

Keeping watch for the shadows' return, or any other sign of them, they picked their way out of the mage school ruins. Asaron led the way, and Victory took over supporting Jarimis' weight from Connor. She summoned a bottle of blood and drained half of it before passing it to her progeny.

Jarimis drained his share even faster, and set the bottle on an outcropping of masonry. "Hell of a thing, isn't it," he said. His tone suggested they were out for a summer's evening stroll, not retreating from the site of a battle.

Victory didn't ask him to elaborate. Her progeny would either get to the point or lead her on a roundabout discussion about the history of two different objects and four theories before he reached it. There was never much between the two extremes.

"We spend our whole lives thinking we're inferior," Jarimis said. "You even tried marrying into a Roman family, and look how that worked out. And this entire time, we're not even a traditional lineage. I wonder what temple in the Qin lands Ahn hailed from."

Victory helped Jarimis climb over a pile of ceiling beams that now resembled stone columns. "I don't think it matters. She didn't seem keen on that life."

"So, are we to assume she is the head of our line?" Jarimis asked. "Establish a family tree of two?"

"Not three, or four?" Or more, if Victory counted Fatima, her long-lost progeny. And she had no idea whether Fatima had ever created more of their kind.

She knew Asaron and Jarimis had not.

Jarimis lifted an elbow, as if to wave his free hand, but flinched and kept it pressed to his wound. "Why carry the weight of dead branches?"

Pain colored his voice, and the debate fizzled. Victory kissed his jawline, the part of her taller progeny in reach.

Jarimis spoke again when the edge of the ruins came into sight. "I'm sorry I lashed out at you, before. There was nothing more you could do with the information you had. You had every reason to believe I was dead."

"But we could have—"

"No." Jarimis stopped, but wouldn't let Victory pull away from him. He met her eyes for one, two, three seconds, until her greater strength forced his gaze to slide away. "You had no reason to think there was anything strange afoot. Remember, I had memories you didn't yet, of meeting you and Toria in Nacostina. At the time, you and the others would have no concept of things like time travel, and whatever the hell these shadows are."

"Okay. You're right." Victory's gnawing sense of guilt, of the undone, might one day morph into a passing "what if?" at his reassurance. One day.

"I know I'm right. Come, the others are waiting."

Jarimis had healed enough to no longer need to rest his weight on her, but Victory helped him around the final corner of what was once the mage school's front door. The others stared beyond. The canyon surrounding the ruins of the mage school had vanished. Instead of a flat plain leading to cliff faces, more ruins had appeared.

"Is that—?" Mikelos broke away from the group and approached the nearest dilapidated building. "Yeah, it's the bakery."

"But it's too close," Victory said. "Where did the school's front yard go?" There should have been the shadowlands equivalent of a rolling expanse of greenery, leading down a long front drive to the main avenue. Instead, Mikelos stood yards away, poking his boot through the pile of bricks that remained of the bakery's old-fashioned oven.

"This is weird." Syri spun in a slow circle. "It's been a few years, and my sense of time is fucked up, but this is not the way Limani is supposed to look."

The girl was right. With Asaron at Victory's back, she passed Mikelos and the bakery and stepped onto the avenue. The pavement was cracked and warped beneath their feet.

"Shouldn't that boutique Toria likes be across the street?" Asaron asked. He pointed to a ramshackle house, almost leaning against its neighbor, a craft store with skeins of yarn spilling out the broken front window.

Victory surveyed the street, until a faded violet sign two blocks away caught her attention. "The boutique is down there. And the yarn store is supposed to be over by city hall."

The others had joined them in the street. "Nothing about this is right," Mikelos said. "What's the hive mind trying to tell us?"

"That it can see our city through its damned minions who have been spying on us for years," Asaron said, "but not put together the intel properly." He scoffed, as if affronted by the poor effort.

The sky had darkened again, to a slate gray. The type of sky where rain was imminent, except the air around them continued to be the same dry, comfortable temperature it had been since Victory arrived here. It was no longer a uniform color, though. Victory pointed toward the horizon, beyond Toria's boutique and a café that should have been a block behind them and a park with broken, rusted playground equipment. "We have to go that way."

A pillar of light broke the sky, a few shades paler than the dark gray. Easy to miss if you weren't searching for it. But now that she'd noticed it, it pulled at Victory like a magnet. A mysterious force that felt right when everything around them, this mockery of her city, was so wrong.

"Ugh, if something is telling me to go one way," Syri said, eyeing the pillar of light with suspicion, "I generally want to go the opposite."

"Same here," Victory said. "But that's the whole point of this, isn't it? Chasing the heart of the darkness?"

"Then show the way." Asaron flicked the tip of Ahn's sword down the street.

Victory lead them past blocks and blocks of collapsed and bedraggled buildings that no longer deserved the name. The city council building, surrounded by warehouses that should have stood over a mile away, appeared as if struck by a bomb. The roof had caved in, and spider-web cracks laced the front steps.

The road they followed continued to be clear, straight toward the light pillar calling to Victory. Potholes and other types of craters spotted the pavement, but they came across no vehicles or other debris that should have dotted an apocalyptic landscape. Soon, they passed the last of the buildings in the incomplete city. The road rolled along through pillars of stone on all sides.

"Where the hell is this leading us?" Connor asked, peering down the length of shattered black pavement.

"Home." The answer burst from Victory before she had time to consider it, but once she'd spoken the words, they fit.

Mikelos brushed a palm over the closest tower of stone. "Jarimis University is in that direction, too."

"Excuse me?" Jarimis snorted, and coughed again in real pain. "Jarimis University? Whose brilliant idea was that?"

"Not the time for this discussion, Zvi," Victory said. Would there be time for it later? Aside from this one certainty, where the road led, nothing was written in stone. "We're headed to the manor house."

She led the way again, along a twisting road between towering boulders that narrowed near the ground and broadened to expand in twisted lengths above. In the real world, these were trees that shaded the southern road and acted like a barrier between city-held property and farmland.

Here, Syri and Asaron ducked off the path and explored the sides. They reported that the emulated forest continued without end, at least as far as they veered.

Mikelos drew a hand over each stone trunk they passed, despite Victory wanting to drag him to the relative safety of the center of the road. "It's like something is trying so hard to make a facsimile of Limani, of our home."

"And failing damned miserably," Syri said. She hunched in on herself, keeping her gaze straight ahead.

Victory drove much more often than walked the three miles into town, but the way the road wound through the false forest appeared to mimic reality down to the last inch. "The house should be around the next bend."

And as she predicted, the road curved to the left and stopped, cut off by an invisible line. The stone trees continued beyond. But to the side, a pristine manor house sat among the rocks. Unlike the buildings in Limani, Victory and Mikelos' home appeared untouched by the ravages of damage or time.

A shimmering wall—some short of magical shielding—surrounded it. It was how Victory often imagined Toria's own shields: a clear wall slicked with color the way oil on water reflected a rainbow sheen.

Victory stepped forward, three paces off the road, and pressed a hand to the barrier. Her palm slid through, with no pressure other than a ghost of a touch she may have imagined.

Next to her, Jarimis sauntered forward. But where Victory's palm passed through the barrier, his stopped short. "Cold. And smooth. Like a glass wall." He lifted his other hand from his closing wound and pressed both against the wall. Still nothing. His bloody palmprint glowed black against the barrier before fading, as if the magic absorbed it.

Asaron approached on Victory's opposite side. "We didn't come this far to be stopped by a magic wall." He pounded on the barrier, striking it with the heel of his palm. It reacted this time, crackling with energy that vibrated across the surface and around the manor house before fading out.

Victory dragged her fingers through the shield again. The tingle against her skin was reminiscent of the shadowy hands that had caressed her both times she traveled through time. "But I can—"

"No." Asaron grabbed Victory's arm and dragged her away from the barrier.

She let herself be led to the road. Though Asaron said nothing more, Victory knew her sire. They were in uncharted territory, so far beyond even the experience his two millennia provided. He would not risk losing Victory so soon after finding and losing Ahn.

But she would not, could not, back down now. "Asaron, if the shadows want to deal with me, that's what they'll get."

"You saw what we faced." Asaron jabbed Ahn's sword down the road, toward the simulacrum of Limani. "You saw how quickly we were overwhelmed. You saw how—" He broke off.

"But this is what we're here for," Victory said. "The whole point of this ridiculous adventure. Confronting the hive mind."

"Wait," Jarimis said. "We don't know yet that Victory is the only one who can pass through."

Asaron turned away, but didn't argue. At Jarimis' urging, Connor approached the barrier. He raised his hands to the shimmering edge. And walked forward.

His forward momentum slowed at once, until it seemed the vampire traveled through some sort of permeable liquid, hazing the outline of his body until the details of his form were indistinguishable. One step, then another. He lifted his foot another time, mere inches above the ground. With a sudden reversal, he fell backward, out of the shield, and rolled away to lie on the packed gravel.

They clustered around Connor. "That was strange."

Victory helped him to his feet. "Sounds like an understatement."

"It is an odd sensation for a vampire to not be able to breathe." Connor furrowed his brow and allowed his gaze to soften, as if he hunted through centuries of memory. "I'd forgotten what it felt like, and I'm not keen to repeat it."

"Next," Syri said, peeling away from the group. She marched toward the barrier.

Though it seemed Syri might pass the barrier through sheer force of attitude, at the last second, a lance of energy lit the shield. Victory threw her arm over her face and turned to the side, and when she was able to blink away the negative after-images, Syri was no longer at the barrier.

Syri picked herself up off the ground, where the shield had thrown her clear across the road and into one of the stone trees. "Fuck." She examined a long scrape along one arm, then prodded at the side of her scalp, where thick blond strands escaped from her bun. "Ouch. That's gonna swell."

Mikelos rushed to her side, and it was a measure of how much she ached when Syri allowed him to help her back across the street. "Do you want me to look at your head?" he asked.

"No, I'll be okay. What are a few more bruises to add to the collection at this point?" Syri sank to the ground and shook out her hair, allowing the strands to hang loose around her face. They hung lank, the way Victory felt.

Mikelos turned toward the barrier and widened his stance. "Guess I might as well try my luck."

Before Victory could discourage the idea, knowing at this point it was fruitless and wanting to spare him any pain or discomfort the shield might throw at him—

—Mikelos passed the invisible line in the grass as if through thin air. He paused, turning to the group. "Interesting." The shield muffled his voice, but the words were clear.

Victory lunged forward, ignoring the tingle that rippled through her when she passed through the shield, and grabbed Mikelos' arm to drag him to the other side. He didn't resist, and they staggered across the grass.

Syri rocketed to her feet. "How—why?"

Mikelos ran both hands through his hair and examined the shield. "I didn't feel a thing."

"Because I'm the target," Victory said. "The hive mind has been drawing me in from the beginning. Not just since we've been here, or since we first saw the shadows. Years. Centuries. My whole damned life."

"And me?" Mikelos asked.

"It's our home. And you're my blood. We're linked."

Connor held his chin high. "I should be mad that I've been replaced, but I couldn't be happier that the woman whose blood mingles in your veins is such a bad-ass."

Mikelos patted Connor's shoulder and laughed. "That she is."

Shadows flickered at the manor windows. The blackout curtains twitched, and Victory's hands flexed in response. She had to go in and confront the hive mind once and for all. This was their last chance. But not for her alone. "Let's go, Mikelos."

"What are you thinking?" Asaron's voice rumbled, echoing against the magical barrier. "It's trying to separate us. You can't protect him and you."

"That's my job, to defend my daywalker." Victory stepped forward, Mikelos matching her pace. "Do you want to waste time trying to dismantle this barrier? Or do you trust me to finish this once and for all?"

Asaron bared his teeth, but when he stormed toward Victory, he grabbed her by the shoulders and lowered his forehead to hers. Victory stilled under his touch, acknowledging the honor she had seen Ahn bestow on her own progeny. He broke away without a word. They'd been together eight hundred years. They didn't need words.

"Good luck," Connor said, Jarimis echoing the phrase a beat later.

"This might be the only way," Syri said. "And if it isn't, we'll try something else."

Victory clutched Mikelos' hand, and they passed through the barrier. This time, no shimmer passed over her skin.

They paused on the other side to take stock. Without the barrier between, the manor house shifted to sharp clarity, standing as Victory remembered it from a few days before, down to the muddy boots Mikelos had left outside the front door.

"I don't know what we'll find in there," Victory said. She dropped Mikelos' hand and drew her sword. "And there was some truth to what Asaron said. Protecting you might be difficult, and we have no idea what the hive mind is, really. It could be like that giant who killed Ahn. You should be armed, too."

"Agreed."

But instead of summoning another ridiculous rifle, created from Mikelos' expectations of what a weapon of the sort should be, his violin and bow appeared. Cradled in his hands, they looked as right as Victory's sword did in her own.

Mikelos cocked a wild smile at her unspoken protest. "This has always been my greatest weapon."

Fruitless to argue. After countless protection details over her mercenary career, Victory knew an untrained fighter at her back in close quarters carried more danger. But Mikelos' music had silenced crowds and stirred up trouble and soothed children and everything in between. "I wouldn't have it any other way."

Side by side, they climbed the porch steps.

Victory resettled her grip on her sword, then pushed open her front door. Mikelos kept close to her. With one last glance at the now indistinguishable figures on the other side of the shield, Victory stepped inside.

The familiar foyer stood empty. She glimpsed coats hanging in the closet, through the door Mikelos never remembered to close. Her daywalker slipped inside behind her.

The snick of the door latching shut, a sound she'd heard thousands, millions of times over her decades in this house, should not have sounded as ominous as it did.

A moment to get their bearings was all they were allowed. A throat cleared to the right, from the former great room Victory had converted to a workout studio. She wasted no more time and pushed through the glass-fronted double doors.

Archer awaited them, resting with arms crossed against a blank space of wall between a tall weapons chest and a display of antique knives. Mikelos tensed, and stepped forward. She needed a significant portion of her self-control not to do the same. Victory latched her free hand onto his arm to stop him.

Seeing Archer die in her last vision ran on repeat through her mind, in counterpoint to the man who stood unscathed before them. This Archer had his full set of dreadlocks, and a trimmed goatee with unblemished skin.

The clothing was wrong, though. To her knowledge, Victory had never seen the water mage in such plain clothing that did nothing to highlight his trim physique.

When she was sure he would stay put, Victory released Mikelos' arm. She asked, "Are you the hive mind?"

The man before them, wearing such a familiar face but staring at them in such unfamiliar curiosity, waited so long to respond that Victory almost believed he was another shade, sent to battle them.

Finally, he said, "I am the present."

An invisible caress swept through the room, sucking the moisture from the air and leaving Victory and Mikelos coughing in the sudden aridity. No time to puzzle through such a strange response, even if it came from Archer's own voice.

Archer lifted one hand and a ball of water congealed above it, hovering and emitting super-heated steam. In a smooth step, he pushed away from the wall and hurled the bolt toward them.

Victory rolled to the side. Glass blew out as the bolt hit the window panes in the room's doors. Mikelos crouched before the scorched remains.

A second ball of water blossomed in Archer's outstretched hand. If it hit either of them, Victory would be in a world of pain and Mikelos would be down for the count.

Archer, or whatever this shadow simulacrum might be, flung another bolt when Victory recovered her feet. She dodged again, the exposed skin of her face tightening with the passing heat. This couldn't go on. Sooner or later, he'd make a lucky shot. Victory lunged forward between the thrown bolts, and Archer backed toward the rear wall.

The representation of the water mage seemed to have this lone weapon in his arsenal, proof it was someone—something—other than Archer. Victory had seen Archer and Toria duke it out in the relative peace of the forests beyond the manor, a gleeful exercise of their abilities where Archer had achieved such feats as summoning quicksand beneath Toria's boots or fog to block her vision and hide his movements.

Behind them, Mikelos began to play. The low hum of bow against strings, as if he didn't want to distract Victory's forward momentum. She placed the song as she dodged another bolt that scattered Asaron's collection of Rus daggers.

She'd never heard the song in instrumental form, but she used to sing it with Toria every night before bed. Toria had learned a ditty she could use to channel the immense amount of magical energy contained in her tiny body as a mage apprentice, receiving short classes at the mage school in the afternoon.

It was a tune the students used to exercise their control. To keep their magic in check.

Archer faltered, and his next bolt flew wide. Victory flinched, but only lukewarm water droplets splashed her. She claimed the advantage to dart forward the final few steps and swung the flat of her blade into the side of Archer's skull.

Before the dull *thunk* of metal against bone rang around the room, the representation of Archer disintegrated into black shards that disappeared into shadow, sinking through the wooden floor.

Mikelos' drew his bow along the strings a final time as Victory turned. "What the hell was that?" he asked.

A simple question with no easy answers. It had already used Archer in a vision once before. If that was the hive mind, why use Archer to fight them now? Why fight them at all?

Victory had no solutions. "Let's keep moving. Maybe we'll find out."

They picked through the shards of glass at the ballroom's entrance, leaving the charred and sodden room behind. Across the foyer, another figure lurked in the least-used room in the house, a formal living room decorated with stiff furniture and artwork Victory couldn't bear to part with but didn't want to see every day.

Like the fist-sized bronze sculpture Liam examined. Toria created it in high school metal-working class, and its value was due to sentimental reasons, not skill or beauty.

The elven historian set the abstract piece on the mantel at their approach. As if her long-term memories of the college professor became confused with her more recent memories of the museum curator in Nacostina's past, this Liam shifted between an unmarked face and one featuring a thin scar that ran the length of his cheek.

This time, Victory didn't speak. She and Mikelos waited inside the living room entrance for Liam to make the first move. The stand-off dragged on for a full minute. Mikelos shifted his weight, resettled his grip on violin and bow, but Victory remained still as a statue, mirroring the shade across the room from them.

Liam grunted in frustration. He stepped away from the mantel. "I am the future." Once again, the voice matched. A perfect replica of the elf left behind at the mage school in Limani. Why would the hive mind choose these men?

Then, their words made a surreal sort of sense.

Victory chose to act as if the man before her was the real Liam. "Does this mean you and Toria are going to make things work together? It's been decades for you, but days for her."

Liam tilted his head to the side, a gesture between curious and noncommittal, but stayed silent.

Mikelos rolled with it. "I feel the urge to give you a lecture about taking care of my little girl, but my little girl can take care of herself. Also, you're not actually Liam, and nothing you say has any bearing on what the real man does in our world."

The shade shifted on his feet, confusion writ on his face. "So, you will not fight me?"

This startled a laugh from Victory. The idea was ridiculous even if she hadn't been recovering from the very real fight she'd feared she might not win against the shadow-Archer. "The real Liam knows I could kick his ass. And my past is full of fighting. If you're the future, why would I want to continue that trend?"

The scar on Liam's face shifted in and out of existence with every breath, as if the darkness could not decide which representation in time this Liam should portray. He seemed to contemplate his next move.

Victory had all the time in the world. Time. Liam's scar stirred a memory deep within her, of Jarimis—or was it Toria?—discussing with delight a theory that all forms of light traveled at a certain speed.

If light had limits, and darkness was its opposite, did that mean darkness had no limits in time and space? That explained the meteorite's ability to transport Victory and Toria through time. And this sudden confusion between which Liam to represent, if he had two faces simultaneously.

Liam bowed to Victory, and shattered into shadow and disappeared. As if the hive mind had put this Liam in her path to send her whirlwind thoughts in this direction, and confirmed them.

"I can't tell if that was better or worse than fighting Archer," Mikelos said.

From his perspective, the disappearance may well have been inexplicable. Victory's mind continued to whirl, and she wasn't sure she had the vocabulary to explain it to Mikelos. "We're getting closer."

"To what?"

"I have no idea."

They returned to the foyer. The workout studio opposite them had returned to its spotless, undamaged state. Proof once again this was not Victory's home, and they could take nothing for granted.

Such as the robed figure in the hallway, blocking their path further into the house. It could have been any woman, from any point in time along the southern edges of the Mare Nostrum waters. But where most woman donned black or dark blue robes, or perhaps white for the richest classes, this one wore a riot of colors, as if dozens of silk scarves sewn together created the layers of protective coverings.

Mikelos did not know this woman. She was centuries before his time, and seeing her in Victory's modern house jarred her senses. "Fatima?"

The woman bowed in silent acknowledgment. The colors in her robe swirled together, like the shadows weren't sure how to represent her. Which made sense, because Victory's progeny never had any problem metamorphosing to be whatever her current surroundings, her current target needed—or wanted.

If Archer and Liam represented the present and future, one option remained. Fatima had been dead for centuries, lost to suicide after the murder of her daywalker Santiago. "I suppose you're the past?" Victory asked.

Another nod. Her hands emerged from the fringes of the robes and drew away the head-covering. Fatima's form flickered, on a larger scale than Liam's scar. Slices out of time. A stunning amber-skinned woman with hair the deepest black. A blackened carcass of ash and soot, the remnants of a vampire who allowed the dawn to claim her.

Mikelos' breath caught, as if the realization of who this must be dawned on him.

Victory preempted any questions he might have, just as she intended to preempt whatever this alternate version of Fatima might throw at them. The woman was a devil of a fighter, quicker than any vampire Victory had ever seen, and she didn't like her odds in the confines of this hallway. In a low voice, she asked, "Did you ever learn any of the old Grecian songs that honor the passing of a loved one?"

A long shot. Such traditional funerary songs hadn't been used in centuries as the customs of the Roman Empire swept through the overtaken Greek city-states. But Mikelos lifted his violin at once to play.

Fatima did not move. Her robes shifted, blown by an invisible wind. But her face stayed in its ruined facade more often than not, and color leeched from her robes, dulling to shades of gray and black, the cloth frayed and decrepit, shredded and rotten.

Victory knelt, placing her sword on the floor before her. Though it grated against every instinct she had to take her attention off a potential enemy, she could play this shadow's game. Especially since this shadow screamed "friend" and "sister" and "loved one" to every fiber of Victory's being. Fatima had been Victory's first progeny. Her first student. The first person she'd loved and trusted aside from Asaron.

She prostrated herself, touching her forehead to the rug running the length of the hall. "I'm sorry I couldn't save Santiago. But I'm not like you. I can't change the past." Victory lifted her face. "I miss you both. Every day."

Jewel colors seeped into Fatima's robes, and her face reverted to unmarred skin from its ruined form, though her hair hung listless and charred around her face. Fatima had been the reason Victory had sworn off ever bonding with a daywalker. She vowed never to make herself so vulnerable—until she'd bound with Mikelos to save his life, a rash decision she'd never once regretted.

The shade solidified into a healthy and hale Fatima, the silk in her robes glowing under the hallway lighting. Their gazes locked. As if Victory needed any proof that this was not, in fact, her progeny, the other woman's eyes did not slide away. The shade's hands drifted, and Victory tensed. But Fatima did not go for any of the multiple weapons she had kept secreted away in the voluminous layers of her robes. She brought her palms together and bowed to Victory.

Instead of shattering, Fatima faded away into a ghost-like image seared onto Victory's retinas. It was as if she'd never been there.

Mikelos eased his bow from the violin, and the silence was almost louder than the melody he'd played. "You hardly ever mention Fatima."

"She was a complicated woman, from a different world. I lost her when she lost Santiago. Even if she is the past, we can't change it."

"Do the shadows know that?"

Victory led him along the hallway, with nary a twinge as they stepped across the spot that had held the shadowy version of Fatima. "Perhaps we are teaching them."

Many doors opened from this long hall that traversed the length of the house, but intuition prompted Victory to stop at one. The library. Jarimis sat behind the broad wooden desk in the rear of the room.

Mikelos brushed past her. "How did you make it pass the shield?"

But Victory snatched his elbow, drawing him away. Because this was not Jarimis. This man was not bloodied, nor wearing combat armor. Instead, he dressed in russet clothing, and a bandoleer of throwing knives crossed his chest.

Jarimis' unofficial uniform from his assassin days, before he became a vampire. Incongruous behind the oak desk, where the Jarimis who had abandoned death for academia once sat.

Victory pitched her voice with intention, keeping her warmth and affection for her progeny out of the words meant for the hive mind. "And what are you supposed to be?"

"I am nothing."

Even expecting some meaningless phrase, the same mystical words she'd received from Archer and Liam, Victory's fingers tightened on her sword hilt as the words pierced her heart. Once upon a time, Jarimis had been everything to her. Jarimis and Allesandra.

Mikelos pulled his arm from Victory's grasp and raised his violin. Unbidden, he set his bow to the strings and produced a sweet melody. It took Victory a moment to place the song. "First Kiss, Last Kiss," a song popularized after the Last War that had stood the test of time. Jarimis' daywalker Allesandra had often sung along to it on the radio, the words drifting into this very library.

It'd been the song playing when Jarimis asked Allesandra to dance with him, in a dirty bar on the edge of the Wasteland. She'd been part of their lives ever since.

The Jarimis that stood before them did not react.

Lost in memory, Victory glanced to the library entrance, as if Allesandra's singing might precede her into the room. She missed their friend too. "Worth a shot."

Mikelos shoved Victory to the side as a knife pierced the doorframe. With another lightning-quick draw, Jarimis flicked a second throwing knife, which deflected against the thick chest piece of Mikelos' combat armor.

Jarimis drew a third knife. They weren't talking their way out of this one. Victory snagged a decorative bowl from the bookshelf next to her and hurled it at Jarimis. He knocked it away, but it gave her the needed second to sprint across the library.

He vaulted the desk. They clashed in the center of the room, Jarimis slipping under the length of Victory's sword and slamming into her. Where Mikelos' shove had been a light punch, this vision of her progeny hit like a truck.

Never bring a sword to a knife fight. Victory flung her blade away and summoned two daggers. Jarimis pulled long knives from his belt and they met in a brutal dance that was more about avoiding strikes than landing them.

Her progeny had always been better with knives, and in the same way she had avoided combat with Fatima, Victory feared she might not win this one. Exhaustion did not limit these creations of shadow.

Music rang out from the corner of the library. Deflecting and dodging Jarimis' blades, Victory did not place Mikelos' choice of song at once. Then, visions of cartoon wolves dashed through her mind. It was the theme to an animated show imported from Britannia Toria used to watch, about real wolves and other animals trained to mimic werecreatures.

But they weren't werewolves. Because this wasn't Jarimis. Victory caught Mikelos' message loud and clear. She threw out every expectation she had about sparring with Jarimis and dropped into a different stance. Now, she moved in the patterns of a Qin martial art learned during a time Jarimis did not travel with her.

The shade stuttered, thrown off by her change in movement. In that brief hesitation, Victory caught him with her blades in two places. One knife slashed across his throat. The second stabbed under the ribcage.

Neither wound would be fatal to a vampire, just damned inconvenient. But the shadow shattered, leaving Victory posed with clean blades in mid-air.

She maintained the fighting stance for the space of three of Mikelos' heavy heartbeats. When the false version of Jarimis didn't return, whole and ready to resume battle, she placed the daggers on the desk and retrieved her sword.

Mikelos lowered his violin, rolling the tension out of his neck and shoulders. "That was brutal. Nothing compared to what I remember of you sparring with him."

"Thanks for the reminder that this wasn't him. Might have been what saved me." Victory was desperate for a break, a chance to catch her metaphorical breath. She'd prefer wandering through an endless rock landscape over being pummeled by memory. The emotional and physical energy of fighting her loved ones sapped her.

But they had to keep going.

No figures from the past blocked the hallway this time, so they proceeded deeper into the house. A quick check revealed Mikelos' music room empty. Two choices—either retreat and climb the stairs to the second floor or keep going into the kitchen.

Victory chose the kitchen. Maybe this echo of her home came complete with a fridge stocked with blood and beer.

Asaron stood proud and tall in the empty space between the cooking area and the large wooden table. Like Jarimis in the library, this was not the Asaron they'd left outside the shield. This man wore armor from their days as wandering mercenaries, in the decades after Victory became a vampire and he molded her into the perfect fighting partner.

But Victory didn't want to fight this Asaron. She wanted to find three beers in the fridge, for all of them to sink into comfortable chairs around the table. To trade stories about their day and exchange teasing quips that showed the depth of their friendship and comfort with each other. A comfort these cold shadows didn't have.

He spoke. "I am the space in between."

Giving her no chance to respond, Asaron's sword appeared in his hand and he lunged at Victory. She raised her blade and the clash rang loud in the kitchen, echoing off the hard surfaces.

Mikelos darted behind the kitchen island, but the room left little space to maneuver with two long blades. Victory considered turning to flee, to attempt to lead Asaron through the house and down to the great room.

Mikelos struck up a tune that transported Victory in time. A bawdy tune whose dirty lyrics had changed over time but kept the same melody. It sometimes accompanied ridiculous combat scenes such as bar fights in modern comedic films—

Because this was a bar fight. Combat in close quarters. Victory had never been considerate of the furnishings when fighting in a seedy drinking establishment, so why be careful of the surroundings when this wasn't her house?

Repurposing the kitchen furniture into additional weapons, Victory hurled chairs and the island bar stools in Asaron's way. His sword caught in the legs of a stool, and Victory found her opening. She scored a nick on Asaron's cheek that glistened with black blood.

Sparks lanced up Victory's sword from the blood she'd drawn, electricity that swept through her body. Asaron lowered his weapon, as if they'd agreed on first blood as the stopping point in a civilized duel.

Victory backed away but kept her sword tip raised. "You're the space in between, because Asaron's blood is my blood. He's always part of me. We're the same line."

The shadow did not speak, and Mikelos ceased his playing. The silence thickened in the kitchen.

Victory filled it. "Everything I am is because of him. Because of you. The shadows may have manipulated my death, but you are the reason I live today. We are of Ahn's line, and I'm so glad I was able to meet her. I'm proud of where we come from."

Confusion crossed Asaron's visage, out of character and odd on the familiar face. And when he spoke, the voice was a lighter tenor, and not her sire's comforting, rumbling bass. "One speaks to us as though one is part of us."

This was the same voice from before, in the space between time when she'd returned from Nacostina in the past. Victory spoke to the hive mind of the shadows.

"I'm not part of you," she said. "We don't belong here. But you seem to want to tell me something by giving me these faces from my life, so I'm doing the best I can to listen."

"One may be able to learn the truth."

At this cryptic phrase, Asaron's shade shimmered into nothing. A force within Victory urged her from the kitchen, toward music playing elsewhere in the house. Piano keys struck unfamiliar chords that rang with taut power.

Mikelos came around to Victory's side of the kitchen, his gaze packed with decades of love and support and trust. He'd follow her anywhere, even if the destination might not be easy. Victory stalked out of the kitchen and toward the music studio.

They found what she expected. At the grand piano that dominated a corner of the room, a copy of Mikelos let his fingers drift over the keys. This Mikelos wore casual jeans and an obscure band T-shirt. His hair was longer, shaggier.

This was Mikelos the first night Victory met him, a man lost and alone, trying to reinvent himself in a new city on the other side of the world.

The hive mind acknowledged their entrance with a dip of the chin but did not stop playing. The tune was unlike anything Victory had ever heard, and though fingers pressed the keys, the tones that emerged from the instrument were too ethereal to be from her own world.

"I—we are everything." The hive mind paused, and the playing slowed. "We were everything. We are no longer sure of the space we encompass in this world. We are no longer sure what our brethren do." Like the shadow of Asaron, a different voice emerged from this portrayal of Mikelos, one that clipped the ends of words and hit a higher vocal register. The hive mind lifted one hand from the keys and examined Mikelos' fingers as if it had never seen the humanoid form before. Or perhaps never had one of its own.

Victory set her sword aside, leaving it against the wall next to the studio doorway. She would bring no violence upon this shade while it wore her daywalker's face. The tug inside her warmed, as if pleased she recognized that killing this shade was not the point of this particular exercise.

With a frantic hiss behind her, Mikelos asked, "What are you doing?"

Victory ignored him and crossed the room with deliberate steps. "Why have you brought me here?"

The shade's eye color faded from Mikelos' warm hazel to gray. The same hue as Toria's eyes, and for a panic-filled second, Victory froze. But it did not shift to a representation of her daughter, for violence to begin anew. So many interactions with the shadows ended in violence and death, so why should this be any different?

Instead, no other change occurred. The hive mind spoke again. "One has always been there. From the days of balance, to this final tipping point. But we knew one would be with us at the end."

"I traveled through time, using one of your artifacts," Victory said. "You spoke to me there."

"We speak to one at all times. It is fitting that one is here to say goodbye."

Mikelos stepped to her side. Victory fought the self-preservation instinct urging her to grab him, to run as far away from this powerful being as possible. Because of it, Jarimis and Connor had been stolen from her and Mikelos before their time. Ahn died before Victory had the chance to learn more about the woman who had given so much to Asaron, and through her sire, to her. So many elves in her own world had been sacrificed to feed its insatiable appetite. Kane died and Toria almost joined him.

The hive mind stared at her. She waited for the power to overwhelm her and force her away, but the moment never came. This being of unimaginable power locked onto her gaze as an equal, and said, "We have lost control, and we need you."

The most straightforward information they'd ever received from the hive mind, in any of its forms. Victory could work with this. It was her nature to see a problem and try to fix it, even if all she could offer to the hive mind was the power of an ant trying to lift the foot of a giant. "What can I do to help?"

The hive mind drifted out from behind the grand piano, treading the air above the wooden floor as if it didn't realize its form didn't coordinate with its surroundings. "We have evolved. Outside of this small realm, the shadows one has encountered no longer answer to us. They have come into their own, and they seek to destroy us. Which is why we have reached to your world, for what meager help we could gather."

173

Mikelos' flinch matched the shock that reverberated through her. They'd been working from information handed down from millennia ago. Everything they knew about the hive mind was out of date.

The shadows were no longer one being. The hive mind never intended to harm Victory, or harm her family. It had searched through space and time to find an ally, and it found her. It had plucked Jarimis, Connor, and Ahn from the real world into this one, giving Victory, Mikelos, and Asaron immediate familiar faces for support and assistance. To a creature for which time had no meaning, what was a thousand years or a moment against Victory's lifespan?

This wasn't a problem for Victory the mercenary, something to kill or defeat. This wasn't even a problem requiring calculated diplomacy for Victory the politician.

This was a problem for Victory the woman. If not for the hive mind, she might never exist at all. The bandits who attacked her caravan and raped and killed her companion may have done the same to her, in another space and time. Instead, the shadows allowed Asaron to slaughter them and rescue her. No matter what else the hive mind did, she might owe her entire existence to it. And Victory paid her debts.

But not unconditionally.

She placed a hand on the warm lacquer of the piano. "What do you need to regain control of the shadows you've lost?"

"Resuming control is not possible."

Victory's hackles raised at the answer, and she flexed the muscles in her hands to avoid backing away. The hive mind's lack of control had resulted in Ahn's death. If the hive mind could not regain charge of the beings swarming the badlands, this realm was doomed.

Syri. Brawleyn. The unnamed woman who had offered Victory a tiny slice of sanctuary when she needed it most. The creatures of light had abandoned Victory's world to protect it from darkness, only to lose the final battle.

But perhaps it meant the hive mind had other potential allies. "What about the others in this world who fight the shadows?" Victory asked. "In the shielded enclaves? Can they help you against the shadows you've lost?"

The hive mind furrowed its brow, in a Mikelos-like manner of bafflement. "That time has far passed." It returned to the piano keys and played a low, dark chord. "When we go, this world will fall to the light. Without the lost ones' ability to draw on my power, the light will vanquish them."

"So, you need us to help you get back to our world," Victory said. "But why do you need us at all? You've reached out on your own. Many of us have seen you." She had no idea how to separate the shadows she'd been glimpsing for the past few years with the presence standing before her.

"We must be with one to leave this place. To rejoin with our lost selves."

Not a precise answer, but perhaps their language didn't have the words to encompass what the hive mind meant. For a creature with the ability to be wherever it wanted, to see whatever it wanted, this method might seem primitive in comparison.

Could the solution be so simple? "You needed me to get home," Victory said. "To join with your fragments we keep seeing."

The hive mind left the piano. He still mimicked Mikelos, but the clothing shifted, fading to a gray tunic and loose pants. His hair shortened and thickened to a wiry texture the same gray as his eyes. Even Mikelos' sun-kissed tan lost its healthy glow and paled to an unhealthy pallor. "One would help us, after everything one has been through in our lands, at the hands of our lost children?"

An empty music stand appeared next to the real Mikelos. He set down his violin and bow. "What will you do if we bring you to our world?"

Victory's vision of the destroyed mage school, Archer dying in her arms, flitted through her mind. Was that their future if they let the hive mind return to their world?

The hive mind examined its pale hands, then spread them wide. "Without the beings of light hunting us, we will reclaim our self. Live in peace, for the first time in too long." The hive mind dipped its chin, as if acknowledging Victory's fears. "What the one saw was a warning of things to come, if our children manage to escape this realm."

If Mikelos disagreed with the hive mind's answer, he'd speak immediately. His silence indicated that he waited for Victory to make the final decision.

With Mikelos by her side, that decision was simple. She may have saved his life first, but they'd saved each other, physically and emotionally, more times than she could count. If it had been a conscious decision, the hive mind might have manipulated events in its favor by accepting Mikelos past the shield with Victory.

Together, they weren't in the business of destruction. She had turned her mercenary hands to building and nurturing, whether her small family or the entire city of Limani. What was one more stray in a city known for its independence?

"Then yes," Victory said. "We will help you."

The pale, colorless being linked the three of them by the hand. Its skin was as cold as hers, and the music studio, and the rest of the manor house, faded around them.

They did not return to the stone forest that had guided them to the manor house. Instead, Victory stood with Mikelos and the hive mind, still wearing the bland face, upon a flat black surface. Smooth, but not shiny or mirrored, so it did not reflect the swirling brilliance above. Lights danced in the metaphorical sky, like the aurora borealis in northern Europa taken to the extreme. The lights included every color of the rainbow, even hues Victory had no name for and others she was certain she'd never seen.

Once she drew her attention away from the spectacle above, she stepped back in alarm. The horizon was closer than it should be. This wasn't another area of the so-called badlands. This was the only area left in the world the shadows controlled. The hive mind's summoned persona listed to one side where it stood, as if keeping even this small sanctuary safe drained it.

Voices erupted behind Victory, and she whirled, the sword she'd left behind in the music studio reappearing in her hands. Asaron and Syri extended blades in return. Even Jarimis pinched a knife between two fingers, poised to throw. A far cry from the way he'd clutched at his healing wound before Victory passed through the barrier around the house. A touch of color in his cheeks had chased away his pallor, and Syri's wrist sported a bandage.

Victory dipped the point of her blade. "No! Stop. We've come to a detente with the shadow's hive mind."

Asaron shook his sword. "It's the reason Ahn is dead."

Despite his furious rumble, Asaron's proper voice comforted Victory. But that comfort stretched thin. She had to keep him from striking down the hive mind before they escaped this world alive.

The hive mind never gave her the chance, heedless of the various weapons trained its way. "And for that, you have our deepest apologies. The loss of the vampire Ahn is a great tragedy. We no longer controlled the fractures of our being who killed her, just as we have lost power over this world now that we are outside our shield."

As if giving credence to his word, the ground shifted beneath their feet. A mild quake, but cracks appeared in the dull blackened surface, spreading like spiderwebs around them.

"As you can see, our power grows ever weaker." The hive mind kept its focus trained on Asaron.

And for the first time in her life, Asaron looked away first. He turned to Victory instead, and she almost flinched away from his fury.

"We can finish it off," Asaron said. "Here. Now."

"No." Victory matched his fury with pure assertiveness. She'd talked her sire out of rages before. He'd see reason. "Those weren't the hive mind. It's been under attack as much as we have. The reason we're even here is because he reached out to us for help. We just didn't understand."

The sword trembled in Asaron's grip. Victory sheathed her sword and crossed the fractured surface until she wrapped both hands around his shoulders. "I've trusted you my entire life. You have to trust me, now."

Asaron pulled out of her grasp. "I always do. Whether I like it or not." He sheathed his weapon with stiff motions.

Oblivious to the tension, or perhaps not cognizant of such emotions, the hive mind broke in as if it commenting on the weather. "I can summon a portal to send all of you home."

"What will happen if you leave this place?" Mikelos asked. He had drifted around the edge of the group, stepping over the cracks crossing the black surface, until he'd circled to a point near Connor.

The hive mind had lost some of Mikelos' height. "If we leave this plane, the balance will tip," the hive mind said. "The light will have full control. Without us as a source of power, the light will be able to destroy our remnants, once and for all." Its skin faded more, until translucent features reflected the swirling lights above them.

They needed that portal before the hive mind had no more substance with which to create it. "Okay, let's do it," Victory said. "Let's go home."

"All of us?" Syri lowered her knives, and hope shone in her face.

"Yes," the hive mind said. "All of you."

A dark whirlwind of power sprang into life behind him. It telescoped outward, and a blank white slate appeared through it, dull compared to the shimmering colors stretching above them.

No, not a white void. A white wall. Victory shifted her weight to one side, and her perspective changed. It was the magical training room in which they'd first met to study the time-travel artifact, devoid of people now. A little wild-eyed, Jarimis also tucked his knife away. He joined Victory with small steps on the solid surface to avoid the fractures.

"Toria will be thrilled to see you," Victory said.

"Is there still a place for me there? You said decades have passed."

"There's always a place for you in my home." Victory glanced at Asaron. "Our home."

The ground rocked again, and they threw their arms wide for balance. The cracks spread, deepened, until the fractures created a patchwork of uneven surface. With low crunches, chunks of the blackened stone fell away in the distance. The horizon shrank, coming closer.

"We cannot maintain this physical link between the worlds much longer," the hive mind said. Concern now tinged its voice, though its facade remained neutral. "One must lead her companions through now."

No further urging necessary. Syri rushed through the portal and traveled to the other side without so much as a pop to give evidence of her passage. She spun on her heel in the training room and waved them through to join her. Victory pushed Jarimis toward Asaron. Jarimis caught the other man by the arm before he balked further and tugged him through.

"Mikelos, Connor, go," Victory said. Excitement plucked at her veins. Toria and Kane and Archer awaited. Along with a proper sky above her. Real blood to drink. A chance to sit. She placed herself next to the hive mind. "I'll pull you through with me. We'll sort the rest out once we get home."

Her mind already spun with plans. How to reintroduce Syri, Jarimis, and Connor to society, to educate them on the years and decades they'd missed. How to incorporate a strange creature of shadow into life in Limani. Jarimis needed a new project, since she knew he'd balk at the idea of returning to the university that now bore his name. The two of them could investigate restoring magic to the world, or maybe Archer had room for him at the mage school—

"But we cannot go through." The hive mind stood firm. "We will use the last of our power to maintain the portal until the one and her companions are through."

Mikelos and Connor had almost reached the portal, but Mikelos whirled on the hive mind. "Then how are we supposed to help you?"

The hive mind bowed, a short incline of respect toward the daywalker. "One has helped us. One has shown us kindness. One has ensured that our violent brethren will be destroyed, never to harm another being."

"But we thought we were saving you!" Mikelos gripped Connor's wrist, his face stricken.

Those who had already passed through clustered on the other side. The room appeared brighter now, full of life, and the group had grown with the addition of Toria, Kane, and Archer. Syri had glued herself between Toria and Kane. Seeing Archer alive and well, so soon after the vision where he died in Victory's arms, summoned a rush of relief that warred with the near panic caused by the hive mind's proclamation.

"I'll stay," Connor said, before Victory even had a chance to work through the problem. "Pull power from me to keep the portal open."

"What?" Mikelos gripped Connor's arm, but the vampire pulled away. "No. You're coming home."

Connor thrust his finger toward the portal. "That's not my home. How long ago did I die? A century? More?"

"I'm your home," Mikelos said.

Connor pushed Mikelos toward Victory, but with gentle care. "You're her home now. And I couldn't be happier." He met Victory's eyes for one, two, three beats. He presented her with a proper gentleman's bow and when he rose, his demeanor shifted. By the time he turned to the hive mind, he stood fierce and tall. "Is this possible? Can I anchor the portal and send you all through?"

The hive mind cocked its head, as if it had never contemplated the option. Without a word, or any sort of motion expected during a magical transfer of power, something about the portal altered. The color around the edge transformed from a silvery hue reflecting the fluctuating color above to the deepest blood-red.

Gasping, Connor fell to one knee. At once, the drain the hive mind had hidden seemed to leech color and energy from the vampire. When Victory and Mikelos hesitated, Connor bared his fangs. "Go!"

But Mikelos would never walk away from Connor. Victory needed to be the strong one. She gripped the hive mind's hand, startled once again by the cool dryness of its palm, and snagged Mikelos by the elbow.

Without a chance for Mikelos to look back, she pulled them through.

She hadn't noticed how silent the other world had been until she fell into the cacophony of her own space and time. Voices around her babbled with exclamations and introductions.

Victory lifted a hand to Connor, allowing Mikelos to sag into Toria's open arms. Connor raised a hand in return, cocked a showman's grin, and vanished when the portal slammed closed.

LIMANI

A multitude of emotions swirled around Victory, as strong as the scent and noise from too many people in too small a space. A piercing whistle stunned them all into silence. Toria pulled two fingers out of her mouth and gestured to the door, now visible behind the vanished portal. "I don't know what the hell is going on or what's happened, but we can at least figure it out somewhere more comfortable."

"Wait." Archer pointed across the room, putting the figure who had been the shadow's hive mind in his cross-hairs. "First I need to know who that is. I recognize everyone else, even the ones who should be dead, and I'm sure you're going to tell us all about that. But him, I don't know. I have kids upstairs who are my responsibility, and buddy, your magic looks whack."

Here in her own world, the hive mind had altered once again. A bit of color had returned to its cheeks, giving it the appearance of a slender, androgynous figure on the shorter side with pale skin and colorless hair between gray and blond. It lurked in a corner of the practice space, presenting an unassuming posture. It seemed to shrink in on itself when all attention turned its way, and its eyes screamed for help.

Victory pitied the being, the remnant, whatever it was. "I take responsibility. It's safe." As far as she knew, at least.

With that confirmation, the group poured out of the cramped space, Victory walking the rear with the hive mind. While Archer ordered a trio of mage apprentices out of a common area, Victory drew the hive mind away. Its skin no longer froze her hand, though it wasn't warm enough to register as human. She ignored how Jarimis targeted half his attention on her, even while Toria talked her brother's ear off. "I'm going to need your assurance, before we enter that room, that you are safe. That's my family in there."

She left the threat unspoken. If the hive mind had tracked Victory her entire life, it knew how dangerous her family could be.

And it was in her world now.

"You have my guarantee." The hive mind managed a bit of a smile when Victory dropped its wrist in surprise at the shift in pronouns. "You saved me. Your family saved me. I'd never imagine turning against you, or them."

"Good to know," Victory said. Footsteps pounded through the mage school at the edge of her hearing. Liam appeared around a corner and pushed past Victory and the hive mind without noticing them. Jarimis lunged out of his seat and the two men exchanged a back-pounding embrace.

Victory stepped through the doorway and waited for the voices to calm. Toria put her hand over Liam's mouth to stop his stream of words to Jarimis. "I'd like you to meet someone."

In another day, another life, Victory could never imagine the story that spilled from her lips. That was before she'd experienced time travel. Now, she spoke of travel to other worlds, instantaneous trips across oceans, and visions of history.

The others broke in with their own tales, shared between pauses to fetch beers and bottles of fresh blood and order pizza. Victory found herself nestled between Mikelos and Jarimis on one couch while the hive mind perched on a stool at the edge of the room. It had accepted water over beer, but nibbled at a slice of cheese pizza, like the food was a foreign delicacy.

It set the half-eaten slice on a napkin when the tale wound its way to it and straightened its shoulders. "The shadows are—were me. Or we were them." It chuckled. "An unimaginable number of lifetimes have passed since I was reduced to a single body, a single mind. Takes some getting used to."

Liam's eyes shimmered in the warm lamplight of the common room, a sign he used the elven equivalent of magesight to inspect the figure across from him. "You're human, then?"

"Or close enough. I suppose you can call me Gray." The hive mind—Gray— touched a finger to its temple. "That's what color my hair ends up when I manifest this form."

"That explains your magic." Archer studied Gray with his own magesight. "Like nothing I've ever seen before."

"I don't imagine I would be."

Asaron set his empty bottle on an end table. "The shadows we saw. Those parts of you. They still going to be around?"

"No." Gray sipped more water, savoring the liquid like a fine wine. "I can exist indefinitely with my power consolidated to this form. That means anything else I'd managed to connect with over the years since my banishment no longer exists, such as the shadows I'd extended into this world."

"Why were they here, anyway?" Unlike Asaron, no judgement colored Toria's voice. "And the artifact that sent us back in time. That was you, too?"

"I sought help on this plane, but I'd stretched myself too thin."

Syri shifted on the other couch between Toria and Kane, studying her hands. She bit her lower lip when she found all attention on her. "I shouldn't have come back, but I'm glad I did. Without the hive mind—without Gray as a source of power, my people will destroy the shadows. It might take a hundred years. It might take ten thousand. I'm not sure what they'll do after that, when a millennia-old war ends. If they return to this world, I'm not sure what will happen."

A problem for tomorrow. Victory had time. Time to pry more information from Gray, and Syri, and any others of Syri's people in this world.

"What about the artifacts?" Liam asked. "We haven't destroyed the one in our possession."

"A fascinating meteorite specimen now," Gray said. "Nothing more."

From his spot on the floor at Toria's feet, Liam curled a hand around her ankle and stroked the bare skin above her sandal. "When your message from Parisii came, we figured we should hold off. Despite some people demanding otherwise."

Toria pantomimed not recognizing to whom Liam referred, while Victory pretended not to see the easy affection. The awkwardness between them had vanished, which reminded Victory—

"How long have we been gone, anyway?" she asked. "We were in Parisii, what, a few nights and days?"

Kane extended a few fingers, counting. "It's been almost a week exactly."

"I'll need to contact David," Mikelos said, "and let him know we won't be returning."

"Zerandan, too." Victory wanted to check on the elven boy they'd rescued. Make sure the elven elders who'd abducted him hadn't turned around and stolen him right back. She also needed to inform Liam of Felix's demise in the Catacombs below Parisii, but she hated to ruin the celebratory mood. And she was exhausted, relaxation suffusing her body after the combined restorative effects of a bottle of hot blood chased by a cold beer. "Tomorrow. Or later today. I don't even know what time it is."

"A bit past sunset." Liam hauled himself to his feet. "We returned your town-car to your house, so we'll need to get you home. Who's going where?"

Exhaustion had claimed Syri, too, and she slouched against Kane's side. Kane patted her hand, and said, "I think we can find room here for this one."

Victory took Jarimis' hand. "Ready to go home, Zvi?" They'd bring Gray with them, for now. Gray needed to find a place in this world the same way Jarimis and Syri needed to be reintegrated.

"Beyond ready."

She heaved herself off the couch and turned to pull Jarimis and Mikelos after her. Her daywalker hadn't said much since their arrival at the mage school, and his movements lacked energy. Asaron's mellowness also hid grief he was unable to hide from his progeny.

For all the joy at Jarimis and Syri's return, they hadn't managed to bring everyone home.

EPILOGUE

At least three decades of paperwork had overwhelmed the desk and filing cabinets in the corner of the library that served as Victory's office. Material Victory had reviewed over the years to vote on in her capacity as Master of the City on Limani's city council, and never disposed of. Years of tax forms. Copies of the paperwork necessary when she sold the bar in town after Allesandra's retirement.

But Jarimis was home. Jarimis had made his former suite on the manor's second floor into his own again. And since he wasn't resuming work at the university (he still complained about the name change) in any official capacity yet, Victory had determined it fair she return his space in the library.

First, however, she had to clear out the detritus of her own time. Culling it all had seemed easy in theory, but now....

The front door slammed, and a new heartbeat echoed in the house. Victory dropped the stack of business cards a decade out of date and pushed her chair away. Not eager to resume her magical training with Toria, but eager to set aside this exercise that neared futility.

Toria wandered into the library after calling greetings to Mikelos, Asaron, and Jarimis, who Victory had left clustered in the kitchen. Instead of prodding Victory into following her out into the yard, she placed two objects on the desk and settled into an armchair.

On one side lay a hunk of weeds, which had scattered dirt on the desk. On the other a tiny vase, containing a delicate rose on the verge of bloom.

Victory groaned and slumped in her seat.

"No, don't think about it," Toria said. "Just—do the thing."

In Gray's first month in Limani, they had set about acquainting Victory with the basics of her abilities. Once secure Victory wouldn't lose control of her power, they had turned her over to Toria's supervision and set off to find themself. Last anyone heard, Gray sent the mage school a message that they were traveling to Europa to see how things had changed in the past millennia or four.

Victory placed her palms flat on the desk. "You sure we shouldn't be doing this outside like usual?"

Toria dismissed the idea with a wave of her hand. "You hit a plateau, so time for a new challenge."

The idea was simple, in theory. In this world, vampiric magic involved the manipulation of life force. This was a step beyond draining a creature of blood to keep her body going. Toria wanted a full transition—kill the weed and force the rose to bloom.

But the reason they practiced outside, deep in the forest around the manor house, was because Victory's magic tended toward the scorched earth method. She could force a flower to bloom, or a butterfly to emerge from a chrysalis, but a surrounding yard of dead grass was the usual price.

The library contained nothing living besides Toria. Her source of power for the rose was the weed—or her daughter. Toria placed her literal life in Victory's hands.

Then again, she'd been doing that for over a quarter of a century. If Toria had faith in Victory....

Victory curled her fingers toward her palms, but otherwise didn't move. She stared at the two plants.

With a sense she didn't have a name for, a shift occurred within Victory. Metallic tendrils rose from the hunk of weed and stretched toward the rose. Power pulsed along the cords until the weeds had shriveled and blackened.

The rose bloomed at once, a vibrant ruby hue. Victory snipped the transfer of power when a single petal drifted to the desk.

Across from her, Toria fist-pumped the air at Victory's accomplishment.

"Did you even have shields up?" Victory asked.

"Of course not." Toria pulled a bandana from her pocket and brushed the dirt and dried husk of weed off the desk. "You and your magic would never hurt me."

Acknowledgements

Once again, this book would not be possible without the help of those around me. Jennifer Della Zanna, Chelsea Stickle, Cara McKinnon, Chris Stout, Kristopher Campa, and Danielle Hinesly all had a hand in making this story and text the best it could be.

Jennifer Barnes and John Edward Lawson continue to be the best support I could have in this crazy world of writing and publishing, and Julia Vilece and David Brawley are the best friends I could have in this crazy thing called life.

And despite much protest on his part, absolutely none of this would be possible without Erik. And the cats.

ABOUT THE AUTHOR

By day, J. L. Gribble is a professional medical editor. By night, she does freelance fiction editing in all genres, along with reading, playing video games, and occasionally even writing.

Previously, Gribble studied English at St. Mary's College of Maryland. She received her Master's degree in Writing Popular Fiction from Seton Hill University in Greensburg, Pennsylvania, where her debut novel *Steel Victory* was her thesis for the program.

She lives in Ellicott City, Maryland, with her husband and three vocal Siamese cats. Find her online (www.jlgribble.com), on Facebook (www.facebook.com/jlgribblewriter), and on Twitter and Instagram (@hannacdits). She is currently working on more tales set in the world of Limani.

www.ingramcontent.com/pod-product-compliance
Lightning Source LLC
Chambersburg PA
CBHW020638250626
47154CB00008B/2721